SO-DMY-666

COUGAR HUNT
COUGAR CHALLENGE

SAMANTHA CAYTO
LEXXIE COUPER
NICOLE AUSTIN

ELLORA'S CAVE
ROMANTICA®
www.ELLORASCAVE.COM

LOCKED AND LOADED
Samantha Cayto

Former army-turned-ER doctor Grace McKinnon is through with going to bed with nothing more than fantasies and a yearning to resurrect her personal life. She's determined instead to take the Cougar Challenge with a flesh and hot-blooded younger man. She discovers the perfect opportunity steaming up the curtain of exam room four.

Captain Mark Bennington has been locked and loaded—ready for action—since meeting Grace. He's on a mission to heat up the Boston nights while on leave. This sexy older woman is lighting his way, fulfilling double-time every sex wish he's ever made. But it's going to be the toughest fight of his life to convince her to take a chance on more than just a fling.

COPPING A FEEL
Lexxie Couper

Darci-Rae Whitlam doesn't know which is more disturbing, receiving scads of obscene phone calls—or getting so turned-on by said phone calls. Then there's the email from her American friend, Rachel, taunting Darci with something called a Cougar Challenge. Just the thought of seducing a younger man is enough to permanently soak her knickers. No wonder her ever-disapproving sister thinks she's oversexed!

Cybercrime Detective Jarrod St. James is investigating a case of stolen identity. He quickly learns the fiery redhead claiming to be Darci-Rae Whitlam is the real deal (his shoulder trapped in the jaws of her gargantuan dog might have sped that decision along). He really should go back to Sydney, continue tracking the imposter who's operating a phone-sex business in Darci's name...but the woman proves too tempting. Job be damned, he has to have her. The fact she's got a titillating challenge to complete only helps his case.

Darci just may be the fastest cougar to snag her cub yet. Being the victim of a crime has never been more fun!

SUMMER OF THE COUGAR
Nicole Austin

With the big four-oh looming, Larissa Cross is more than ready to shed the roles that have defined her and make drastic changes. Gone are the widowed Army wife, soccer mom and empty nester. She's even setting aside the schoolteacher until fall.

A naughty challenge issued by fellow erotic romance booklovers on their blog, *Tempt the Cougar*, has come at the perfect time and ignited Rissa's competitive drive. It's going to be a glorious summer full of hot younger man lovin' for a new cougar on the prowl. Rawr!

Tattooed and pierced fireman JD Harmon is tempting prey but there's much more to the hunk than his bad boy good looks. A one-night stand isn't in his plans, and sex—no matter how mind-blowing—won't distract him from his goals. JD intends to tame the wicked cougar and stake a claim on her heart.

An Ellora's Cave Publication

www.ellorascave.com

Cougar Hunt

ISBN 9781419963681
ALL RIGHTS RESERVED.
Locked and Loaded Copyright © 2010 Samantha Cayto
Copping a Feel Copyright © 2010 Lexxie Couper
Summer of the Cougar Copyright © 2010 Nicole Austin
Edited by Helen Woodall, Kelli Collins and Jillian Bell.
Cover art by Syneca.

Trade paperback publication 2011

With the exception of quotes used in reviews, this book may not be reproduced or used in whole or in part by any means existing without written permission from the publisher, Ellora's Cave Publishing, Inc.® 1056 Home Avenue, Akron OH 44310-3502.

Warning: The unauthorized reproduction or distribution of this copyrighted work is illegal. Criminal copyright infringement, including infringement without monetary gain, is investigated by the FBI and is punishable by up to 5 years in federal prison and a fine of $250,000.
(http://www.fbi.gov/ipr/)

This book is a work of fiction and any resemblance to persons, living or dead, or places, events or locales is purely coincidental. The characters are productions of the author's imagination and used fictitiously.

COUGAR HUNT

LOCKED AND LOADED

Samantha Cayto

ജ

Dedication

ଛର

This book is dedicated to the original Cougar Challenge ladies: my dear friend, Dalton Diaz, and my new great friends, Ciana Stone, Desiree Holt, Mari Freeman, Samantha Kane, Mari Carr and Lynne Connolly. I'm so grateful to be a part of such a wonderful group of writers. Cougar Growl!

This book is also dedicated to my maternal grandmother, Cecelia. She didn't live to see this story, but I think she would have appreciated it given that she was a cougar long before the term was coined.

Author Note

ଛର

You'll find the women of Cougar Challenge and the Tempt the Cougar blog at www.temptthecougar.blogspot.com.

Trademarks Acknowledgement

The author acknowledges the trademarked status and trademark owners of the following wordmarks mentioned in this work of fiction:

30 Rock: NBC Universal, Inc.

Bombay Safire: The Bombay Spirits Company

G.I. Joe: Hasbro, Inc.

Kevlar: E.I. du Pont de Nemours and Company

Lauren Hutton: Lauren Hutton Good Stuff LLC.

Sam Adams: The Boston Beer Company

Spanx: Spanx, Inc.

Chapter One

ॐ

"Here you go, Doc Mac, the film for your next patient."

Dr. Grace McKinnon took the x-rays from the emergency room nurse and flipped through the patient's file. She raised her eyebrows. "Drunk and hitting walls at four o'clock in the afternoon. My, my, this young man is ambitious."

Silvie, a veteran of the ER, merely shook her head. "I don't think he's drunk."

Grace frowned and took another look at the patient's chart. "It says he's acting belligerent and had to be persuaded to get the x-ray."

"That's right. His friend brought him in under protest and cajoled him into being seen. There's a lot of tension in that young man, but the good news is that the friend not only seems to have the upper hand, he's also totally ripped. I didn't feel the need to call in security or anything."

"Great," Grace replied with a complete lack of enthusiasm. She was at the end of her shift. Tackling an angry guy who may or may not have been drinking, and who was not happy to have her help was not something to look forward to. She braced for confrontation as she entered the treatment cubicle.

She stopped short when a set of hard eyes locked onto her. Light blue and crystal clear, they were set deep into a square-jawed face right above a strong nose with bit of a crook from a long-ago break. Every detail stood out starkly because the man's blond hair was cropped short. Not quite a buzz cut, but close. He was tall and muscular, his impressive biceps visible under his t-shirt, and his hands jammed inside the pockets of his jeans.

The sight of this man took her aback. She stood staring at him, drinking in the primal perfection he provided. Her tired body perked up with interest, and she forgot what she was doing for an instant. He was military, had to be given his bearing and the hint of a dog tag chain around his neck. Seeing him brought her back to her own army days. A wistfulness joined the heat flaring in her belly. She had loved serving and loved soldiers, too. But the doctor in her couldn't ignore the look on the young man's face. His expression was both weary and concerned.

"Finally!"

Grace pulled away from the lure of the man in front of her and turned to the man who had spoken. He was sitting on the examination table, an ice pack over his right hand. This was her patient, not the guy she'd spent a second or two, or hell three, ogling. This one was equally well-built and made her think military, too. His face, though, was haggard and angry, his hair a shaggy mass of reddish curls and his clothes were worn. His expression was pure mad. She worked to be patient.

"Mr. Conroy? I'm Dr. McKinnon." She put her best doctor tone into her voice, the one that said she was both the detached professional and the caring one. When he didn't answer, she continued anyway, talking the film out of its folder and shoving it into the light box.

"I have your x-rays here." She stood back to take a look at the film and bumped into something hard. Blue Eyes had moved up behind her for a closer look. He pulled back with an apology.

"Sorry, ma'am." There was a slight Southern drawl to his voice. "I'm worried about Sean's hand."

"I understand we have you to thank for getting him in here," she replied, keeping her tone even, trying not to show how his proximity unnerved her. He was only a kid, for goodness' sake. She could have fifteen years on him, and damn her soul if that point didn't tickle her deep inside.

14

Hands still in his pockets, he shrugged and glanced at his friend who stared at the floor, petulant look still plastered on his face. "I was afraid he'd broken it." With a nod toward the x-ray, he asked, "Did he?"

Grace pulled away from the lure of the unnamed friend and concentrated on her patient's test results. "No, fortunately not."

"Shit, Mark, I told you so." Conroy was surly and ungrateful. He was also suffering emotionally. It didn't take a doctor to see it.

"Watch your language, mister," the friend, Mark, retorted. "Sorry, ma'am," he added with a rueful grimace aimed at Grace.

"Not a problem," she assured him. "I've heard the word before. I served in the army for over fifteen years." Now why had she gone and told him something so personal? It was unlike her, unprofessional. Mark's face lit up at the news, however.

"Really, ma'am?"

"Who cares?" muttered Conroy, but he shut up and stared at the floor again when Mark shot him a stern look.

Okay, time for her to get her head out of her ass and get these guys on their way. Besides, there was something far more important for her to speak to this Mark about than her military service. "Mr. Conroy, I'm sending in a nurse to bandage your hand." Turning to Mark, she added, "May I speak with you a moment?"

"Yes, ma'am." He gave his friend another look that said, "Behave yourself" before following Grace out.

She gave the high sign to Sylvie before continuing farther away from the cubicle so she could talk freely. When she judged they were far enough away from Conroy, she turned and hit that wall again. Mark muttered another apology as he backed up a pace. He acted as flustered by the contact as she felt. But that was ridiculous. Her reaction was normal. He was young and ripped and designed by God to get a woman's juices flowing. She was forty-two and while pretty and fit, also ragged from a tough shift in the ER. No way this guy was into her. A pity because as a younger man, he fitted her idea of a fantasy lover. This wasn't one of those erotic romance stories she loved to read, however. She put aside her growing attraction and tackled the important issue at hand.

"Why isn't your friend being seen at the VA hospital?" She crossed her arms as she demanded the answer, trying to put emotional distance between them. This wasn't a bar, after all.

Mark opened his mouth and then shut it again. A few seconds ticked by before he finally answered. The look on his face told her he had waged some inner battle before picking a reply. "I had a hard enough time getting him to come here and it's right around the corner from his apartment."

"I'm not talking about his hand, Mr...." She paused waiting for an answer. She was surprised at how interested she was.

"Bennington. Mark Bennington." He cleared his throat. "It's ah, Captain Bennington, actually, of the United States Army." He grinned briefly, a boyish grin with a cute-as-a-button dimple on the left side. The kind of grin that said he was proud as punch. As well he should be because God, if he was older than his late twenties, he wore it well, and to have the rank of captain was a real achievement.

He extended his hand and she took it. "Grace McKinnon," she supplied which was stupid because she had already announced that she was Dr. McKinnon. Everybody knew that doctors stressed the title because they were proud as punch, too, of their achievement and needed to maintain a professional detachment from their patients. Of course this was not her patient. Still.

His hand was warm and rough and squeezed hers with just the right amount of pressure before he let it go. In fact if she used a little bit of imagination, she'd think he held her hand a few seconds longer than necessary. Wow, she must be really tired to think a thing like that. *Focus, Grace.*

"Okay, as I was saying, Captain Bennington, why isn't Mr. Conroy being treated at the VA for PTSD? You do know he's suffering from it?"

His expression turned pained. He stared at his feet and rocked back and forth on his heels a few times before heaving a big sigh. "Yes, ma'am." When he looked at her again, his eyes were clouded with worry.

It was a kick to her gut. Hot and vulnerable, a deadly combination. She wanted to wrap him in her arms and hold him tight, make everything better. Crazy but the urge was strong. Instead she went with the mundane. "You don't have to ma'am me. I'm not in the army anymore."

He shrugged. "I am. Habit. Besides, I'm from the South so I grew up calling every woman ma'am, from my mother to the gal serving me fries with my burger."

"I understand." To be honest, being called ma'am by this guy turned her on even more. Best not to think about it. She was revved up enough. "How long has your friend been out?" *Yes, talk about your patient, Grace. That's your job, remember?*

"Almost a year. He was up and didn't reenlist. I had hoped being a civilian would help him. The emails he's been sending me said otherwise. I've got twelve days left of a two-week leave before I deploy again. I'm worried about him."

"Does he have family around here?"

"Yes, ma'am. Sean's from Boston, but they're not much help. His father has always told him to man up and deal, you know?"

She did know. It was hard for men, especially military men, to face emotional problems. Yes, she had seen plenty of good, strong men fall prey to post-traumatic stress while serving. She was worried. It helped, though, to have a friend who cared. Sean was lucky to have Mark, if only for a few

17

days. Reaching into her pocket, she pulled out her business card and handed it to him.

"Here. I'm not a psychiatrist, and I'd really like your friend to get the help he needs from the right people. But call me if things get worse and you need to talk to someone."

He took the card and studied it for a moment before putting it into his own pocket. "Thanks, I will."

He smiled and man it made him even more attractive and younger looking. Her body jolted in reaction, arousal erupting in all the usual places. Good thing she had crossed her arms. As a doctor, she understood she couldn't help her body's response. Her female parts were capable of imaging how good the captain's male parts would make them feel. They didn't care that his body wasn't looking for her middle-aged one with its wrinkles and sags. It wanted an equally young, hard female body to rub against. Even if she was wrong about that and this was the perfect chance for her to take the Cougar Challenge that her friend, Elizabeth Winters, kept urging her to do, the situation was all wrong. Captain Bennington was not her patient, but his friend was and hitting on a guy in the ER was unethical if not downright illegal.

The really dumb part was how much her brain was getting in on the act. Images of her tangled with all those perfect male muscles popped up unbidden. Her body didn't care about the practical or the ethical. It only knew what it wanted and what it wanted at that moment was Captain Perfect naked in her bed. She mentally shook herself. The whole attraction was ridiculous under the circumstances. This was reality, not a romance story.

She was tired, that was all. All she really needed was to clock out, go home, order delivery from her favorite Chinese restaurant and catch up on episodes of *30 Rock*. Then she could retire to her comfy, albeit empty, bed and read her latest book until her body exploded with a sleep-inducing orgasm. Wow that sounded pathetic. A little self-help once in a while was fine, but it had become her way of life. She needed to get out more and date real men, age-appropriate real men. Or, maybe she did need to take the Cougar Challenge. She'd been lurking for a while on the Cougars' blog site. Those women were obviously happy with the way their challenges worked out. They inspired her, although she was still uncertain. She had always been such a sensible, duty-bound woman. Throwing caution to the wind and having a fling with a younger man was so unlike her. Could she do it? She didn't know. Hanging around any longer with the tempting Captain Bennington wasn't making her head any clearer. Seeing Sylvie leave the cubicle, she jumped on the opportunity to make a getaway.

"Looks like your friend is all set. Take care and good luck."

Mark glanced over his shoulder, his mouth tugged in a hard line. "Thanks." Wagging her card, he added, "For everything."

"You're welcome." Grace wheeled around and walked away, trying not to hurry. It was hard. She sensed Mark's eyes on her all the way down the hall. Damn, maybe she'd better pull out her DVDs and run a Johnny Depp marathon. She needed to put this guy out of her mind and fast.

* * * * *

"What's that?"

Mark yanked the business card out of Sean's reach before he could snatch it. "Nothing," he replied. Pocketing the thing, he took the bottle of beer his friend offered. Drinking wasn't necessarily the best idea, but alcohol did seem to mellow Sean at least for a while. If the guy drank too many, he turned aggressive again. Man, taking care of his friend was getting harder and harder. What was going to happen when he had to leave? His head hurt thinking about it so he let it go for the moment. Sean slouched on the couch, staring at him, waiting for a better answer. Mark played it cool, sank farther back in his chair and took a healthy slug of his drink.

"It's the contact info for the doctor who saw you today, is all."

Sean scowled. "Shit, dude, I told you I don't need to see anyone. Toss it."

"I'm not keeping it for you." That was the truth. Not the whole truth, but at least half of the truth.

Sean scoffed around another swallow. "Like you need a doctor, Mr. Tough As Nails."

Mark winced. The guys in his unit thought he was too tough to be bothered by anything. They didn't realize how much he withheld from them because he was their leader. They needed to think he wasn't affected by what they saw, what they did. He was. Of course, he was. He had his moments of fear and doubt and wanted to punch walls now and again just like they did. He had to keep it together, though, for the sake of his men. That was what being a leader was all about. He was proud he did it so well. Not that he wanted to share this part of him with Sean. Maybe he should. Maybe it would help his friend open up. He didn't feel up to it now, so he confided something else.

"I like her."

His friend stared at him blankly. "Like her, as in want to bang her?" he asked incredulously.

"Jeez, dude, get your mind out of the gutter." Mark took another long pull of his beer. Images of the woman in question sprang forth in his mind, her body wrapped around his, hugging him close, rubbing him hard. She was soft and warm and welcoming. Blood flowed to his cock and he gripped the cool beer bottle tightly to try to ease the sudden ache.

"Okay, like her as in making respectful love to her?"

"I'm thinking of asking her out, that's all."

"Dude, she's like, old enough to be your mother."

Mark eyed the other man over the rim of his bottle, a strange surge of anger welling up. The hell she was, and regardless of the woman's age, she most definitely did not remind him of his mother. Dr. Grace McKinnon was a tall woman, shapely, yet fit-looking under her doctor's coat. Her skin was smooth and pale, her hair very dark, almost black. She had worn it straight back from her forehead in a ponytail, and if there had been any silver in it, he couldn't tell. Her eyes were green with specks of gold. She was pretty, not stunningly beautiful or anything, but pretty. And hot. Definitely hot. His body had reacted to her the moment she entered the cubicle. His little soldier had saluted immediately. Thank God for tight jeans, otherwise he would have died from embarrassment. Best of all, there had been no wedding ring. He hoped it meant what it usually meant and wasn't because of where she worked. He wanted to see her again and this time somewhere more romantic than an emergency room.

Mark glared back at his friend. "She'd only be old enough to be my mother if this were the Dark Ages or something. Give me a break. She's pretty and sexy and very nice. I'm only here for less than two more weeks. I'm looking for some fun."

"Damn straight, so let's go down to Hooligans and hook up with some young ass who will drool over Captain Hero and throw you some out of patriotic duty."

"Wow, how is it you manage to make sex sound so unappealing?"

Sean shrugged. "I'm just telling it like it is. I know it won't be like cuddling up with Miss Head Cheerleader from bumfuck North Carolina, but dude, she dumped your uniformed ass during your first tour of duty, remember? She married the class nerd who served his country by working his way up middle management."

Mark sprang from his chair, nervous energy suddenly demanding he move around. "This isn't about Meghan," he insisted. "Meghan was a million years ago and I'm over it. All I'm looking for is to have a decent meal in a nice restaurant without having to worry about suicide bombers. I want to have an interesting conversation with an intelligent woman who doesn't ask me how many people I've killed and what

21

does it feel like to be over there. God, I really get tired of that shit. Grace McKinnon is ex-army. She won't ask me those questions. She'll ask me other things like what's my favorite movie, or something, and I'll ask her the same stuff back."

"And, then you'll bang her."

Mark gave up and barked out a laugh. "If there is a God." His friend was hopeless. At least he wasn't hitting walls or crying. Shit, he was in over his head with Sean. Maybe one of the questions he would ask Grace was what more he could do.

"So, what are you going to do, bro, call her at her the hospital or something and ask for Dr. Mom?"

Mark rolled his eyes, taking the business card out of his pocket. "Don't have to. Her mobile number is on this."

"Whatever." Sean drained his beer and headed for the kitchen. "Bet you don't have the balls to call her."

The thought of actually dialing the number and asking an older, more sophisticated woman out did make his blood run cold and his belly quake. It was kind of like getting shot at if he thought about it. So he did what he always did, he manned up. Pulling out his phone, he punched in the numbers.

Chapter Two

ဢ

"Another night of takeout?"

Grace finished paying the delivery guy before she answered her neighbor's question. Danny stood in his own doorway, shirtless as usual, jeans slung low. It was an awesome sight and given that he was around Grace's age, the right kind of guy for her to ogle. Too bad he was gay. She made a face and went back into her apartment, leaving the door open, her arms filled with a bag of spring rolls, crab Rangoon and General Gau's chicken.

"I've had a long day and given that I can only cook food that kids like to eat, this seemed the best option."

"Yeah, except that it's too often your best option these days, girlfriend." Danny had followed her as she knew he would, shutting the door behind him.

"I have enough for two if you're interested."

He stopped just inside her kitchen, hands shoved in his back pockets, hip cocked. "What are we watching?"

"I was thinking Johnny Depp," she replied as she unpacked her meal.

"I prefer Orlando Bloom."

"That's because you are a child molester."

"Please, the man's in his thirties."

"Barely. Those of us past forty should be casting our net toward an older crowd."

Danny suppressed a shudder. "I thought we agreed to forget my last birthday ever happened."

"Sorry." A flashing light caught her attention and Grace glanced at her answering machine. She had a message. She was afraid she knew who it was from. Ignoring it wouldn't help, though. Stepping around her friend, she went to listen.

"Hi Grace, it's me, Aaron." There was a small chuckle. "Guess I always say that even though I know you know my voice. Anyway, I was wondering what you're up to tomorrow night. I know you have the weekend off and I thought you'd like to do some window shopping on Newbury Street and catch some dinner at Cammy's." A long pause ensued. "So, ah give me a call. Bye."

Grace hit delete and closed her eyes. Warm hands descended onto her shoulders and squeezed the tension building there. "When do you think your brother-in-law is going to realize you hate shopping, window or otherwise, and find the food at Cammy's mediocre at best?"

Grace moaned at the relief the impromptu massage gave her aching muscles. "Never," she answered in a weary voice. "Because he thinks I'm Mary, or rather he thinks I'm like Mary."

"Which you're not."

"Which I'm not," she agreed. There was a brief stab of grief at the thought of her sister. Five years later and it still hurt, although not as much. Time did help, not enough, but some. "He thinks we should get married."

Danny stopped his fingers and whirled her around to face him, hands clutching her upper arms. "He proposed?" Alarm shot through his words.

Damn, why had she said that? "Not in so many words," she clarified and moved back to the kitchen. She took plates and utensils out. "He's mentioned a few times how nice it is to be with me, how we've done such a good job together these last few years, and how he doesn't think he'll ever be able to go out and start dating again."

Danny, as familiar with her kitchen as she, selected a bottle of wine and popped it open. He filled two glasses and plopped one down in front of her while cradling his own. "Why should he bother when he has a convenient sister-in-law to play the role?"

"It's not like that." Divvying up the food, she took the plates to the living room and placed them on the coffee table. She shuffled through her movie collection, ignoring Danny's critical eye.

"It is like that. For heaven's sake, Grace, you gave up your career in the army and put your life on hold to help him through rehab and raise his daughters."

"My sister's daughters," she reminded him with a scowl. Damn, no movie appealed to her. Maybe she should go back to Plan A and watch *30 Rock*. She needed a good laugh, a really good laugh.

"Yes, your sister's kids, and your sister's husband," Danny agreed. "You did your duty, the right thing, but it's over now. The girls are in college and Aaron's a big boy, completely healed. He doesn't need you anymore." Plopping down on the couch, he picked up his plate of food. "Why don't we just catch up on episodes of *30 Rock*?"

Bless Danny, he was the perfect friend. Grace joined him and used the remote to find the show on demand. "His hip was crushed. It left him with a little bit of a limp."

"He's gorgeous. Women will overlook a limp."

"I know he's gorgeous and nice and generous. I could do worse."

"Sure," Danny agreed around a mouthful of General Gau's. "You could do worse, but why should you settle? You're a hot babe, Grace, and a doctor. You have options out there, believe me."

She did, sort of. The problem was she had been out of commission for five years, longer when you considered she had been deployed when Mary died in the accident. Dating was ancient history for her. She wasn't sure she had it in her to go back out there. A face popped into her head, square jaw, chiseled cheekbones with piercing blue eyes. Her nipples tingled at the image. Her thighs squeezed tight involuntarily to stroke the arousal budding between them. Okay, she wasn't dead. Thinking about that young man was proof her fears were well-founded, however. She was stuck in her past or in erotic romance fantasyland if she thought a guy so young was dating material.

And yet she recalled the stimulating talk she'd shared with Elizabeth Winters over lunch some months ago. An OR nurse who had been part of Aaron's surgical team, Elizabeth was the reason she worked at the hospital. The two had met and formed a fast friendship. The day Elizabeth confessed she not only loved erotic romance, but younger men/older women romance, was when Grace realized how much they truly were alike.

* * * * *

Elizabeth Winters leaned over the cafeteria table with a gleam in her eye. "It's called the Cougar Challenge."

Grace wrinkled her brow. "Isn't cougar a derogatory term, like 'pathetic older woman'?"

Her friend shook her head in reply. "You have to embrace the concept and the term. What's wrong with going after hot, younger men? We're not our mothers or our grandmothers. We work hard to stay in shape and remain attractive. Our lives don't end just because we've turned forty."

"I suppose." Grace couldn't keep the skepticism out her voice.

Stabbing a tomato with her fork, Elizabeth waved it as she made her point. "You don't have to think in terms of forever. There's nothing wrong with a fling. You deserve it, Grace." She plopped the food in her mouth, chewed and grinned.

"Think of a hard and handsome young man, then imagine running your hands over all that firm flesh."

Grace did and nearly choked on her own mouthful of salad. "I'll consider it," she said in a strangled voice.

Elizabeth smiled knowingly. "You do that. In the meantime, check out the blog. You won't be sorry."

* * * * *

Grace had taken Elizabeth's advice, signed onto the Cougar Challenge website and certainly wasn't sorry she had. It was fun to see how things were working out for the other women. She needed to think about it some more and to maybe go out with Elizabeth and cast her net. Elizabeth had found her younger man, Kevin, but she'd be willing to be Grace's wingwoman. Maybe Grace would get lucky and find someone like Kevin, or Mark, who try as she may, was not leaving her thoughts.

Her friend had encouraged her to imagine touching a younger man. Well Grace had no trouble with that kind of image, not with the memory of Mark's hard body planted firmly in her mind. It took no effort at all to remember how his clothes molded his sculpted muscles and to imagine what his body looked like underneath. What if he had been her patient? What if he had been the only man waiting for her in the examination room?

She could picture him sitting on top of the examination table, legs dangling over the end. He is wearing combat fatigues. No, not completely. His shirt would be off, his camouflage pants unbuttoned at the waist, his feet bare. Wisps of blond hair, darker than what is on his head, peep out from his waistband. His large hands grip the end of the table, the corded muscles of his arms bunch with impatience. The moment she enters the cubicle, he nails her with his gaze.

She stops, clutching the clipboard to her chest. Her breath hitches. She takes a deep lungful of air to steady herself and lets it out on a long, slow sigh. Her body flushes with the heat rising within her. The coolness of the hospital's air-conditioning slaps at her hot skin because she is wearing nothing but her lab coat and a pair of high heels, red ones. His eyes apprise her in one long sweep. She can see the hunger in them and feels the same. She wants to pounce, but takes it slowly, sauntering toward him.

She steps inside the space between his open legs. Her gaze lingers on the impressive bulge that greets her. Her hands are magically free when she reaches him, reaches for him. She runs them up his smooth front to palm his pecs. His back straightens and arches at the touch. His chest rises with a deep breath. His eyes are slits as he stares down at her. The small brown nipples are sharp points. She leans over to lap at one and then the other. A low moan vibrates at the back of his throat. His hands shoot out to clasp her waist and pull her closer. His lips find hers and he swallows her up in a savage kiss. Her nails dig into his shoulders as she returns his passion.

A finger slides down and slips between her wet folds. She hums into his mouth at the feel of her clit being tickled and teased. Her juices slick his finger, letting it glide smooth and quick between her pussy and her clit. Her hips wiggle to urge him to go faster. His finger abandons her suddenly and she mews her displeasure, but it returns with his hand sweeping across her ass to cup the cheek and squeeze. It is her turn to moan and then gasp as that wet finger wanders over to circle the puckered hole in-between.

She deepens the kiss even as she works a hand between their bodies to find his cock head pushing out of his pants. With her thumb, she mimics his movements, making small circles around the weeping slit. He picks up speed while grinding his hips against her body. She holds on tight and presses closer, too. But she wants more, she needs more. She wants his cock inside her. She needs him to lie back on the table with her straddling him, with his cock pushing inside her aching pussy. It's been too long. This is not enough.

Summoning her full strength, she pushes away from him. Startled, hurt eyes stare at her. "Why?" they ask. She smiles and wags a finger at him before shoving against his chest with the palm of her hand. Down he goes to lie flat on the table, legs still hanging over the edge. Now he's hers for the taking. First she has to get rid of her lab coat. It binds her body too much. Her nipples, painfully hard, rasp against the stiff fabric as it floats against her. She yanks it off, tosses it aside, and reaches for the man waiting for her. His chest rises and falls with quickening breaths. His cock, red and glistening, beckons her.

She slides her hands up his thighs and pulls the zipper of his pants all the way down. He's gone commando, nothing covers how hard he is, how ready he is for her. She licks him from base to glans and is rewarded with a groan and a thrust of his hips. So she does it again and again until he is begging her to climb up and ride him. When she raises her leg to do just that, his strong arms reach down to help haul her on top of his hot body.

She straddles his legs, clinging to the table edge to steady herself, while he grasps her waist to hold her in place. She positions her cleft against his erection and rocks her hips. The slide of his flesh against her clit sends her heart racing. The climax builds within her. She could come like this if she tried. But that is not what she wants. She wants his cock inside her now. Freeing one hand, she clasps his hard length and raises it toward her body. With one fluid motion, she buries him inside her aching core. A cry of pleasure tears from her throat. Yes, God, yes, this is what she has missed for so long.

She pushes up and drops back down. Then again. She rides her fantasy man as hard and as fast as she can. His fingers dig into the sides of her waist as he aids her in her ride. He thrusts his hips up to meet her as she descends, their bodies slamming together in perfect rhythm. Her breath comes out in short, harsh pants as the orgasm builds in her. She cries out each time their bodies meet. His voice joins her. She can't hold back, she can't stand the tension anymore. She's coming, it's bursting through her.

His body is heaving against hers. "Grace!" he yells her name.

"Grace," he said her name again, but his tone is amused. "Grace, hello, Grace?"

* * * * *

Grace blinked her eyes as she snapped out of her fantasy. Danny stared at her with a knowing grin on his face. "Are you still with me, sweetie?"

She nodded slowly, still a little dazed by her bout of hot fantasy sex. Wow, she really did need to get out and find a man. But not tonight. Pressing play, she said to Danny, "Let's drop the whole depressing topic and let Liz Lemon make us feel like we're totally together people."

Danny heaved a big, long-suffering sigh. "Fine."

A second later, Grace heard her mobile phone ring. "Crap." Putting down her plate, she got up to answer it.

"Let it go," Danny advised pushing pause.

"No, it might be a patient."

"You're crazy to put the number on your card," he called back.

She looked at the number calling before answering it. The area code said it wasn't local, but then you could never tell with mobile numbers. "Grace McKinnon."

There was a brief silence, then, "Um, Dr. McKinnon, Grace, hi, it's Mark, Mark Bennington."

Her jaw dropped open, her heart skipped a beat, and her clit throbbed. For long seconds she fought to reorient her mind. Mark Bennington as in Captain Mark Bennington? The guy she had been thinking about? Well, drooling over really. Then her brain kicked in and she rolled her eyes. His friend, he was calling about his friend. "Is Mr. Conroy all right?" she asked, a concerned doctor once more instead of a love-starved ninny.

"Oh, ah, yeah, Sean's fine." He cleared his throat. "I'm not calling about him at all, actually." Funny, the guy sounded like she felt. "I just wondered what you were doing tonight for dinner." There was a pause and an awkward laugh. "You know, if you're not married or engaged or in a committed relationship, or anything."

Dinner? Grace looked over at her plate of Chinese food and glass of wine. Danny was staring back at her mouthing, "Who is it?" She ignored him and worked to get her tongue moving properly. "As a matter of fact, I'm eating now. With a friend," she added. "I'm not any of those situations you mentioned." She laughed awkwardly herself. God, what was the matter with her?

"Oh." He sounded disappointed. "I was hoping we could get together sometime. Tonight's obviously out. How about tomorrow?"

This young man was asking her out on a date. A date! As in, he wanted to see her again without her lab coat on, or maybe, with just her lab coat on. Holy shit! "Um," was all she could think to say.

"If you're not busy, that is." Now he sounded hopeful. He really wanted to go out with her. Holy shit, again!

She must have mouthed the words because Danny was all over her like white on rice, making inquisitive faces and mouthing questions. She batted him away and turned to look at the wall. What to say, what to say? No, of course, the idea was absurd. He was too young. The situation was weird. She wasn't ready to take the challenge.

"I'm free tomorrow night." It was if someone else's tongue had moved into her mouth. She had not intended to say that. Yet, in the back of her mind, she could see Elizabeth cheering her on.

Samantha Cayto

"Great, that's great." He was nervous. How sweet—and hot, can't forget that piece of information. The man was supernova hot. "There's a restaurant on Newbury Street I hear is good."

"Cammy's?" she asked, heart sinking.

"No, it's called Edge, but we can go to Cammy's if you prefer."

"No," she assured him quickly. "Edge is fine."

"Great," he said again *because you know kids today have such limited vocabulary.*

Stop it, she chided herself. *This was not, repeat, not a kid.* "How about we meet there around seven," she suggested because she really needed to step up and act like the assertive woman she was. She had always had a sensible policy not to have guys pick her up at her place on the first date. You never knew who the crazy ones were.

"Great, I mean sounds like a plan. Do you want directions to the restaurant?"

"No, it's okay. Newbury Street isn't very long. I'll find it."

"Okay, then, see you tomorrow at seven."

"Seven," she confirmed.

There was a pause. "Bye, Grace."

"Bye, Mark."

She hung up and Danny pounced. "Spill!" he barked.

"There's nothing to spill," she replied coolly, putting her phone back in her purse. She walked calmly to the couch. Her heart was racing and her legs were weak. What had she done? "I have a date for tomorrow night, if you must know."

Danny slid in beside her and grabbed the remote before she could restart the program. "I must. I want details. Who is this guy?"

Grace strived for casual. It took a big swig of her wine to achieve it. "He's someone I met today in the ER. He brought

32

his friend in with an injured hand. I gave him my card because the friend's suffering from combat-induced PTSD."

"They're military?" Danny shoveled food in his mouth as he watched her avidly for answers.

"Army, yes, although the patient is ex. The guy who asked me out is still active duty."

"I bet he's totally jacked."

"He is," she confirmed with a sigh. "Totally."

"More," Danny prompted when she fell silent.

He wasn't going to shut up until she told it all. "Okay, he's like Orlando's little brother, only blonder and with a more muscular build."

Danny swallowed hard and downed his wine. "Oh, my God, that's fantastic. I can't believe we were just talking about your lack of love life and G.I. Joe calls out of nowhere. That's kismet."

"You're not listening to me," she chided. "I said Orlando's younger brother. He's a baby."

"What's his rank?"

"Captain."

"How young can he be? They don't exactly recognize savants in the military. Rank has to be earned through years of service. He's probably in his early thirties."

"He doesn't look it, but even if he is, it's still too young for me."

"Bullshit. This is your fantasy."

"No, it's not!" She hadn't dared share the whole notion of the Cougar Challenge with her male friend.

"Oh, really? Let's take a look at your reading selection, shall we?" Danny sauntered over to her book shelf and pulled out a few of her paperbacks. "*The Cougar Takes a Bite. Cougar Love. Young Man/Hot Love.*" He grinned slyly at her. "Ding, ding, we have a winner. *Soldier Boy.*"

Grace groaned and threw her head back. "Okay, you're right," she said. "Anyway, I'm going. I said I would and I will. I think it's a mistake but apparently my tongue and my clit think otherwise."

Danny put the books back and returned to the couch. "Finish eating, we're going shopping tonight."

"What? No we're not."

"Yes, we are. You need an outfit for your date."

"I have clothes."

"No you don't. I've seen your wardrobe, remember?"

"Fine. If we need to shop why can't we do it tomorrow during the day? I'm bushed."

"Because tomorrow we'll need time to have your hair done and for waxing." Danny had the same tone of voice one uses for small children.

"I'll give you the hair." It had been months since she'd had a cut and color. No sense in letting the gray hair shine like a beacon during dinner. "Except I doubt Jenna has time for a last-minute appointment on a Saturday."

"For this, she'll find time. Trust me."

"Does everyone I know think I'm pathetic in the romance department?"

"Pretty much, yes."

"Great," she sighed channeling Mark and his apparently favorite word. The thought of him sent blood rushing to her clit. She took a deep breath and savored the feeling. It had been so long since a man had turned her on. She had almost forgotten how good it was. Danny was staring at her, so she refocused her attention on him. "I don't need waxing, though."

Without warning, Danny shoved up her pant leg. "I can only imagine what it looks like at the beginning of these tracks," he intoned.

"It doesn't matter because he won't see any of it."

"A girl can hope, can't she?"

Yes she could, she thought, but said instead, "Could you be any more stereotypically gay?"

Danny swept up her glass of wine and finished it off. "I doubt it."

* * * * *

Great. How many times had he said the word when he asked Grace out? He couldn't remember. He only knew he must have sounded like some dopey teenager with a ten-word vocabulary. Man, he was lucky she had agreed to go out with him. He was usually smoother than that with women. Since the big kiss-off from Meghan, he had kept it on the cool and casual side with the women he met and dated. Having had the charming experience of his heart being stomped to pieces once, he wasn't in the market for a repeat. A couple of drinks, a little dinner, some good conversation and all topped off with hot and sweaty sex was all he looked for.

So how come he didn't pounce on those things at the moment? They were right there for the taking in this local dive bar that Sean dragged him to night after night. Well the conversation part wasn't quite there. The women who frequented the place weren't much for talking and even when they did speak, he could barely understand them. It was a combination of their thick Boston accents and how utterly trashed they were already. Drinking started early in Hooligans. Drinking started early in Sean's apartment, too. There was no way he could convince his friend to stay in for the night, however, so his only choice was to go to the bar with him.

"You want another beer?" the bartender asked. Mark shook his head. He'd had enough.

Sean rapped his knuckles on the bar top. "Another round over here," he demanded. He was sandwiched between two young women in too-tight clothes and with too much makeup. There was a lot of loud laughing and grab ass going on. The women rubbed against Sean appreciatively when he ordered the drinks as if he had just given them their favorite thing, which he probably had.

The one facing Mark was giving him the come-hither look, practically licking her lips even while she felt up his friend. She was definitely his for the taking. A crook of his finger, and she'd drop Sean like the proverbial hot potato, or as the woman would no doubt say, podado. The thing was, he didn't want a quick fuck with a drunk young woman. He wanted his quiet date with Grace, which would hopefully end with a long, slow fuck. Christ, his cock certainly hoped so. Ever since he'd heard her voice over the phone, he had been locked and loaded. Just the thought of seeing her the next night made the blood pool low and his head light. He hoped she'd wear her hair down and maybe a dress. She was tall so he bet her legs went on forever. Her thighs were probably slender and strong, the kind that could wrap around a man and squeeze him to death, a good death.

Okay, those thoughts needed to stop. His jeans were snug enough to hurt. He didn't need a case of blue balls. He didn't need to sit in this place and get quietly drunk, either. All he wanted to do was go back to Sean's and take a cool shower to wash the sweat of the day away. A little self-help under the water spray might take the edge off, too.

Leaving Sean on his own was risky, though. The guy didn't know when to shut himself off. Mark had talked to the bartender before about it, and the guy was on board where Sean was concerned. Still it didn't mean Sean couldn't end up in another bar or someone else's place. The way the women were pawing the guy, likely he'd end up sleeping somewhere other than his own apartment. For sure Mark wasn't going to volunteer to wade in and make it a foursome. Maybe it was being thirty or maybe it was being promoted to captain, but he was looking for something or someone more mature.

He was looking for someone like Grace. He wanted tomorrow night to be a good one and he hoped she would like him well enough to see him more than once. He didn't have much time left and spending it with a nice, hot woman was just the ticket before being deployed back to Hell on Earth. Standing up, he drained his glass and put enough money on the bar to handle his drink and the ones already poured for Sean and the limpet twins.

Sean looked at him. "What the fuck, dude, you're not leaving already?"

"Sorry, but yeah. I'm tired, hot and need a shower. I'm heading back to your place." He paused. "You should come, too."

There was a loud duet of protest from the women. They sounded like cats being beaten. "Dude, no way. It's too early. You're acting like an old man."

Mark shrugged. "I guess that's what happens when you turn thirty."

Sean laughed and tossed back his beer. "That must be why you're chasing such old pussy."

Mark's hand shot out and grabbed the back of Sean's neck. "Don't talk about her like that, or I'll knock that grin right into the ground." He wasn't sure where the anger came from. He only knew he couldn't let go of his friend until he nodded in understanding.

"Sorry, Jesus, what's got into you?"

Mark unclenched his hand and shrugged. "Told you I was hot and tired. You sure you're not coming with me?"

"Why would I when I have such lovely company to keep?" Grabbing both women by the waist, he pulled them close to his body and nuzzled first one and then the other. The cats yowled again.

Mark shook his head and turned without another word. Part of him feared leaving his friend and felt responsible for looking out for him. A bigger part was too tired to do more than he had already in one day. This was more than he could handle, and he was selfish enough to want a little fun for himself. Less than twenty-four hours from now he would see Grace. His cock twitched at the thought.

A shower. He definitely needed that shower.

Chapter Three

ဢ

Hi Ladies! This is my first time blogging. I'm a friend of Elizabeth Winters. She's been trying to get me to take the Cougar Challenge for a while now, and guess what? I'm doing it. I have an honest-to-God date with a younger man, and a soldier no less. I was going to turn him down and yet I found myself saying yes. How often do you get a chance to fulfill a fantasy? I can be sensible some other time. Wish me luck.

Grace

Welcome Grace! After meeting these ladies, I learned that fantasies come along as often as you make them. Go for it!

Stevie

Grab on with both hands, Grace, if you'll pardon the double meaning. I did and got more than I ever thought I would. Without the cougar challenge I wouldn't have the great life I do now. Go on. Take that first step.

Autumn

Grace stopped outside the restaurant for a quick look at her reflection in the window. Jenna had worked her usual magic with her hair, chestnut with caramel highlights. The highlights had been Danny's idea and enthusiastically embraced by the stylist. Grace hadn't stood a chance. She didn't want to look like she was trying too hard to be younger than she was. But she had to admit the color gave her some much needed pizzazz. In fact, she looked damn good. If her goal was to be a successful cougar, and it was, then she was locked and loaded. She wasn't sure what she thought of the word, though. Certainly Elizabeth and the other women of the Cougar Challenge had embraced the designation and made it their own. There was power in that, and now she was one of them. The support helped even if it was only cyber support.

Her hair was down in gentle waves, which was a little uncomfortable for a warm June night. It softened her face, though, and her Lauren Hutton makeup did its job. It evened out her features, giving her a healthy glow without sending in the clowns. She tugged at her dress hem. It was shorter than she liked, but she had deferred once more to the master. Danny had assured her she looked hot, not slutty, and she had won the argument over whether she should slip on her Spanx underneath, so that was something. She did feel sexy with the filmy material of the skirt swishing around her thighs. Her legs were waxed and bare, and she was wearing silver sandals with Baby Louis heels. Red toes winked back at her when she looked down, a perfect match to her nails.

Her friends had done an awesome job making her pretty for her date. Now it was up to her to actually go inside and meet the guy instead of stalling out on the sidewalk. As soon as she stepped inside Edge, she spotted him. He was already seated at a booth facing the door. He didn't see her right away because he was playing with the salt and pepper shakers and the sugar container, moving the objects around the table top as if lining up soldiers for a battle. His hands moved in quick, jerky gestures. *Holy crap, he is nervous!* The realization helped ease her own jitters. She stepped forward and was intercepted by the hostess.

"Table for one?" the young, perky woman asked.

"Actually I see my date right over there," Grace replied.

She watched the other woman's eyes follow her finger. Her eyebrows shot up when she saw Mark, but she kept her smile in place. "Right this way."

Even before they reached the table, Mark looked up. He smiled broadly at her and stood. He was still as gorgeous as she had remembered. In fact he was more so. Those eyes fixed on her drove up the heat index. She wanted to lift her hair from her neck and fan her hot skin. Her Spanx constricted her now aroused body like a reticulated python. Still she noticed he was clean-shaven and wore a pair of crisp khakis and a button-down shirt. He had obviously made an effort to look nice for her. It increased her confidence.

"Hi, Grace. You look fabulous." He held out his hand as if to shake. When she took it, he merely held onto hers for long seconds, staring into her eyes, before letting it go. The warmth of his fingers clung to her skin. She flushed at his scrutiny and was unable to hold his gaze.

The hostess left with a low murmur about enjoying their meals. Grace and Mark remained standing. He stared at her. She stared at a spot beyond his shoulder trying to think of something to say. They stood that way for a few awkward seconds before she realized he was waiting for her to sit down first. She slid into her side of the booth and when he had joined her, she returned his compliment.

"You look great yourself." They both winced at her choice of words.

"Please believe me when I say I'm not usually that tongue-tied when I ask a woman out."

"I didn't notice any awkwardness," she lied, picking up the menu. "Unless you count my own."

Before he could reply, a waiter stepped up. "Hi, I'm Josh. I'll be your server for tonight. Can I start you off with a drink?"

The plan had been to stick with soda water, to keep a cool head. She tossed the plan without conscious thought. "I'll have a dirty martini with Bombay Safire gin, dry, straight up with two olives, please." What the hell, better to be hung for a sheep as for a lamb. Either this date was going to be spectacular or a

41

spectacular failure. Might as well be a little buzzed. Dutch courage wasn't always a bad thing.

Mark's eyes popped open at her order and she grinned back at him with a shrug. He looked at Josh. "Do you have Sam Adams on tap?" When he confirmed they did, Mark ordered a pint.

Alone once more, Grace and Mark did what every couple did on a first date, they hid behind their menus. "What looks good to you?" Mark asked, eyes peering over the large laminated booklet.

Hmm, this was part of the date she forgot to plan for. If Mark were a guy her age, she would assume he wanted to pay. She would protest, and mean it, but she wasn't sure how it went with younger people. Did he assume they would split the bill? No way to tell, so the safest bet was the old standby, ordering the cheapest thing on the menu. She'd either be saving her wallet or his or maybe both. Whatever, it worked. "The roast chicken looks good."

"It does," he agreed. "The surf and turf looks better, I think."

Lobster tail and filet mignon, one of the priciest selections. She shrugged. "I'm from the Boston area. I practically have lobster swimming in my veins. Chicken will make for a nice change." She looked at him with the sincerest smile she could muster.

Frowning, he closed him menu. "Grace, I'm going to be perfectly blunt here. This dinner is on me. No arguments," he added when she opened her mouth to do just that. "If roast chicken is what will make you happy tonight, then I want you to get it. For myself, I'm going for a bowl of clam chowder, a Caesar salad and the surf and turf. I'd be delighted if you joined me, but the choice is obviously yours. I don't want you to pick based on price. The army pays me plenty well enough to afford to take a gorgeous woman out."

Grace smiled at the compliment, inordinately pleased to hear him say he found her attractive even though it was clear given he had asked her out. She also knew the army didn't pay that well and a pricey Newbury Street dinner was not in his everyday budget. Still he was obviously sincere in his offer and she wanted to make him comfortable. So when their drinks came, she let him order two of everything, right down to the filet being cooked medium rare. He smiled at her once the server was gone. It was bone-melting and her heart beat picked up pace. She took a healthy swallow of her drink trying to think of something to say. It had been so long. Small talk eluded her. Mark, bless him, beat her to it.

"So, why the ER? You know, instead of going into private practice or a specialty?"

Grace smiled, a nice buzz starting already. She was more relaxed. "I get that question quite a bit. I'm asked even more why I decided to join the army in the first place." She waved her drink at him. "It was money pure and simple. I needed to finance medical school so I enlisted." With a more dainty sip of her martini, she continued. "Now you may wonder why a Boston girl would join the army instead of the navy. The answer, sadly, is motion sickness. I'm very prone, which left out the navy and the air force. The marines were a little too, um, mariney, for me. So that left the army. As for the ER, it was a natural fit after tending to battle victims." She shut up and gulped down more of her drink, afraid she had run off at the mouth.

Mark watched her, though, attentive. His eyes hadn't wandered in that telltale sign of boredom. In fact he was nodding at her. "Now that you say it, it's obvious. Did you like being in the army?"

"I did, actually. I liked the discipline and the challenge."

"I like those things too, although I joined the army because that's what you're obligated to do when you go to West Point."

"Oh," she responded. West Point was impressive. They only accepted smart, ambitious people.

He grinned shyly and dropped his gaze. "Yeah, well it was kind of obligatory to go. Men in my family have gone since before the Civil War. They don't always make the military their career. My father didn't, but it works for me. I'm good at being a soldier and it feels right serving my country. More often than not, I go to bed thinking I've made a difference."

Grace drained her glass. Before she could speak, their chowder came and they dug in. It was good and as it was one of her favorite foods, she savored the experience before picking up the conversational ball. It wasn't so hard anymore. She felt more at ease with Mark. He really was a nice guy as well as an incredibly sexy one.

"You must be good," she observed. "Being a captain at your age says as much."

He paused mid-spoonful. "How old do you think I am, Grace?"

Oops. The martini was a mistake. It had loosened her tongue. Bringing up age was definitely a dumb move. "Oh, thirty-ish," she hedged.

He laughed. "I'm thirty. Not so young."

"Not so old, either," she replied in a low voice.

Putting down his spoon, he crossed his arms and gave her a hard stare. "Okay, age is the elephant in the room so why don't we admit we can see it. Honestly it doesn't bother me and I don't want it bothering you." He leaned toward her. "How old are you?"

She considered lying for about two seconds. "Forty-two." She couldn't hold back the grimace. Mark simply nodded and went back to his chowder. "That's twelve years," she added.

"I can count."

"It's a big difference. Why doesn't it bother you?" He wasn't the only person at the table who could tackle things head-on. Best to know now if the date was heading nowhere. She didn't trust his casual dismissal of the matter.

Mark put his spoon in his now-empty bowl and shoved it aside. "Grace, I knew you were older when I asked you out. If it mattered to me, I wouldn't have asked you out. If it mattered to you, you wouldn't have accepted."

As she mulled over how to respond, Josh returned to take their bowls and hand them their salads. "I can't say I haven't thought about it," she confessed. "I can only say it doesn't bother me enough not to be here." She could have, should have, confessed right then and there how much the idea of a younger man turned her on. She chickened out.

He grinned at her over a forkful of salad. "The judges say we can accept that answer." Shoving the food in his mouth, he chewed and swallowed, the grin never fading. "The food here's good, don't you think?"

The flush ran up Grace's body and stained her cheeks. God, she wanted this man. "Yes," she answered in a breathless voice. "It's wonderful."

Dinner was great, and if use of the word showed a lack of vocabulary, he didn't give a damn. It was everything he had hoped for, an excellent meal with a hot woman. Grace had been tense when she'd first sat down and so had he. A little alcohol and honesty, though, had done the trick. Once the age thing had been settled, they'd both moved on to the kind of small talk that marked a first date just as he'd envisioned. He had to admit she was older than he had expected but what did it matter when she sent his blood zinging through his veins. With her hair down, *thank you God*, her face was soft and inviting. Her dress's neckline dipped provocatively low. He could see the swell of her breasts peeping out, although he was careful not to let his gaze linger. What he wouldn't give to cup his palms around those soft globes. Instead he grasped his coffee mug and contented himself with watching her lick the last of a piece of chocolate cake off her fork. Her enticing chest rose and fell on a deep breath.

"I'm stuffed. That was a wonderful meal. Thank you."

She smiled at him. She had done that quite a bit over the course of the evening. It made him ache. He took a gulp of hot coffee to distract himself. "I'm glad you enjoyed it. I did, too. Sean said it was a good place." At the mention of his friend, his happy dipped. No telling what his friend was getting himself into at the moment.

Grace's happy dipped too. She frowned. "Is he okay? Do you need to get back to him?"

"I don't know if he's okay. I mean he obviously isn't okay. But I don't need to get back to him. There's only so much I can do, and right now, selfishly, I'm sorry I even mentioned him. Let's talk about you instead. Why'd you leave the army?" As soon as the question left his lips, he knew he had asked the wrong question. A tremendous sadness overtook her expression. "Sorry," he hastened to backpedal. "I can see you don't want to talk about it. Forget I asked."

Grace shook her head. "No, it's fine, really. Not talking about the things that upset us or make us sad is what can lead to exactly what Sean is going through. I left the army because my sister died." Leaning forward, she played with her coffee mug while she continued. There was a faraway look to her eyes. "I was on my third tour in Iraq when I got called into my CO's office. You know that's never good, and the look on his face when I entered told me it was really bad. I knew he was going to tell me someone had died, but I assumed it was a service member or even a civilian I worked with. I didn't think of back home. You never think of bad things happening back here.

She paused, taking a sip of coffee. When she put the mug down, he reached for her hand, clasping it in his own. It wasn't something he thought about. He simply did it. Her skin was incredibly soft and warm. To his relief, she didn't pull away. Instead she twined her fingers with his and continued talking.

"My sister Mary and her husband were coming home one Saturday night from a party and some guy crossed the divider. He wasn't even drunk, simply tired. Mary was killed instantly. Aaron, her husband, ended up in a coma for a few days and so badly injured it took months of PT and OT to function properly again. He'll never be a hundred percent physically."

He squeezed her hand. "I'm sorry." They were always inadequate words.

With eyes only a little misty, she finished her story. "Even though my two nieces were already teenagers, they still needed a parent. I was all there was for a long while. I mustered out based on a hardship." She looked at him, looked at their clasped hands and smiled. "They're both grown now. The younger one started college last year. It's time for me to live my life again. I haven't been on a date in over six years."

Wow, he hadn't seen that confession coming. There was uncertainty in her eyes, as if she had told him some big turnoff. Raising their still joined hands to his lips, he kissed the back of her fingers. "It's been over a year for me, actually. I'm glad we did this for both our sakes."

Further conversation was interrupted by Josh with the bill. Reluctantly Mark released Grace in order to pay. He grinned and shook his head when she sweetly tried to cover the tip. Once they were outside, he snatched her hand up. Again she didn't resist. The contact put his body on full alert. It was as if he were on patrol, adrenaline pumped, every sense straining. God, he wanted this woman, but it was early enough that the sun hadn't fully set. Too early to go back to her place which is what they'd have to do for any full body contact. There was no way he could take her back to Sean's dump even with Sean absent.

"I hear there are a couple of good clubs nearby. You want to go?" He strived for casual, to keep the "I want to rub my body up against yours in a major way" out of his voice. He could tell instantly his suggestion was a bad one.

47

"Um, sure, club hopping sounds good." Her eyes were wide open and looking straight at him.

"You are a really bad liar, Grace. You don't want to go club hopping."

She laughed and tossed her hair back, exposing her lovely long neck. He wanted to lean over and bite it. "No, I don't. Sorry."

"Not a problem, but I have to be honest here. I really don't want our date to end yet. Is there something else you'd like to do? How about taking a walk in the Public Garden?" Which would be boring unless he could talk her into making out behind a bush or something. Her call, though. As long as she didn't let go of him.

Agonizing seconds ticked by as she weighed the question. Just when he was afraid she was going to call it a night after all. She rocked him back on his heels.

"I bought a condo last fall not too far from here. A few minutes' walk, in fact. Would you like to come back and have some more coffee, or wine or beer? I have beer." The way she said it meant she didn't normally have it on hand and was proud she could offer it. It also meant she'd planned on asking him back if things went well. Obviously things went well. Damn if his little soldier didn't salute the idea.

"Going back to your place sounds like a *great* idea."

She laughed, getting how he had deliberately used the word "great" and led him down Newbury Street.

She hadn't exaggerated when she said it was only a few minutes away. Before he knew it, they were inside a nice condo in an old brownstone building. The place was simple and as neat as a pin. It didn't have the usual girly stuff which told him either she was more army than not or hadn't had time to buy a lot. As soon as she locked the door, she leaned against the wall and slipped off her sandals.

"Sorry, I have to get these things off my feet."

His gaze riveted on her small, dainty feet and slender calves, he merely nodded. "No problem. How had he missed the red toenails? What would they look like pressed against his ass while he dove into her hot body? Her fingernails were a matching color. Those he had noticed and had already wondered if they'd scratch his back when he made her come. "Excuse me?" She had asked him something but the blood roaring from his fantasy had stopped up his ears.

She cocked her head at him. "I asked what you'd like to drink."

"Oh, ah whatever you're having is fine with me, ma'am." He winced. Way to make her feel old.

She rolled her eyes at him and grinned, taking it like a good sport. The living room and kitchen were separated by an open counter, so he had no trouble watching her saunter to the refrigerator. Her dress clung to her shapely ass. He could stare at it all day, but thought better of it. No sense in being too obvious. The woman had been untouched in years. She needed wooing, not leering. He looked around the condo and spotted her bedroom through an open door. He could see a neatly made bed and because that sight tested his resolve to go slow, he turned his attention to the living room. He wandered the small space, pretending to be interested in her book collection, and then he did spot something of interest. On one shelf there was a small rectangular box he recognized only too well. He opened it up before he could think better of the breach of privacy it might mean and stared open-mouthed.

"One Sam Adams." Grace held an open bottle out to him, another one in her hand. She looked at what he held and blinked back at him. She obviously wasn't going to tell him, so taking the beer from her, he asked.

"How did you earn a bronze star?"

Her mouth formed a thin line. Snatching the box from him, she shut it with a sharp snap and put it back where he found it. "It was nothing." She turned and sat down on the arm of her couch. She took a small sip of her beer, clearly not intending to say more.

He knew he should let it go, but hell she had the thing out where anyone could see it. "It couldn't have been nothing, Grace. They don't give out bronze stars, with a V device no less, with your mess kit. You got that for combat bravery. How did a doctor end up in combat?"

"You were over there, you know the whole country is a battlefield."

"Yeah, but still." He couldn't wrap his mind around it. It wasn't that Grace was a woman. He had fought alongside women in battle. He knew the "no women in the front line" rule was bullshit. It was that she was a doctor. Doctors were awarded the bronze star for being outstanding doctors in wartime. The Valor Device added to the medal, though, piqued his curiosity.

"I was doing my job, no more, no less, just like everyone else," she responded in a clipped tone.

Sensing her discomfort, he let it go. "And you don't want to talk about it."

"And I don't want to talk about it," she confirmed with another small sip of her beer. He could tell she didn't like beer. She must be only drinking it to make him feel at home.

Damn, she was a wonderful woman, and he wanted her. The way she was sitting, he could see more of her legs. They were shapely and long. He wanted them wrapped around him badly enough to throw caution to the wind. Downing a healthy slug of his beer for courage, he went over to her. She didn't flinch when he ran the fingers of his free hand through the soft waves of her hair.

"You could make a man forget his own name."

A pretty blush stained her cheeks. Her gaze dropped. "That's very sweet of you."

"No ma'am, that's my line. You're very sweet and beautiful and desirable. I intend to kiss you, just so you know."

Her mouth opened in a silent "oh". Plucking the beer that neither of them wanted from her hand, he set both bottles down on the coffee table before gathering her in his arms. She went willingly, hugging his waist as he cupped the back of her head to guide her mouth to his. The moment their lips met, she sighed and opened to him. Her tongue welcomed his inside and twirled around it.

He moaned at the contact and slanted his head to deepen the kiss. He clasped her body tighter, letting her feel his hard cock straining against his pants. He wanted her to know how much he desired her, how much she turned him on. Twelve years meant nothing. All that mattered was the need raging through him, through them both. Grace didn't remain passive or try to push away. She grabbed him harder, rubbing against his erection. He moaned again and dropped a hand to gather up the hem of her skirt. Soft firm skin greeted him before he touched something that felt like a Kevlar vest.

Mark pulled out of the kiss enough to see her face. "What's this?" Running his hand up, he could tell the thing plastered her skin all the way past her lovely ass and to her bra.

Grace's eyes opened to tiny slits. She bit her lip before saying, "Shit, my Spanx."

Spanks? "Huh? Did you just say you want me to spank you?" The thought nearly made him come.

Grace groaned and dropped her forehead against his chest. "No," she said in a muffled tone. "It's a modern day girdle."

A girdle, like what his granny would wear? That was stupid, but he knew enough not to say what he was thinking. He felt around all the body parts the thing covered, intrigued by thoughts of what it hid. His fingers slid between her thighs and to his delight, he found a slit in the armor. Grace gasped when his finger slipped inside. Oh, man, he hit naked flesh. Moist, hot, plump flesh.

"This is convenient," he grunted into her ear because all he could think about was releasing his cock to replace his finger.

But Grace laughed. "It's not for what you're thinking. You try slipping anything besides your finger in there and we'll be heading for the ER." She gasped again when is finger flicked her clit. "Yes," she sighed.

That was all he needed for encouragement. Pulling his finger out, he released her enough to slide both hands up under her dress. When he had a firm grip on the top of the girdle thing, he pulled it down and off. He ended up on his knees in front of her. The perfect place to go exploring. With a firm, yet gentle grip, he clasped the back of her thighs and licked a trail with his tongue from the side of a knee to the sweet juncture he had probed before. His head was under her dress, covered with darkness and heat. He could smell her arousal and planted his tongue between her folds, desperate for a taste.

Her body jerked at the first lick. Hands clasped his head, urging him closer. He lapped at her clit, long and slow. Grace moaned and bucked against his face. He held her more firmly, determined to make her come now that he knew how much she wanted it, wanted him. Her fingers dug into his skull as he picked up speed. His tongue flicked her clit. His lips sucked and tugged at the nub. She yelled his name and writhed. He hung on tight, not stopping until she started to collapse. Wrapping his arm around her legs, he stood up to carry her on one shoulder. She squealed in surprise, but didn't struggle as he hauled her toward her bedroom.

Chapter Four

ဢ

Grace's head spun as Mark carried her into her bedroom, yanked off her comforter and laid her down on her bed. He was breathing hard, and she doubted it had anything to do with the effort of carrying her. His eyes were darker, and pinning her to the spot with a hunger she hadn't seen in years. The front of his pants was tented with the magnificent erection she had felt when they kissed. Despite her fabulous orgasm minutes ago, she was dying to have that cock inside her.

"If you're going to say no, Grace, please do it now," he begged.

"Silly man." To make herself perfectly clear, she sat up enough to pull her dress over her head. Her bra went next and she sank back down and let him look. It was hard. She wanted to cover up, insecure about her older body, yet she knew he would have none of it and if he was going to be turned off, now was the time to know. She held her breath as his gaze slid slowly down her body. She willed herself to be confident the way the other cougars were.

"My God, you're gorgeous," he said in a low voice. "Why you'd want to bind yourself in that contraption, I'll never understand." He swallowed visibly. "I want to be inside you right now. May I?"

His words and the obvious sincerity of them did almost more to turn her on than his tongue. The dull throbbing of her clit picked up speed. Her nipples tingled and hardened even more. "Please," she invited.

Mark grinned as he toed off his shoes and yanked at his belt. It wasn't his usual boyish grin, more of a wolfish, "I'm going to eat you" kind of grin. Except that he already had eaten her and she was the one who was starving for more. His clothes disappeared in seconds. He stood by her bed, naked and beautiful. His body was honed to perfection, every muscle sculpted. His cock jutted out ready for action and glistened with pre-cum. He fished through his wallet and pulling out a condom, tossed the wallet aside.

"I promise this is new and reliable," he said as he covered himself. His head jerked up. "Which sounds like I was planning on this happening, and I sort of was, but it was more like a hope than an assumption."

Grace laughed to set him at ease, and opened her nightstand to show him the box of condoms she had put there the previous night. It was all Danny's idea, but no need to tell Mark that. He laughed too.

"Excellent." He joined her on the bed, on his side, facing her. He caressed her hair before leaning down to kiss her. His tongue danced with hers, and she sank farther into her mattress with boneless pleasure as the heat slowly built within her once more. Mark trailed his fingers down her face and neck, stopping when he reached her breast. His thumb flicked at her hard nipple, making her moan deep into his mouth. He moaned back.

Not wanting him to have all the fun, she reached between them to encircle his cock with her fingers. It jumped in her hand, and his hips bucked forward when she tugged his stiff flesh. Groaning, he nudged her hand away and rolled onto her. He released her mouth. "Sorry, Grace, but I can't wait."

"I don't want you to," she replied and inhaled sharply when he entered her.

He stilled. "Did I hurt you?"

"No, don't stop," was her strangled reply. It had been so long. Her body had almost forgotten what it felt like to be filled by a man. But she was slick from her earlier orgasm and primed for another. She opened her legs as wide as she could and welcomed him deep inside her aching pussy.

He moved slowly at first, his strokes long and easy. He was trying to be gentle with her, yet now that she was acclimated to the invasion of his cock, she wanted it faster and harder. Pressing her heels against his tight ass, she urged him on. He got her message, picking up the pace, his cock thrusting in quick, short strokes. His mouth found hers again. His tongue mimicked the rapid movements below. Grace's climax crested, crashed, her pussy clamped down tight. Her fingers dug into his shoulders. She cried out and heard Mark echo her. His body slammed into hers a few more times before he collapsed on top of her, a dead weight.

Right away he tried to move off her, but she held him tight. She loved the sensation of a man lying on her. She had missed it, she had missed all of it. Hugging her lover closer to her, she closed her eyes and simply enjoyed herself. Tonight her life had started again. Sleep claimed her, and she let it, a smile on her face.

* * * * *

Grace opened her eyes to sunlight peeking from behind her curtains. The clock on her nightstand said it was five past nine. Her body told her she'd had one hell of a night. She winced at the ache in her lower back and inner thighs. But she smiled at the sight of the large, strong body lying beside her. Mark was turned toward the wall, still sleeping. He had spent the night and had woken her once during it to coax her into another round. She had been more than willing. Now all she could think of was how morning was not her best look. Quietly as she could, she snuck into the bathroom to pee and touch up her makeup. She was in the middle of hiding her bags, when the door opened. Mark lounged against the doorjamb, looking at her through the mirror with sleepy eyes. His cock was fully locked and loaded with a condom on.

"Hope you're not going to that trouble for me," he drawled.

Grace spoke to his reflection. "Well I'm not doing it for me."

He shook his head and came all the way in. He hugged her from behind and nuzzled her throat. "You don't have to put that gunk on. I find you plenty hot the way you are." For emphasis, he rubbed his cock against her ass.

Grace gave up. Turning in his arms, she gave him a shove. He stood back with eyebrows raised and a concerned look. She ran her hands up his pecs and circled his hard brown nipples with her thumb. "I think I owe you something," she teased.

"Huh?"

She licked a nipple before dropping to her knees. His cock waved in front of her. Clasping its base, she swallowed the hardness as far down as she could.

"Holy fuck!" Mark braced his legs farther apart and entwined the fingers from both hands in her hair. "You do not have to do this," he whispered. "But damn that feels good."

Grace grinned around the mouthful and tugged and lapped while her other hand played with his balls. She wanted to take him in completely, but he was just too big so she contented them both by working the head of his cock. As a doctor, she knew a man's pleasure spots better than most women. She flicked the skin underneath the glans with her tongue. Mark rewarded her with grunts and jerks until suddenly, he pulled her up literally by her hair.

He spun her around and bent her over the countertop. "Watch," he commanded as he slowly impaled her pussy from behind. Eyes wide open, she watched him as he watched her. She gnawed at her lower lip as he filled her and gasped as he went as deep as he could. "I'm going to fuck you nice and slow until we both can't stand it anymore," he promised.

Sliding his hands down to her waist, he held her firm as he began to thrust with long strokes. He acted as if he were lazy and had all the time in the world, the way his cock slid in and out with maddening slowness. But his face told a different story. His eyes blazed and his jaw was clenched. His chest rose and fell in ever more labored breaths. Her breathing had picked up, too. Not enough, though.

"I need more," she gasped.

"Easy, darlin', I've got you." He reached around to slide a couple of fingers between her labia. As he rubbed her clit, her climax climbed higher and faster, and the position forced him to enter her with shorter, harder thrusts.

"Yes, that's it," she encouraged. "Come on, Captain, make me come."

"Yes ma'am." His fingers twirled around her clit until she doubled over even more, forehead pressed against the counter. The climax burst throughout her body like a flower blossoming, radiating from the center. It left her limp and breathless and only vaguely aware of Mark pressed against her back, arms braced beside her head. He clamped his teeth on the back of her neck, shuddering at his own orgasm. When he was still, he let go of her neck only to press his forehead against her shoulder. "Got any plans for today?"

* * * * *

Mark eyed his objective with grim determination. This was going to be a tough assignment, but he needed to man up and get the job done. No way he'd let Grace see him fail. Not that he had anything to prove to her. He knew he had satisfied her in bed and out of it. Still, a man had his pride. He nodded once. "Okay, I'm ready."

"All you have to do is watch me," Grace assured him. "It's really very simple. I mean we're eating a lobster, not performing neurosurgery. If you can clean a rifle, you can get meat out of a boiled crustacean. These are soft shelled, too. A snap."

Mark remained unconvinced. Nevertheless, he wasn't about to look like a wimp or an idiot in front of the most fantastic woman he had ever met. Man, this was turning out to be the best leave of his life. Grace was amazing and the sex was mind-blowing. They were both making up for lost time, having made love twice in bed and twice in the bathroom, one of those times in the shower. That was a fantasy of his that he hadn't quite managed before today. He could cross it off the list and try for another. He was certainly ready for more action. But first, there was the little matter of the lobster. The tail on his plate last night had been plucked from the shell already. Grace had insisted he had to eat an entire boiled one at least once while in town. She had also talked him into going to the aquarium. It had been fun, although honestly doing anything with this woman was fine by him.

"Mark, you need to pay attention," she admonished gently.

"Sorry." He picked up his lobster with both hands the way she was.

"Fan out the tail and twist the shell where it meets the body. Like this." With a deft flick of her wrist, the lobster was now in two pieces.

Mark mimicked her motion, although his results were less impressive. He had rendered it in two, but had also crushed a bit of the shell at the same time, causing liquid to spurt on him.

Grace chuckled. "Not bad. Now you know what the bib is for."

Looking down at the tacky plastic tied around his neck, he saw the picture of the lobster mocking him. He tossed his chin toward Grace. "How come you're not wearing one of these?"

"I don't need one," she replied. "I'm what you'd call an expert." She couldn't finish the sentence without laughing. "Come on, the claws are next."

They dismembered their meals and she showed him how to use the crackers and pick. Every move was precise and confident. She knew what she was doing and he was fascinated by her. Plucking meat from one of the arms, she swirled it in drawn butter and held it out provocatively between two fingers. "This is the best kept secret of a lobster, the knuckle meat."

He leaned over the table and took the offered morsel in his mouth, sucking a couple of her knuckles in too. "Hmm. That is sweet," he agreed when he released her.

Her eyes sparkled with amusement. She yanked a lobster leg free and held it up to him. "This is the second best kept secret." Sucking it into her mouth, she clamped her teeth down on the shell as she slid the leg out slowly.

Holy Mother of God, if she kept this up, he was going to have to leave wearing the bib around his waist. He groaned softly. "You are killing me here, Grace."

She laughed again and nodded. "I know. I'm sorry. I don't know what got into me."

He grinned. "I did, Grace. I got into you. Would you like me to get into you again?"

It was her turn to groan. "Eat your lobster, Captain Bennington," she retorted primly.

Clamping down on a lobster leg, he mumbled, "Yes, ma'am."

* * * * *

It was probably a bad idea to spend what was left of their now weekend date by going to check up on Conroy. Grace just couldn't shake the nagging feeling about the guy. She could tell, too, that it was weighing on Mark even though he insisted he wasn't worried. If they didn't check up on the vet, he was going to figuratively end up in bed with them anyway. Might as well see how things were going with the guy. Maybe everything was fine and they could continue to enjoy what was left of the weekend. She didn't think so, but she could hope.

The area of Boston where Mark said Conroy's favorite bar was located, the area where Conroy himself lived, was not the sort of place she would wander around alone at night. She was with Mark, though. She felt safe with him, his strong arm wrapped around her waist, hugging her close. He wore the same clothes as on their date, with the sleeves rolled up because of the heat. It had the effect of showing the world his impressive biceps. Guys were giving them a wide berth as they sauntered down the sidewalk. He stopped in front of a rundown bar that was trying to look like a quaint Irish pub.

"This is the most likely place," Mark said as they eyed the front door. "It's pretty rough inside. I'd leave you out here, but it's pretty rough out here too. Sorry."

"There's nothing to apologize for. I pressed for this and I'm not worried about the inside or the outside as long as we stick together. I trust you to keep me safe."

He swung her closer for a quick kiss. "Why thank you, ma'am." He took a deep breath and exhaled slowly. "Let's see if he's here."

It took a few seconds for her eyes to adjust to the gloom of the place. Before the smoking ban, it must have been even more dark and bleak. In any event, there was not much to see. It was pretty packed for a Sunday night, people sitting around and drinking, standing around and drinking, and shooting pool way in the back and drinking. From the looks of the patrons and the raucous wall of sound that hit Grace the moment she entered, it was clear drinking had been going on for a while. She clung close to Mark as he cut their way through the crowd to the bar. It was easy to spot Conroy's red hair. He sat way at one end, a couple of young women hanging on him.

Mark stopped behind his friend and tapped him on the shoulder. Conroy whirled around, fist raised. Mark dropped Grace's hand to put both of his up in surrender. "Whoa, sorry, buddy. I wasn't thinking."

Conroy's expression was fierce and he didn't change it or lower his fist for long seconds. Mark stood patiently, waiting for his friend to process what was going on. It was obvious he had experienced this before. If Grace had had any doubt about Conroy's PTSD, it was gone now. She waited, tense, ready to intervene if Conroy followed through with his threat.

He didn't. Lowering his hand, he grinned. "Hey, look who's back. How'd your date with Doctor Mom go?" His gaze flicked to Grace as Mark silently lowered his hands. "Shit, I guess you got lucky. Hey, Doc." He raised a beer bottle toward Grace in greeting.

Mark's arm curved around her waist again. He tugged her close and glared at his friend. "Try not to be such an asshole, Sean. We're here to let you know that I'm hanging with Grace for the rest of the night. You didn't answer your cell."

Conroy shrugged and tipped his beer back to drain it. The women with him gave Grace the once-over and dismissed her. They were not dismissing Mark, however. "Why don'tcha stay and play with us, Mahk?" one of them offered, thrusting her barely clad breast forward.

Grace rolled her eyes.

"You got something to say, moms?" her friend challenged. Grace raised her eyebrows at the woman, at a loss for words. *Am I supposed to get into some kind of cat fight?*

She was saved the trouble by Conroy, of all people. He laughed. "Easy, Kerry, the doc here was in the army. She'll beat your pretty ass for sure." He rapped his knuckles on the countertop. "Another beer, Joey."

Mark shook his head. "We're leaving. I need to go back to your place and get clean clothes. I don't suppose you'll come with us."

Conroy just laughed and turned away. Without another word, Mark spun around and headed for the door, Grace in tow. Once they were outside, he grabbed her for another quick kiss. "I'm sorry about that." He turned to lead her down the sidewalk, still clinging tight to her waist.

"Why are you apologizing? It was my idea. That man needs help."

"I know." He sounded frustrated, and she realized she was dumping too much on him.

"He's not your responsibility. You've done as much as you can."

"Maybe." He gave her a slight smile. "Anyway, let's get my stuff and go back to your place. I've had a great day, Grace, and I want to have another great evening. No more Sean for now."

"No more Sean," she agreed.

* * * * *

It was wonderful to get back to the quiet and peace of her home. Mark's presence didn't detract from the feeling, either. He made it better because her body was already aroused with thoughts of how they might spend the evening and the night. The way he eyed her, he had to be thinking along similar lines. Because he had changed into jeans, she couldn't tell as well if he was aroused. Still, there was a good-sized ridge behind his zipper. It promised delightful possibilities.

"You keep looking at me that way, Dr. McKinnon, and I'm going to take you right here and now."

The breath whooshed out of her lungs. Her clit throbbed and her nipples tingled at the thought. She pictured him shoving her against the wall, lifting her leg and driving his cock inside her. She imagined clinging to him and sobbing as the climax overtook her. She wanted it. She wanted him. Now.

Grace took a step toward Mark and the doorbell rang. She stopped and frowned. Who would come over on a Sunday night? Oh, God, not Aaron? She had left him a message about being busy the previous night. He wouldn't be so bold as to simply drop by. Raising a finger up to Mark, she said, "Hold that thought." When she opened the door, she found Danny on the other side with a small bowl in his hand. She narrowed her eyes at him.

He smiled broadly, not even trying to hide his effort to see past her. "Hey, there. I was hoping to borrow a cup of sugar."

"Sugar?"

"Yup," he replied, pushing his way gently into the apartment. "I'm making chocolate chip cookies and wouldn't you know I forgot to get more sugar at the store. Hi, I'm Danny Briggs, Grace's neighbor." He stood in front of Mark, with a shit-eating grin on his face, one hand extended.

"Mark Bennington." He took the offered hand and was nearly knocked off balance when Danny gave a vigorous shake.

"My," Danny practically cooed. "The army does keep our boys fit."

Mark stared at the other man, with a deer-in-the-headlights look.

"Ugh," Grace exclaimed under her breath. Damn her nosy friend, although she did have him to thank for the waxing and the condoms and the beer. She hadn't intended her questionable date to turn into a night of marathon sex, but given that it had, she was very glad to have been prepared. The day had been fantastic, too. She was relaxed and happy with Mark, as if they were old friends. His presence by her side kept her in a constant state of arousal, as well. Never in her life had she gone for two nights in a row with a guy, but she was raring to go with Mark.

"Don't get comfortable, Danny," she called over her shoulder as she opened the cabinet door for the sugar.

"Isn't she delightful? I've known her for less than a year, but if I weren't gay, I'd have proposed already."

Oh. My. God. Grace tore out of the kitchen and shoved a five-pound bag of sugar at Danny. "Here." She gave him the evil eye, hoping he'd take the hint and leave before she killed him.

Taking a second to juggle the bowl and the bag, Danny grinned back at her. "Thanks, girlfriend. I'll be baking 'til the cows come home with this."

"Enjoy." Grace grabbed one of Danny's elbows and propelled him to the door.

"Nice meeting you, Mark," Danny called as he was shoved out into the hallway.

"Ah, yeah, you too," Mark replied, uncertainty in his tone.

Grace whirled around and pressed her back against the closed door. "Sorry about Hurricane Danny. He can leave a lot of destruction in his wake."

Mark grinned. "Naw, he was just checking me out. That's what friends do. Think I passed inspection?"

"His drool factor was pretty high, so I'd say yes."

"That's good," he replied coming toward her at a lazy pace. "Although what really matters to me, is passing it with you." Reaching her, he tugged her into his arms and kissed her long and slow. When they came up for air, he rested his forehead against hers and spoke quietly. "This has been one of the best days of my life."

The confession startled her. This was only a fling, wasn't it? Of course, what else could it be given the difference in their ages and the fact that he would be gone in a week or so. She pulled back a little to look him in the eye. She saw sincerity there as well as desire. His gaze was blazing hot, pupils wide and dark. Seeing the intensity of arousal there, she relaxed and bathed in the attention. He was only a man trying to get a woman into bed. That's what made him say something so strong. No problem given how much she wanted to get him back into her bed, too.

"It's not over," she teased, nipping at his lower lip. "What would you like to do?"

"Oh, Doc," he moaned. "I've got a list that would take us a year. We've already knocked off one item." When she looked at him quizzically, he explained. "The shower."

She raised her eyebrows and squeezed his behind. Such a nice firm handful. "Really? That was so tame. Surely you've had sex in a shower before?"

Wincing, he shook his head. "Nope. That was a first for me. I have to confess I haven't been with a lot of women."

She pressed her lower half against him and rubbed the ridge straining within his jeans. "You could have fooled me."

"Oh!" he grunted and returned the rub. "You are killing me here, and thanks, I aim to please. Honestly, though, you're like number six. I was with my first girlfriend throughout high school and West Point. She was pretty conservative, so we didn't do much experimenting. Then she dumped me halfway through my first deployment."

"Oh, the bitch!"

Mark laughed. "I think I may have referred to her as such for awhile, but really it was for the best. Not everyone is cut out to serve or to wait at home for those who do serve. You know how it is."

"I do." Grace moved her hands to his front and worked them under his t-shirt. Running her fingers up his chest, she cupped his pecs. "Her loss."

"Yeah, well, what with other deployments, I haven't dated much since her and haven't had any relationships that lasted long enough for me to feel comfortable pulling out the list." He leaned over and traced her outer ear with his tongue. "It was a happy coincidence that you fulfilled one this morning."

"So what's at the top of that list? What's the one thing you'd really like to try?"

"Hmm," he replied with a frown. "No, I don't think so. If you have any chocolate sauce, we can try one farther down," he added with a grin.

She wanted to argue, but she could see he was uncomfortable. With a sly grin of her own, she nodded.

Picking her up, he twirled her around. "Hot, damn! This is the best day of my life."

Grace held on tight, enjoying the ride and the image of what they would do with the chocolate sauce. Maybe Mark was right. Maybe this was the best day of her life, too.

* * * * *

Mark watched the ribbon of chocolate slowly envelope one of Grace's dusky nipples. Half gone when they started, the bottle of syrup was almost empty. He had squeezed it and lapped chocolate up one side of Grace's body and down the other. He had almost had his fill of the sweet, but he doubted he would ever be done tasting this woman.

She was pinned under his body, her arms stretched over her head, held there by his hand clasped around her wrists. He hadn't intended to dominate her physically, that hadn't been part of the fantasy at first. But the way she writhed and bucked as his tongue and lips licked and sucked at her sensitive skin risked the fun ending too soon. If he let her go, she had made it clear she would get his cock inside her pussy as fast as she could. She was begging for release, but he wasn't done yet, not by a long shot.

With a snap of the bottle's cap, he tossed the container aside and latched onto her chocolate-covered nipple. He sucked hard and was rewarded with a cry from Grace. She arched her back up off the bed, pressing closer to him. With his free hand, he helped her effort to give him even better leverage to lave and nip the hard nub inside his mouth. Her legs moved restlessly, entwining his, trying to move him so that his cock would slide between her legs. He chuckled against her flesh, amused at her efforts and damn pleased at his control of her body. His cock was more than ready for her—hard, aching, sheathed for action. It lay heavy against her thigh. When she writhed as she was now, it twitched with impatience. It wanted in her hot, tight core, too. Almost, not yet. He wanted to make this last.

"Mark," Grace groaned, "please, I can't stand it."

With a final tug, he let go of her nipple and grinned down at her. "You have to stand it, darlin'. Remember this is my fantasy."

"Fuck that," she ground out. "Fuck me, now."

He answered her with a kiss, tongue thrust deep inside her welcoming mouth, letting her taste the chocolate that lingered. His hand cupped her breast, rubbing her distended nipple with his thumb. Her skin was sticky. He let the friction drive her arousal even higher. She thrashed harder against his hold, her need spiraling out of control. He wouldn't be able to hold her much longer without hurting her, and that was not in his plans. His own climax was building fast and hard, too. If he didn't slide into her soon, he would disappoint them both. So he shifted to lie flat on top of her. He released her breast to use both hands to hold hers. Palm to palm, he held her arms over her head and pressed her body deeper into the mattress. His mouth never wavered in its assault. With his knee, he pushed her legs farther apart, spreading them as wide as he could. He settled between them, cocked his hips back and thrust home.

Grace screamed inside his mouth. The walls of her pussy clasped his rigid flesh in repeated spasms as her orgasm overtook her. She lifted her legs and tilted her hips to take him in deeper. She met each push with one of her own. He was embedded into her tight pussy so far his balls slapped against her ass. Her heels dug into his backside urging him on, riding the climax for long seconds. When her cries turned into short, quick whimpers of pleasure, he kept going, taking her with steady thrusts, trying to make it last, hoping to make her come again. He concentrated on keeping the semen from exploding out of him. He didn't have long to wait, thank God. As soon as her movements slowed, they picked up again. He could feel the tension rise within her once more. She moaned deep and low. Her teeth clamped down to bite his tongue as her body bucked against him. Mark let go. The climax burst out of him. He pounded hard and fast as the waves of pleasure surfed his whole body.

When he was spent, he collapsed on top of Grace. The two of them lay boneless, arms and legs tangled, chests heaving as they caught their breaths. Neither spoke, but they didn't have to. And he had been right. It had been the best day of his life.

Chapter Five

ℳ

Happy Monday morning, ladies! I have three words for you. Hot. Heavy. Sex. Thank you all for your support. Any time I started to doubt myself, I thought of your encouraging words. I've got a week of fun to look forward to. I'll keep you posted.

Grace

I am so glad I issued that challenge. :-) It brings a tear to my eye to think how many people are having Hot. Heavy. Sex. because of me. Sniff.

Monica

Grace tried to concentrate on the chief of staff's lecture, but all she could think about was Mark's sex list and what they were going to try that night. They had spent the better part of a week together, meeting after her shift ended, trying things that were new to him and sometimes new to her too. As sex acts went, they were pretty tame. They had licked chocolate off each other, sixty-nined, had sex on the dining table, sex on the couch and sex in her office. Okay that last one had been on her list.

She didn't want to think about how his leave was up in a couple of days. He would go back to his base, deploy to Afghanistan, and she'd return to her blasé life. It was a depressing thought. She preferred to scheme about the best way to get him to tell her his biggest fantasy. So far he had demurred and her curiosity was really piqued. How kinky could it be? She wanted to give him something to remember her by, something that he might pull out along with his cock from time to time to enjoy. At least he could until the real thing came his way. It would. He'd find a woman, younger than she, who would willingly retry the list. It was the right thing for all concerned, yet the thought of him with another woman bothered her. Stupid. He was a young man. He should be with a young woman, while she, Grace, would have to decide whether settling for Aaron was the best plan for the rest of her life. After the intense pleasure of Mark, she was even less sure settling for anyone was tolerable.

As soon as the lecture was over, she ran out of the hospital and into Mark's arms. He had taken to meeting her there after her shift. They both wanted to wring as much out of their time together as they could. She kissed him hungrily, not caring if people she worked with saw her. There was nothing wrong with living a little. Mark looked younger than he really was, but she had never cared what other people thought anyway.

"God, kissing you sweeps away the life-sapping tedium of a staff meeting."

Hugging her close, he echoed the sentiment. "Kissing you chases away the irritation of spending the day with Sean. He used to be a fun guy," he added with a frown.

"How is he?" They had pretty much agreed to keep Sean out of their time together after the previous Sunday night. It was hard to completely ignore, though, the reason she and Mark had met.

"The same. He drinks too much and is testy and jumpy and morose when he's sober. He won't listen to me. I can't convince him he needs help." He shrugged. "What shall we do for dinner?" Arm around her waist, he steered toward the T station. Although she had a car garaged in the city, the public transportation system was more convenient.

"How about pizza?"

He stopped. "Really. Pizza's okay?"

"Of course. It's the one thing we haven't had yet together, and my generation eats it too you know. You kids didn't invent it or anything."

They continued on. "Shit, Grace, you are not of a different generation. Do you have a place in mind? Can we call ahead and pick it up, eat it at your place?" He pinched her side. "'Cause, honestly darlin' I can't wait to get you naked."

Grace gasped then laughed and pulled out her phone to call her favorite pizza place. "What do you want on it?"

"Anything you like."

"You might regret that." The restaurant picked up and she ordered mushrooms, green peppers and anchovies. Mark grimaced at the last item, but said nothing. When she was done, she asked, "Is there anything on your list involving pizza?"

He gave her a sly look. "Maybe."

* * * * *

Mark couldn't believe his good fortune. Here he was sitting stark naked on a beautiful woman's bed eating pizza and drinking beer. Life had never been better, except he was leaving soon and wouldn't see Grace for a year or more. He wasn't even sure he'd be able to see her when he got back. Neither had brought it up, but he would tonight or tomorrow morning because it was too important to let go. This had started out as a fling, made more stimulating by the age difference. A few days in Grace's company, however, had changed the rules of the game. He was taken with her in way he hadn't experienced since Meghan. In fact, when he thought of the childish love he had felt for his old girlfriend, it was nothing like the feelings bubbling inside him now. Things were different. Grace was different. The thought of leaving her hurt. The thought that she might see this only as a fling, and nothing more, hurt worse.

He needed to put these thoughts aside. At the moment, the pizza was half gone and the last of his beer was sliding down his throat. His cock was stiff and had been since he first held Grace in his arms that evening. Part of this particular fantasy was waiting while they ate. He wanted to draw out the anticipation, make them both crazy with need. If the ache in his balls was any indication, it was working. Grace sat propped up against the headboard, facing him with her legs spread. He could see her nether lips were wet from her arousal. Seeing the evidence of her desire made him even more hard.

"What are you staring at?" she asked and sipped lazily at a glass of wine.

"I'm staring at how much you want me."

"Oh, really?" she drawled.

"Yes, ma'am. Makes for a nice change given that my erection always gives me away."

"Men are simple creatures." She paused. "Your list is pretty tame, too, I have to tell you. Can't I convince you to share the big one?"

Oh, no. No way he was going to ask for that. It was something a woman gave to a man she trusted. He couldn't expect her to feel that way about him. It was too soon. But it was sweet for her to ask. "No, ma'am."

"How bad could it be? I mean does it involve rubber?"

He rolled his eyes. "No."

"Whips?"

He debated a second. "No, but if you want you could try it on me. I do not hurt women, ever."

"Good to know, and for the record, I could warm up to the whip thing." She heaved a sigh. "So not BDSM. Farm animals?"

He barked out a laugh. "Good God, no!" Grace grew pensive and when the silence dragged on, he prodded her.

"What could you possibly be thinking that's worse than farm animals?"

She looked him in the eye. "Not worse, but another woman? You want a threesome. Maybe with a younger woman?"

Shoving the pizza box aside, he kneeled between her legs and put their drinks on the nightstand. He cupped her face with both hands, determined to make sure she believed him. "No, Grace," he answered in a low voice. "That is not on my list. One woman is plenty for me, and I do not, I repeat, *do not* fantasize about being with a younger woman when I'm with you."

"Okay, then you really need to tell me what's at the top of your list because my imagination can run wild."

Shit. It was embarrassing and presumptuous, she'd tell him no, and then maybe they could get down to fucking. *Big deal, just say it.* "Anal." He grimaced as soon as he said it and waited for her reply. She surprised the hell out of him.

"That's it? Anal? You want to have anal sex?" When he nodded, she added, "Who fucks whom?"

Oh wow, it had been so obvious to him. Clearing his throat, he answered. "I do you?" Even now he was freaked out about saying it, about asking for it. Hell, if she wanted to fuck him with something, then okay. It would not be on any list he would ever draw up from now until the end of time, but whatever Grace wanted, he'd give her.

"Okay."

What? His brain froze. "I don't think you understand me, here. I'm talking about sticking my cock up your lovely ass." Crude, yet clear. He'd be lucky if she didn't toss him out on *his* ass.

"I get it. I'm a doctor, remember. Human anatomy is my profession. I said okay." Wrapping her hands around his, she added, "I've done it before."

"Really?" She nodded. "And you liked it well enough to do it again?" She nodded once more and released his hand to grab his cock. It jumped.

"I think your cock is rooting for this."

Mark closed his eyes and moaned his appreciation. "If it liked it any better, I'd be coming in your hand."

"Can't have that. Scoot back." Eyes open, he complied. Grace kneeled on the side of the bed and pulled a condom and a tube of lube out of the nightstand drawer. She turned to him. "We have to do this slowly."

"Yes, ma'am." He was afraid to speak, afraid to breathe. He couldn't believe this was happening. "Whatever you say."

"Lie down." He dropped down onto his back and steadied her when she straddled him. "We start with getting me as worked up as we can."

"I can do that."

"Yes, you can. Give me your right hand." When he complied, she squeezed a dollop of lube on his index and middle fingers. "Use that to massage my sphincter while you eat me out. Can you do that?"

"I'm an excellent multi-tasker."

"We'll see." She shifted so that her pussy was hovering above his mouth and squatted low enough to give his tongue access. He lapped at her clit with long, slow strokes while his finger played with the puckered hole of her luscious bottom. Just touching her there while licking her was enough to send him over the edge. To ward off the climax, he pictured taking his rifle apart. *Oh, man, I have to hold on.*

Grace clung to her headboard, writhing and moaning. He picked up the pace, and when she pressed her pussy lips against his body and shouted out her release, he poked his finger inside her. "Yes, that's it, don't stop," she gasped.

Her anal passage welcomed his finger with a tight heat that he had never felt before. He could only imagine what it was going to be like to have his cock there instead. His hardness increased with expectation. His balls pulled up tighter. He changed his rhythm, sucking her clit with gentle pressure, while his finger stroked inside Grace.

She bounced slowly down to take him in more. "Try two."

He thought it was too soon, but didn't argue. His cock was dying to replace the finger. It wanted in and he had to trust Grace to set the right pace. He added the second finger and was thrilled by how relaxed she was. It wasn't long before she came again. Her body swayed and she gave a low moan. He kept sucking and thrusting until she pulled away from his face and reached around to still his hand.

"Are you all right?" he demanded, worried he had been too rough.

"Shh," she quieted his concern and picking up the condom, covered his aching, straining cock. Then she slathered on the lube.

"Are you sure?" He hardly dared breathe, but he had to be sure.

"Shh," she admonished again, and eyes closed she lowered herself onto his rod.

Her descent was slow, agonizingly slow. The head of his cock popped past her sphincter and entered that amazing world of heat and pressure. It was unlike anything he had ever experienced. The fit was tighter than a pussy, tight enough to almost make him come immediately. He fought back the tide, wanting to make the experience and the pleasure last. He wanted to thrust up inside Grace hard and fast. Not being able to do that, having to stay still, kicked the heat up. He groaned. "God, Grace."

"Like this?" she teased in a husky voice.

"You're killing me." He opened his eyes enough to see her grinning down at him as she impaled her body on his. She pumped using short strokes. He wasn't going to last much longer. He had to make this good for her, too. He used the palm of his left hand to circle her clit and thrust his thumb inside her pussy. He could feel his own cock inside her other channel and that was it for him. Arching his neck, he yelled as the orgasm claimed him. His body quivered with the effort not to writhe. The blood roared in his ears but not so much he didn't hear Grace call out his name.

She collapsed on top of him. His cock slid out of her ass. He could do nothing more than cradle her in his arms as sleep claimed them both.

* * * * *

Grace stepped out of the shower and stretched. The heat had helped ease muscles sore from the heavy workout they had received the past few days. She had no complaints, though. She had taken the challenge and now it was over. The memories of her time with Mark would stay with her for the rest of her life. She would never forget in particular the look on his face when she lowered herself onto him last night. It had made him so blissfully happy. Such an easy thing to give. She was glad she had pressed for his number one fantasy.

She entered her bedroom quietly, hoping Mark was still asleep. He wasn't. He was lying in bed, grinning at her. "Why didn't you wake me?"

"You're on vacation. You should be able to sleep in. Besides," she added grabbing underwear from a drawer, "I'm afraid I wasn't up for another round this morning."

He shot up to a sitting position. "Did I hurt you?"

"No," she assured him because he hadn't. She was fine and even felt delightfully wicked about what they had done. "You worry too much."

He dropped his eyes and his voice. "I care about you, Grace."

Her heart did a slow roll, ending with a stab of pain. He would be gone soon. She wished it weren't so and it was stupid for her to feel that way. He was a young man on leave.

He would get on with his life with a pleasant memory of his somewhat wild time with an older woman. Briskly getting dressed, she said, "I care about you, too, Mark." There was a brief silence while she rummaged in her closet for something to wear.

"I'd like to keep in touch while I'm deployed," he said in an uncertain tone.

Her breath hitched as she strived for a casual reply. "Sure. I'll give you my email address. Let me know where to send care packages. My sister used to send them to me all the time. I know what a difference they make." She shoved her body into pants and a shirt, blinking back tears. Stupid. So stupid. What was the matter with her? She forced a smile on her face and turned to look at him.

He stared back at her, frowning. "I'll appreciate the care packages, believe me, but just being able to talk to you would be awesome." He looked away briefly. "I mean I'd like to keep in touch and maybe see you again when my tour is done. I know that's a lot to ask," he added quickly. "We haven't known each other long and there'll be lots of other guys who'll ask you out. I'm just hoping, that's all."

Stunned and confused, Grace grabbed her hair brush. With harsh strokes, she took out tangles and braided her wet hair. She couldn't look at him and wasn't sure how to respond.

"Grace? Say something, please."

She turned to face him. His feelings were plain to see on his face. It didn't mean anything. He was caught up in the moment. She had fulfilled his biggest sex fantasy. His hormones and maybe some sense of gentlemanliness were putting words in his mouth. Once he was back on base, among his peers, he'd see things differently.

"I've had a wonderful time with you, Mark." Her chest was so tight she could barely get the words out. "But we need to keep this in perspective."

"Shit," he said quietly. Closing his eyes briefly, he laid back down.

"No," she hastened to ease his upset. "Don't feel bad. I'm trying to be the realistic one here. I am older and I need to be rational about this."

"Fuck that." His soft tone took the edge off his words, but the bitterness underscored them nevertheless. "I don't care about your age."

Grace shoved on shoes. She was going to be late for work. She had not intended to have this talk until later. It was for the best, she supposed. "You will care about it eventually. You'll come back and start thinking about the future, about getting married and having children. You'll need a younger woman for that."

"I'm not even sure I want to have kids, but are you saying you can't have them?"

"Technically I can, but the odds at my age, the odds for the age I'll be at the time we could even begin to consider something like that? Not so good."

"Well, damn it, Grace, I'm not proposing. I want to see you again, is all. Can't we just see where this may lead?"

She shook her head and grabbed her purse. "I can't see stringing either of us along when it's most likely a no-go in the long run. It's foolish. Look, I'm sorry. I have to get to work."

"Okay. We'll talk about this later when I pick you up."

She stopped at the doorway and took a deep breath. This was hard, horribly hard, harder than what she had done to earn that bronze star. "I don't think you should. I think it's best if we say goodbye now. You only have a couple of days left anyway."

He shot up and made to get out of bed. "No!"

Holding up her hand, she said, "Yes." Her tone was firm, final. She waited for his acquiescence.

The hurt she caused him was plain to see. His gaze was set firmly at a point beyond her, his jaw locked in a grimace. After a few tense seconds, he gave in. "Whatever you say, ma'am."

Not trusting her voice, Grace turned and walked away.

* * * * *

Grace shifted a bag of groceries and opened up her apartment door. Not having Mark with her made everything quiet and lonely. Work had dragged on, too, without the prospect of seeing him. Damn, how had things gotten so out of hand? She needed to pull herself together and put the hot young man out of her mind. He was not for her. He was never going to be for her. She shouldn't have lost sight of that obvious fact. Entering her place, she didn't bother to shut the door because she heard Danny opening his. Great, that's all she needed, a tongue-lashing from her friend.

"Where's G.I. Joe?"

Grace closed her eyes and prayed for patience. "I have no idea," she replied pulling her meager food out of the bag.

Danny propped himself against the kitchen counter. "Don't tell me you had a fight."

She shrugged. "Not so much a fight as a reality check." When Danny raised his eyebrows at her, she explained. "He wanted to keep in touch and see each other again when he got back."

"The bastard!"

Smiling despite her misery, she gave her friend the details he was looking for. "I reminded him of the folly of staying together long term. Our age difference could survive a fling, but happily ever after?" She shook head and shoved the last of the groceries into the refrigerator. There was still some beer in there, beer she had bought for the first date only because Danny had insisted. In the days that followed, she had been glad to have it for Mark and had tried to enjoy it herself. Now it would sit untouched, a reminder of her time with him. "You should take the beer with you."

Danny followed her into the living room and flopped down on the couch beside her. "You're being an idiot, you know."

"I'm being realistic. I know this is not one of my erotic romance stories. This is real life. Once Mark is back among people closer to his own age, he will realize for himself that it won't work between us."

"Yeah, because he spent his leave in the retirement village known as the City of Boston and you happened to be the youngest piece of ass he could hook up with." She blinked at him. What was he talking about? Danny sighed. "See, your problem is that you forget he was hanging with his age-appropriate friend already and that they were perfectly capable of prowling for hot, young things. And yet, he asked you out. It says something about the two of you."

Grace opened her mouth to argue. The phone rang, taking her attention instead. She got up to see the caller ID and groaned. It was Aaron. Just what she needed. Then she realized, that *was* just what she needed. Aaron, sensible, safe Aaron, man who already fitted neatly into her life. She picked up the phone. "Hi Aaron."

"Hey, hi Grace." Her brother-in-law sounded happy she'd answered. "I'm glad I caught you."

"I just got home from my shift." Turning her back on Danny and his face of horror, she said, "I'm sorry about missing out on dinner the other night."

"That's okay, I know you're busy. I was hoping for another chance tonight. Are you free?"

"Yes, I am, actually. I'd love to meet you for dinner."

"Wonderful. Let's say Cammy's in a half hour."

Grace closed her eyes. "Yes, great." There was a kick to her heart. She ignored it. "See you in a bit."

* * * * *

Mark used his key to let himself into Sean's apartment. He had pizza and cola in the hope of keeping his friend inside and sober that night. He knew it was a long shot, but hell, what else was there for him to do? Grace. Shit, lovely Grace had kicked him in the balls in the nicest possible way of course. He felt kind of like he had after reading Meghan's Dear John email, a little sick, a little lost. It was stupid of him given how little time he had spent with this woman. They hadn't been going out for years or even weeks. It had only been a week really, hardly enough time to hurt as much as it did. If he had only kept his mouth shut, he could be with her now. Then he could have kept up with her by email and maybe she'd be so taken with him by the end of his deployment, she'd have welcomed him back. Maybe. It was too late now.

"Sean?" he called out, putting the food on the kitchen counter. Man, it was hot in the tiny apartment even with the window wide open. "Dude, where are you? I have pizza." Knocking on the bedroom door, he peered in and saw nothing but the unmade bed that was always in that condition. A quick look in the bathroom came up empty, too. Crap, had Sean gone drinking already? Of course he had. It was dinner time.

There was a noise outside the window. Mark frowned and crossed the room. He stuck his head out to see what was out there and his heart stopped for a second before pounding back to life. "Holy fuck, what are you doing out here!"

Sean was sitting over the edge of the fire escape, a bottle of beer in his hand. When he turned, Mark could see his friend carried more than a drink. He had a pistol. The seriousness of the situation sent Mark into high alert. At the same time, he knew he needed to keep it cool the same as he did in battle. He lowered his tone of voice. "Sean, what are you doing?"

"Thinking," his friend replied before taking a swig of the beer.

81

"Thinking? Well, why don't you come inside and we can think together without the gun."

"Naw, the gun is part of the thinking."

Mark took a deep breath. "Dude, you are seriously freaking me out here. Please come inside."

Sean shook his head and stared straight ahead. "Go away, Mark. Go fuck your cougar pussy. This doesn't concern you."

Ignoring the slam at Grace, Mark searched desperately for the right words. "This does concern me. You're my friend, Sean. I want to help. You can talk to me. I understand how you feel."

"No!" The shout made Mark jump. "You don't know," Sean continued in a quieter tone. "No one really knows, least of all a guy like you who always has his shit together."

Not always. Mark's shit was definitely not together at that moment. What the hell was he going to do? Call the police, he supposed. They had people trained to deal with suicides. "Okay, man, chill out. I'm leaving."

Sean turned to look at him. His expression was fierce. "Don't call the cops on me. Right now I'm just thinking. I hear or see cops and I'm going to stop thinking. You understand me."

Holding his hands up, Mark said, "I understand. I promise I won't call the cops." He pulled his head back inside the apartment and took his phone out of his pocket. No cops, but he needed help. There was only one person he could think to call.

Chapter Six

සා

"How's your salad?" Aaron peered at Grace over his fork and smiled.

"It's very good," she lied. He was so happy to have her go out with him, she didn't want to spoil it. It wasn't a bad salad, really, and they were having a pleasant evening out. They had covered their respective jobs and how disappointed they both were about the girls electing to spend the summer working near their college. It was the usual stuff they talked about, nothing particularly interesting, yet easy.

"You know, I was thinking maybe we could take a week in August and go visit the girls." He looked at her hopefully. Danny was right. Aaron was a handsome man with curly dark hair with a touch of grey. He was shorter and beefier than she liked, but virile in his own way. If she put a little effort into it, she could enjoy sleeping with him. Couldn't she?

"Oh," she hedged, not ready yet to make a decision. "I'll have to check my rotation schedule."

"Sure. Let me know and I'll take care of everything. This is all on me."

"Aaron, you don't have to pay my way."

"I want to. After all you've done for the girls and me, it's the least I can do."

She opened her mouth to argue and her phone rang. "Sorry, this could be a patient." Rummaging around in her bag, she found the phone and frowned at the number. Damn. She considered ignoring the call for about a second before caving. "Hi, Mark." Instinctively she turned away from Aaron. She didn't want him to see her expression.

"Grace, thank God. I wasn't sure you'd take my call."

His alarm was obvious. "What is it? What's the matter?"

"Sean's out on the fire escape, drinking and holding a pistol."

"What!" She stood up and slung her purse over her shoulder. "Have you called the police?"

"He said he'd off himself if I do. Grace, I'm scared shitless here. I don't know what to do."

"I'm on my way."

"Really?"

"Yes, of course. Sit tight and try not to do anything to antagonize him."

"Believe me I couldn't be sitting any tighter if I had tracers flying overhead. Thanks, Grace."

"I'll be there as soon as I can." Hanging up, she took a step toward the door before remembering where she was. "I'm sorry, Aaron, I have an emergency."

"Of course, don't worry about a thing. Should I come with you?"

"No," she called over her shoulder. "I'll call you later." She stopped and before she could think better of it, she turned back to him. "Aaron, you're a wonderful man. You should find someone to enjoy the rest of your life with. Mary would want you to. You don't have to settle for what's comfortable."

Neither do I, she realized as she rushed to Mark.

* * * * *

Grace flew through the front door of Sean's building and sprinted up the steps. The guy lived on the third floor, which meant he had a likely killing distance if he jumped. She didn't have to call or knock because Mark was waiting for her at the open door of the apartment.

"I was listening for you. That was fast."

"I got lucky with the cab." They were both speaking softly. She jerked her chin toward the window. "Out there?" When he nodded, she dropped her bag down on the couch and took a deep breath. "Okay, I'm going to see if I can talk to him. You need to call the police."

"I promised I wouldn't."

When she simply stared back at him with her eyebrows raised, he said, "Right, I'll call the police. Good luck and thanks again. I didn't know who else to turn to. Sean's family doesn't get him."

She put her hand on his arm and the warmth of his skin did wonders to calm her nerves. He was strong and it made her feel safe and strong in return. "I'm glad you called me."

She went to the window and poked her head out. There was Sean draining a bottle and cradling his gun. He had a faraway look on his face. "Hi, Sean." She kept her voice as low and soothing as she could. The last thing she wanted to do was startle him off his perch.

"Go away," he ordered without even looking at her.

Flinging a leg over the sill, she straddled it to see him better and to talk more easily. She only had to keep him focused on her and not on killing himself long enough for the right professional to get there. "Sorry, Sean, but I'm too worried about you and so is Mark. You're freaking him out here."

Sean shrugged. "Sorry but I can't think about anyone but myself right now. Mark doesn't understand. He's like Mr. Perfect. Nothing gets to him."

"I doubt that. We all have different ways of dealing with the stress of combat. Maybe Mark is better at hiding what bothers him than we are."

"No offense, Doc, but you don't understand, either. Not like I do."

"Oh, really?" She was going with her gut, which was killing her, but her gut told her to open up. She had something to say that might help this man. It was probably long past time for her to talk about what bothered her, too. It was uncomfortable talking about it in front of Mark, though. It shouldn't be considering what they had shared of themselves. But that had been about bodies and sex. This was far more intimate.

"I have a bronze star with a V Device." She said it as a matter of fact, not pride.

Sean snorted. "No way. You're a doctor. How'd you end up in battle?"

Grace closed her eyes briefly to gather her thoughts and courage. "My story's not remarkable. What happened to me happened to hundreds of other people. I was part of a small convoy heading out to a remote village to set up a one-day medical clinic. I was in the second vehicle and you know how it is. There's this interminable stretch of nothing, boring dusty nothing, and you get caught up in your own thoughts. Then it happens."

"I.E.D.," Sean said before she could. His voice was as dull as her trip had been until that moment.

"Yes. It was an improvised explosive device and it took out the first vehicle and part of mine. Then there was shouting and gunfire. One of the men in the vehicle in front survived the explosion, but as soon as he got out, he was cut down." She swallowed hard and forced herself to continue. "So, it was all this chaos and you freeze for a moment, not sure what to do. Then I grabbed my pack and jumped out, sure I was going to get hit. But by then, we were returning fire. The nurse with me was a young guy on his first tour. We got out on my side because it was the farthest from where the enemy was shooting. I could tell our driver and the man riding shotgun were hurt. We needed to get them out, but before we could, I saw the man who had been shot was still alive. He had crawled under the first vehicle."

The memories, and her emotions, the fear in particular, swamped her. She paused to catch a breath, pull herself together. Strong, warm fingers curled around the hand by her right side. She spared a glance in that direction and saw Mark kneeling by the window. He looked at her intently, nodded once in encouragement. Sean was looking at her now, too, instead of the street and his gun. His attention meant she had to continue. The solid presence of Mark gave her the power to do so. She took a deep breath.

"I ran to him and the nurse followed. Together we pulled the guy up and carried him over to an outcrop of rocks. It wasn't much, but it afforded some cover. My nurse started working on the guy. When I looked back, I could see one of the injured men stir in the cab. Those two guys were sitting ducks where they were. Someone had to go back for them. Someone had to confirm, too, that the others were beyond help."

"You could have sent the nurse," Sean muttered.

"I could have." She shook her head. "He was so young and newly married, and Christ, there was a baby on the way. So I ordered him to stay put and I went back."

"Gutsy." This was Mark. She glanced at him and saw admiration in his gaze. She rolled her eyes at him.

"It's what I had to do. You do what you have to do."

"Yeah, that's the hell of it." It came out of Sean as more of a sob, but it showed he was listening. If he listened, hopefully he wouldn't jump or shoot.

She licked her lips and took another deep breath. "I checked first on the ones I thought were already dead. They were, poor bastards. I knew them both. Bullets hit close enough to feel the heat of them. I wanted to run. I wanted to cry. No time for that, so I ran to the guys who were still alive. The first one was tough but doable. He wasn't that tall or heavy. I had to carry him because he was unconscious. I can't describe how scared I was. I don't expect I have to."

"No, ma'am." Both men said it, Mark's voice barely a whisper.

"Anyway, I made it back to the rock, left him with the nurse and went back. The driver needed help too only he was this big, burly sergeant. Carrying the first guy had already wrenched my back as I would later realize. The big problem, however, was how I was going to get this second man out. I was pretty sure I couldn't carry him and dragging him was going to expose us both to greater danger."

"You did it." Mark's voice was louder this time. There was pride in his tone. She was afraid to look at him for fear of breaking into tears.

"Sort of. When I got back to the truck, I was able to pull him out and then by some miracle one of the guys returning fire made his way over to me and we both carried him. I was never so relieved in my life as to see that guy come up by my side."

She went silent, the memories barraging her faster and harder than she had even imagined they would. It wasn't clear she was doing any good, although Sean at least was still listening. In the distance, she heard sirens. Help was on its way. She had to keep him distracted enough not to make good on his threat to Mark.

"I'm sorry, I'm not telling the whole truth."

Sean squinted at her. "Yeah?"

She kept her focus on him, but Mark squeezed her hand. He was giving her his total support. "Yeah, see the guy who came to help did all the carrying. He gave me his M16 so that I could cover him while he hauled the injured man to safety. At first I fired at nothing in particular, just creating noise and distraction. Then a group of insurgents broke past the truck and headed toward us."

"How many did you kill?" Sean's question was blunt. His tone weary.

Grace's sigh was weary, too. Mark's warm, firm lips pressed a kiss into her palm. It calmed her and helped her continue in her effort to distract Sean. She heard doors shutting and footsteps from around the building. Any minute now and her job would be done. "I don't know. Four," she amended. Continuing to lie to him was hardly going to help the situation.

"Do you see their faces at night?"

"Sometimes, but the thing that really gives me nightmares is how close I came to not being able to save that second man. In my dreams, no one comes to help and I try and I fail." She stole another glance at Mark. His expression was sympathetic and encouraging. She bathed in the sight for long seconds, the memories of her experience not so bad when she had his support.

"You're afraid you're going to screw up, let people down, your combat brothers and sisters, your family. You can't handle the pressure." Tears ran down Sean's face. "It never goes away. The fear never goes away."

"It helps to talk about it. I've said that a million times to others but this is the first time I've taken the advice myself. Thank you, Sean." She meant it. She turned to Mark and mouthed "thank you" to him too.

"I want the fear to go away." The guy was crying in earnest now. The bottle slipped from his grip and shattered below. There was the sound of running feet.

"Sean, there is help. Please put the gun down and come inside."

She didn't think he was going to do it, and then he did. Putting the gun on the fire escape, Sean crawled over to her. She climbed back into the room and was enveloped instantly by Mark's arms. As safe and wonderful it was, she understood when he let her go and hugged his friend close as soon as Sean was inside. The two men collapsed on the floor, Sean clinging to Mark, sobbing.

Mark looked up at Grace. There were tears in his eyes, as well, and something else. He was looking at her with love.

* * * * *

Mark sat in the waiting room, sipping a cola to steady his nerves. Images of the past few hours of his life kept flashing by. He tried to concentrate on the most important ones, the ones featuring Grace. She was helping to admit Sean temporarily to the psychiatric unit of her hospital. She had advised him to go home because it could take a while, and he had politely said "no fucking way". He was not going without her and where would he go anyway, back to Sean's? Yeah that's where he wanted to be, the place where he had almost seen his friend die and where he had heard the woman he was falling in love with bare her soul.

In truth, though, the second part he didn't mind. He only regretted that it took an extreme situation to get her to open up and that while she had included him in the telling, she hadn't been comfortable enough to tell him directly. There wasn't enough time, is all. If he had all the time in the world to spend with her, he was sure he could convince her they were good together. The age difference didn't matter. He wanted Grace. He needed Grace, and if what he had left with her was a couple more days, he'd take it. He'd convince her to take him back until his leave was up. If he had to beg, he'd beg. He would even play the "my best friend just tried to kill himself" card. And, yeah he was desperate, a man who was about to lose the woman he was falling in love with.

"Mark."

Engrossed in his thoughts, he had missed Grace's approach. He jumped up. "Hey, how's Sean?" She looked tired, but she was smiling.

"He's sedated. I've made arrangements for him to be transferred tomorrow morning to the VA hospital. His family's on their way. I think they finally understand how serious this all is and how much help he needs."

"Thank you. I don't know what would have happened if you hadn't been there."

She waved him away. "I'm glad I could help. I have to admit all of this helped me, too."

Mark nodded. "Getting stuff out is good. I knew you held something inside about how you earned the medal. I had no idea it was so rough."

"I don't think I really appreciated how much it bothered me, either. It was easy to brush aside the nightmares in the cold light of day. I had so much else to worry about, I kept burying it deeper and deeper."

She took a quick, harsh breath and moved closer to him. She clasped her hand in his and looked deeply into his eyes. The intensity of her gaze took his own breath away. "There's another reason why this whole thing helped me. It made me realize how much you matter to me. I thought I could have a nice, no-strings fling with a gorgeous younger man. I thought of it as my last hurrah before settling down for the rest of my life with someone safe that I don't love. I was wrong. At least my heart tells me I was wrong."

His breath came back in a whoosh. Raising both their hands, he kissed the back of hers, his gaze never leaving her face. "I want to say something here, but I'm terrified of saying the wrong thing, of pushing you away again."

She chuckled. "You can't. I promise you can't. I'm not sure if what I feel is love. I'm not sure we have a future together, age notwithstanding. There hasn't been enough time."

"Time doesn't always matter."

"No, not always. Still, we only have a couple of days and then you're gone. It will likely be a year or more before we see each other again. So why don't we take the days we have and see how it goes."

Mark didn't answer. He didn't think he needed to. This had been his plan all along. Instead of saying anything, he pulled Grace into his arms and kissed her long and slow. When they broke, he pressed his mouth to her ear. "You up for a list item?" When she nodded, he asked, "Know any closets close by?"

She gasped, but then she broke away from him, and tugging him by the hand, brought him around the corner and through a door. As soon as it was shut again, they were in near total darkness. Perfect. "Sorry, sweetheart," he whispered. "I need fast."

He needed fast? Well, so did she. Grace nearly giggled with delight as Mark spun her around and pressed her against the wall of the utility closet. She stayed where he put her and heard the rustling of clothes, heard the crinkle of a condom wrapper. Then his hands were on her, unbuttoning her pants, exposing her aroused bottom to the air. His fingers probed her labia, ran circles around her already wet clit. She gasped in pleasure when his cock entered her in one hard thrust. Her arms braced against the wall, she pushed back as he surged forward. He wrapped his arm around her firmly to hold her against him while his finger and thumb pinched her plump nipple through her shirt. As she writhed against his hold, he continued to set the wild pace, his fingers working her clit to a fury. His teeth sunk into the back of her neck while his body bucked harder, faster. He growled into her skin and her harsh breaths filled the small room. She wanted to shout as the climax overtook her. The need for quiet made the wave of pleasure all the more intense. Her body thrashed against her lover's, his embrace tightening as tremors racked him.

When it was over, when the last of their pleasure rumbled through their bodies, Mark held her tight against his chest until their breathing evened out. Then he redressed them both, and checking through a crack in the door, led her back out to the empty hallway.

She looked at him wide-eyed. "Wow, I'd really like to get a look at that list of yours."

He pulled her in for another quick kiss. "I promise to email it to you, one item at a time. And when I'm back, we can start checking them off one by one. I bet you have a list, too. We should start that one first."

Grace smiled and wrapped her arms around her soldier. "We already did the moment I met you."

Hey, Cougars. I'm sniffling over my keyboard. Mark left today. I gave him one hell of a send-off! I'm going to worry about him. I'm going to worry about us, too, and maybe he isn't the "one". If it doesn't work, though, I'm not going to blame it on age. I'm over that bull. We need to spread the word. Cougars of the world, take the challenge! You won't regret it.

Grace

It sounds like he might be the "one". But no matter what, he's important to you. So worry all you want, and come here for moral support. Send him lots of care packages with naughty letters. I'd want that if I were a soldier. Hmm, actually I want that anyway. Off to call my man.

Monica

Nobody knows what the future is going to bring. You have now, and now is pretty damn good. All you can do is enjoy the time you can carve with emails and letters, and hopefully a phone call or two, and then take it from there when he comes home. Oh, and when you come up for air, Kevin and I would love to have the two of you over for dinner.

I'm so proud of you for taking the risk with Mark. This is the biggest, best "told you so" I've ever had the pleasure of yelling from a rooftop. Please give him our best, or better yet, give us his addy to send some care packages.

Elizabeth

COPPING A FEEL

Lexxie Couper

&

Dedication

For my mutt, Hudson, who died while I was writing this tale. For eleven years you made me smile with your unconditional love, goofy doggy grin, wagging stubby tail and protective, unwavering loyalty. Writing without you curled up at my feet will somehow feel wrong. Thank you for being a part of our family for so long. Will miss you like crazy, mate.

Just try not to cock your leg on the Pearly Gates, okay?

Author Note

You'll find the women of Cougar Challenge and the Tempt the Cougar blog at

www.temptthecougar.blogspot.com

Trademarks Acknowledgement

The author acknowledges the trademarked status and trademark owners of the following wordmarks mentioned in this work of fiction:

Bugs Bunny: Time Warner Entertainment Company, L.P.

Glock: Glock, Inc.

Hells Angels: Hells Angels, Frisco, Inc.

iChat: Apple, Inc.

Law & Order: Universal TV Distribution Holdings LLC

Speedos: Speedo International B.V.

Volvo: AB Volvo and Volvo Car Corporation

Chapter One
Newcastle, Australia

ॐ

Darci Whitlam stared at the handset of her phone as if it had grown a set of arms and was trying to feel her up. Well, not feel her up as such, but grab her nipples through her t-shirt and bra and twist them until she cried uncle. What the hell had she just heard?

Her frown pulling hard at her eyebrows, she returned the handset to her ear and said, "Excuse me?"

"I want to bend you over the sofa and pump your sweet, tight cunt full of my hot cum."

Darci blinked. "Umm, yeah, that's what I thought you said."

Face igniting in red heat, she clunked the handset of her phone back in its cradle and chewed on her bottom lip. Bloody hell, that was the third dirty phone call she'd had this morning! Each from a different man, each describing in great detail what the caller wanted to do to her. What the hell was going on?

Turning back to the phone, she picked up the handset again and stared at it.

It's not going to give you the answer, Darci.

That was true, but she had to do something. For starters, find out why three men thought she, Darci-Rae Whitlam, an unassuming high-school English teacher in a small city on the East Coast of Australia, was, in fact, a telephone sex worker. How the hell did they get her private number? Not even the smartest student at school had unearthed that number, and Terry Cahill had been trying since year nine.

Shouldn't you be more worried about how everything that last caller said made you feel?

She pulled a face, dropping the handset back into the cradle once more and blowing at the fringe of her bangs. Probably yes, but two things kept the worry at bay.

A) She was a black belt in Tae Kwon Do and could, if needed, kick some serious ass.

And B) The explicit nature of the phone calls made her, well...kinda horny.

Okay, that's it. You're officially insane. This is why Vivian calls you oversexed. You get, let's face it, a mildly disturbing call and instead of being scared, you're bloody well excited.

Darci blew into her fringe again, a frustrated exhalation that did nothing except contribute to the unruly mess of curls falling over her forehead. She shouldn't have thought of her older sister. Whenever she thought of Viv, she got antsy. Viv was the achiever in the family – the famous literary novelist who followed in their father's famous shoes. Viv had the doting doctor husband, the two med-school-grad children, the well-trained, pedigreed King Cavalier Spaniel and the three-story mansion overlooking Sydney Harbor.

Darci, as Viv often pointed out, was a forty-year-old, unmarried high-school teacher who still went out to bars on the weekend, wrestled on the beach with her totally untrained mutt, Jay Jay Jones, ate carbohydrates until they came out her ears, drank beer straight from the bottle and often forgot where she'd left her one tube of lipstick.

Darci also, much to Viv's dismay and shame, had no qualms about her relationship with Mr. Tibbs, her rabbit (the vibrating variety, not the furry kind), and still enjoyed flirting when given the chance – especially with sexy young men.

Which is why she calls you oversexed. God, if she knew you were getting excited over an obvious case of mistaken identity, she'd throw a pink fit.

With one more huff into her fringe, Darci walked away from the phone. She probably should do something about the calls, but not now. Now she wanted to connect with someone who didn't care if she flirted with strange—but always handsome—men in bars.

Dropping into the worn, comfortable leather recliner tucked under a low reading lamp in the far corner of her living room, Darci woke her laptop and opened iChat. If she was lucky, Rachel would be online. The American knew how to make her laugh and didn't care one iota if she owned a rabbit. In fact, Darci was pretty damn certain the physical therapist owned one herself.

Rachel, however, wasn't online, her little Bugs Bunny avatar just a ghosty-gray image in the buddies list, which probably meant Rach was still in bed. Darci grimaced. "Bum." She dragged her hands through her hair, which disturbed the curls even more than her earlier melodramatic hyperventilating. She should close her laptop and get to marking assignments. She had a pile the size of Ayres Rock waiting for her, itching at her subconscious, but she just wasn't in the mood. For starters, the three phone calls this morning were still affecting her and she just felt...unsettled.

Don't you mean horny?

Rolling her eyes at her own ridiculousness—*oh yeah, that's an elegant word for an English teacher should use, Darc*—she shut down iChat and opened her email instead. She'd check her inbox, answer what needed to be answered and then give Jay Jay a bath. The pair of them had spent yesterday afternoon surfing and the dog still smelled like a seaweed farm.

"Ah," she murmured, spying Rachel's name in the From column. "Talk about freaky." Wriggling her butt deeper into the recliner, Darci toed off her flip-flops and opened Rachel's email, the mysterious subject header making her grin—*Go here now!*

The email opened and Darci's eyebrows lifted. Unlike Rachel's normal emails, which provided lovingly detailed descriptions of what Rach had been up to, what book she was currently reading as well as what hero she was currently in lust with, all info Darci loved to read, this email contained just two things.

A web address.

http://temptthecougar.blogspot.com/

And the words, *You're invited to become a Cougar, Darci. Join us.*

Darci frowned. "What the hell?"

Moving her finger over the laptop's trackpad, she clicked on the link.

And double blinked when a website unlike any she'd been to opened.

"Bloody hell, Rach," she muttered, her gaze flicking over the various images of very hunky, very naked men filling her screen. "Where have you sent me?"

She studied the men before her, her pulse quickening. There was text to go with the images, but for the moment it may as well have been ancient Mandarin for all it meant to Darci. What held her attention were the men.

The *young* men.

She shook her head, unable to drag her stare from her screen. "Oh my..." Sculpted muscles Michelangelo would have been proud to create defined bodies devoid of any middle-age spread. Artfully messy hair tumbled over foreheads free of wrinkles, not a gray strand to be seen in the thick, glossy locks. Clear, direct eyes gazed out at her—blue, black, green, hazel. Eyes smoldering with open desire and seduction.

Darci sucked in a sharp breath. "Twenties. Can't be any older than mid-twenties."

And so yummy your knickers are growing damper by the second.

The unexpected thought took her by surprise and she sucked in another breath, this one a little less sharp and a little more...ragged. Pulling at her bottom lip with her teeth, Darci read the blog's header — Tempt The Cougar — and then the first post. She half-frowned, half-grinned at a section of the first paragraph.

"...women who dare to take the challenge and experience the delights of sex with a younger man. Women who cast off their cloaks of conventionality and indulge their inner wild woman.

"Stay tuned for updates!"

"Oh, Rachel Bridges," she chuckled, returning her attention to the gorgeous men clearly a decade younger than her. "You bloody naughty girl."

The last time she and Rachel spoke, Darci had mentioned — in passing, mind you — how cute the fresh-out-of-university Phys. Ed. teacher just appointed to her school was. Rachel had giggled, her broad New York accent still evident in the joyful sound, and changed the subject. Until this very moment, Darci thought she'd embarrassed her friend. Now...

She shifted in the recliner, pressing her thighs together in a vain attempt to squelch the growing throb between her legs. The young men on her laptop screen were delicious. She couldn't think of another word.

Oversexed and now under-vocabbed? What would Viv say?

"For starters, she'd point out there's no such word as under-vocabbed," Darci muttered, gazing at one particularly fine young thing with bulging muscles, piercing blues eyes, skin the color of toasted honey and thick, black hair messed-up in such a way her fingers itched to mess it some more. She swallowed, the throb between her legs growing more insistent. Demanding attention.

Closing her eyes, Darci leaned back in her chair, her pussy constricting with impatient want. An image popped into her mind of the dark-haired young man from the site and she let out a soft moan.

Jay Jay was outside gnawing on an old bone. The house was hers alone for a good half hour. All she needed to do was imagine how wonderfully smooth and taut Mr. God I'm Gorgeous' skin was under her palms, how hard and perfect his biceps, how sublime the undulations of his abs beneath her lips and she'd be more than halfway to an orgasm. With a little help from her fingers, she'd be at the moaning destination with some extra mileage thrown in for gasping, heart-hammering fun.

She slid her fingertips under the waistline of her shorts—

And her phone rang.

"Oh, you've got to be kidding me!" The exclamation burst from her on a strangled breath. She jolted to her feet, her pulse pounding, her sex thick and heavy with expectation. Hurrying to the phone, she snatched it from its cradle and rammed it to her ear. "What?"

"Is that the thanks I get, Ms. Whitlam?" Rachel's accented chuckle slipped through the connection and Darci bit back a curse. "Or have I interrupted something?"

"Ha," she shot back, fighting to get her heart rate back under control. At her age, she couldn't afford to get too excited.

God, now you sound like Viv. What the hell is wrong with you, Darci? You're forty, not eighty.

"Ha?" Rachel echoed, her voice slightly tinny with the miles between them. "That's it? Where's the sarcastic Australian wit I know and love so much?"

"Busy." Darci shot her still-open laptop a quick look, a pang of disappointment stabbing into her core at the sight of her screensaver activating. She caught a fraction-of-a-microsecond glimpse of her man, with his sculpted muscles and piercing eyes, and then an image of Jay Jay jumping into the surf after a seagull filled her screen and she let out a frustrated sigh. "Sorry, Rach," she said, turning her back on her laptop to give her American friend her full concentration. "That wasn't nice of me."

Rachel laughed, the sound throaty and infectious. "I recognize that tone, Darci-Rae. You *have* received my email, haven't you?"

Darci rolled her eyes. "Bloody hell, am I really that much of a deviant? What made you think I—"

"Because I did almost the very same thing when Cam first sent me the link." Rachel laughed again. "It's okay, hon. There's nothing wrong with tending to your needs. Especially when the view is oh so fine."

Darci suppressed a snort. Rachel was a true wordsmith. She'd love to see her uptight sister have a conversation with the New Yorker. "The view was very fine indeed," she admitted, feeling her cheeks heat. Blushing? For the second time in one morning? There really was something wrong with her.

Rachel burst out laughing. Really laughing. If Darci didn't know it was physically and geographically impossible, she'd have sworn she felt the planet shaking with Rachel's mirth. "I knew it! Aren't they gorgeous? Tell me, which one took your fancy?"

Darci dropped to the floor and stretched out on her back, crossing her ankles on the edge of the phone table. "Black hair, the bluest eyes I've ever seen, a body so divinely perfect it must be illegal and shoulders so broad I doubt he'd fit through my door."

"Ah," Rachel answered. "Rico. Yeah, he was Monica's favorite too."

Darci rolled her eyes. Rico. Of course. What were the odds she'd fall in depraved lust with someone called George or James or...or...Jim? None.

Oversexed, under-vocabbed and now exotically clichéd? Viv's sniffed voice whispered through Darci's head. *Where will all this end, sister of mine?*

"In the bedroom with Mr. Tibbs. Now shut up."

"What?"

Rachel's laughing question made Darci blink and she slapped a palm to her face. Damn it, she'd said that aloud?

"Sorry, Rach," she hurried, dropping her ankles from the table and pulling herself into a sitting position. Who was she kidding? Lying on the floor? Like a teenager?

"Is that your absent sister you're talking to, Darc?"

Rachel's question tickled her ear through the connection, the American's obvious enjoyment at the situation turning each word to a husky chuckle. She let out a sigh, giving her laptop a lingering look. Images of Jay Jay running about on the beach slowly scrolled over the screen, hiding from view the delightful Rico and his young, firm, entirely too-desirable body.

And that's the way it has to stay, Darci Whitlam. Fantasies are all well and good, but you have to live in reality.

She pulled a face once again. "How is it you know me better than my own flesh and blood, Rach," she began, crossing her legs, "and yet we've never met? Are you stalking me?"

Rachel laughed again. "Stalking? No. Giving you a kick up the— How do you Aussies put it? Aah-ss, yes."

"A kick up the arse?" Darci's eyebrows rose. "About what?"

"There's a reason I sent you the invite to join the blog, Ms. Whitlam," Rachel answered, and for a second Darci swore she could hear something close to pride in her friend's voice. "It's time I laid down a challenge."

Darci's eyebrows shot up higher. "A challenge?"

"You are one of the most flippant, unconventional women I know, Darci-Rae. You have multiple degrees in literature and yet you devour erotic romances and pulp horror books like they're becoming extinct. You look like a model and wear jeans tighter than a teenager, you can probably kick anyone's ass and still have enough breath left to sing an opera—but you're afraid to *live*."

Before Darci could respond to the ludicrous statement, Rachel continued, her American accent broader with each word. "The shadow of your famous family keeps you trapped in the dark; the voice of your older sister prevents you *truly* going after what you long to experience and it's about freakin' time someone did something about it. I've decided that someone is me. So here's the challenge, Darci. As of this very moment—three a.m. New York time—you are on the hunt. I *dare you* to find yourself a younger man and live the fuck out of every fantasy you've ever had and be damned what Vivian thinks.

"I dare you, Darci-Rae, to become a cougar." She chuckled. "And blog about it."

For the second time that morning, Darci stared in dumbstruck disbelief at the phone in her hand. For about the fourth time that morning, her sex constricted at the words she heard.

Find yourself a younger man...live the fuck out of every fantasy...

"A cougar?" she echoed, throat tight. "As in—"

"A woman ready to show a younger man exactly what it's like to *really* make love. A woman not afraid of the years she's lived and the mileage she's traveled. As in, *you*."

For a moment, Darci didn't know what to say. And then she did. "You're out of your bloody mind, Rach."

Rachel laughed one last time. "Tempt the cougar, Darci. Take a long look at the blog, take a long look at your innermost desires and then take a long look at the lifeguards down on that beach you spend so much time at with your dog. I want a full report by the time I'm having my bagel and juice."

"And when's that?"

"In about four hours. Jump on the blog, introduce yourself and share with all of us a piccie of one of those sexy lifeguards you've told me about."

Darci opened her mouth. To say what, she wasn't sure.

"Oh, and by the way," Rachel said, filling the silence with confident ease. "Did I ever tell you how old Ethan is?" She disconnected the call before Darci could find whatever words were tumbling around in her head, leaving her to stare at the telephone handset for the third time that morning.

She blinked, the conversation whirling through her head. What the hell was Rachel up to? What was going on? Why was Rachel up at three in the morning on a weekday? How old *was* Ethan? And just *what the hell was going on?*

Tempt the cougar, Darci.

Mouth dry, pulse pounding, Darci hung up the phone and shuffled on her knees over to her recliner and sleeping laptop. She pressed the tip of her right index finger to the space bar, staring at the image of Rico returning in delicious color to her screen. Young, perfectly formed, gloriously endowed Rico. Her pussy fluttered and she swallowed the lump in her throat.

Tempt the cougar, Darci.

Scrunching her eyes closed, she thought of the secret fantasies she'd long harbored but never shared with anyone. Fantasies involving the experience of her age and the stamina and enthusiasm of a younger man. Fantasies she'd flirted with in the safety of the local pub but never dared dream to fulfill.

Fantasies her friend on the other side of the world had picked from her brain and placed in front of her when she, herself, had been too worried about what her famous sister would say.

She let out a sigh and shook her head. Rachel was right. Viv spoke too often in Darci's ear. Too often and too loudly.

"So, are you going to do anything about it?"

The answer to her own muttered question didn't come.

Instead, she found herself moving her cursor to the invitation link Rachel had sent...and clicking.

Ten minutes later, she sat back and read the very first blog post she'd ever written.

Hello. My name is Darci and I'm a cougar. Well, a cougar wannabe. Actually, that's not right either. Let me start again.

G'day. I'm Darci, I'm Australian and my friend Rachel Bridges just laid down a challenge I can't possibly refuse. Before I even knew I had a thing for younger men, Rach did (she's quite intelligent, isn't she?). After only a few telephone conversations, Rachel realized what I needed and sent me the best kick up the butt I could ask for (although I'm still in shock that she did *grin*)—an invitation to join this blog and the amazing women on it.

Why the hell can't a woman in her forties have the best sex of her life with a man in his twenties? Who decided we have to settle for the saggy-bottomed, remote-hogging men of our own age? Why the hell do I feel guilty when I flirt with a younger man?

Enough, I say! I want what society has long said I can't have, dammit!

Rachel, I accept your challenge. This Cougar Down Under is ready to be tempted.

(BTW—I hope you like the pictures of some very delicious Aussie "cubs" I've included.)

(BTW, again. Is it PC to use the term "cub" or am I just bowing to the media's latest manipulation of the English language?)

(BTW, one last time. I babble. A lot. Sorry.)

She looked at the two images she'd included. Both gorgeous Australian lifeguards, their bodies muscled to perfection, their smooth skin bronzed by the sun, their bright red Speedos leaving little to the imagination.

A deep ripple of excitement shot through her and she let out a sigh. Damn, she really was insane. Vivian was going to have a field day with this.

Delete it, Darc. Stop this insanity now!

The shocked voice in her head could've been her sister's. Or hers.

She leaned forward, placing her finger on the trackpad.

And the phone rang.

Her heart smashed into her throat and, face aflame once more, as if she'd been caught redhanded doing something far too naughty, she slammed her laptop shut. But not before quickly hitting Publish on the blog entry.

Storming across to the phone, she snatched up the phone and rammed it to her ear. "Bloody hell, give me a chance, will you?" she laughed.

Silence answered her. For a second. "Is this Darci-Rae Whitlam?" a deep male voice asked on the other end of the connection.

Darci's heart smashed harder into her throat. "Yes."

Silence again for a split second, followed by, "I want to press you against the wall and make love to you with my tongue."

Darci closed her eyes, her sex flooding with damp heat. *Oh God...*

"I want to eat out your pussy and fill my mouth with your cream," the man continued. "I want you to ride my face until you scream and then I want to flip you onto your stomach and fuck your sweet cunt with my dick."

He stopped. Waited.

Pulse pounding, mouth dry, Darci opened her eyes and looked at her closed laptop, her sex constricting. She licked her lips and pressed her thighs together. "And then what do you want to do?" she asked.

Chapter Two

ဢ

Detective Jarrod St. James stood in the cool shadow of a massive eucalyptus tree and frowned at the view before him. That his investigations had led him to *this* house, in a quiet suburban street complete with front-yard tire swings, children playing in the sprinklers and old men mowing their lawns in brightly colored shorts and straw hats, still didn't sit right with him.

He might be a suspicious big-city cop, he might be hardened from dealing with Sydney's bastard crooks, but everything in his gut told him the house in front of him, with its rambling beds of native wildflowers, its granite birdbath teeming with raucous magpies, its neatly trimmed edges and perfectly painted gutters, was *not* the home of an illegal phone-sex worker.

And yet, when you called the number listed for this address, that's exactly what you got. A very sexy female voice more than willing to talk very sexy things.

Jarrod let out a silent breath. Cybercrime detectives rarely stepped away from their computers, let alone *physically* tracked their perps. It wasn't the done thing. Cybercrime detectives did all their work with a keyboard and mouse and let the blokes with the guns round up the bad guys.

Trouble was, Jarrod hadn't always *been* a cybercrime detective, and this case—a stolen-identity case with hundreds of unsuspecting victims—had struck too close to home. He knew what it was like to have your identity stolen and used by someone else for less-than-honest reasons. Shit, he'd needed to resort to changing his name to escape the debt collectors hounding him after he'd been the victim of identity theft five years ago. One innocent purchase over the net, one not-so-safe use of his credit card and BAM! Sydney homicide cop James Dubois-Jarrodson is suddenly also Melbournian James Dubois-Jarrodson, a man with very dubious moral ethics and a penchant for very illegal buying habits.

It was the reason Jarrod had moved to cybercrime. Catch the bastards before they fucked up someone's unsuspecting life. His head always worked its best when it was focused on computers. Shit, he'd been offered a full IT scholarship to the University of New South Wales six months before finishing school.

His fists, however...well, they always worked their best breaking some lowlife's jaw, a situation probably due to the fact he'd been a bully's favorite target—a geek. He'd answered the call to the police force straight after graduating high school and somewhere along the line became a homicide detective. And then came the theft of James Dubois-Jarrodson's identity—and he transferred divisions as the newly known Jarrod St. James.

As right as that choice was, however, the move to cybercrime had left him restless.

Pursuing a case of identity theft beyond the computer lab was exciting—but wasn't meant to end up in a quiet street in coastal Newcastle. What kind of criminal mastermind lived in a neat little two-story surrounded by gum trees, wattle and tree ferns? With a 1996 Volvo in the driveway? A Volvo wearing a "Public Education. It's Our Future" bumper sticker, no less?

Jarrod breathed another drawn-out sigh. Maybe he'd been too long in front of a computer after all. This couldn't be right. This felt wrong.

"But this *is* the only address for someone claiming to be Darci-Rae Whitlam," he muttered, scanning the front windows, the gauzy curtains and wide awnings concealing the interior from his inspection. "And it *was* someone claiming to be Darci-Rae Whitlam who spoke to you on the phone a mere three hours ago."

With alarming ease, his cock twitched at the memory. The woman—whoever she really was—had the most amazing voice. A voice created to send a man wild. She'd said very little that could condemn her. Asked a very husky question about what he would do with his tongue after he brought her to orgasm with his fingers, wondered if he had staying power, pondered what it would be like to be tied up by him. But in that voice of hers, like smoke and velvet playing in the back of her throat…it was enough to set his groin on rock-hard alert and his pulse quickening beyond fast.

Is that the real reason you're here? 'Cause a possible crook got you horny with just her voice?

For the third time he let out a protracted sigh, this one tainted with deprecating disgust. Fuck, what was he doing?

"Catching a criminal, Detective." His growled whisper rumbled deep in his chest. "That's it. Catching a criminal who's stolen the real Ms. Whitlam's life—and making her pay."

He forced away the sensation of stirring steel in his cock, narrowed his stare on the front door of the house and crossed the front yard, the delicate perfume of the native violet ambling through the flowerbeds wafting into each breath he took.

Climbing the five steps leading to the front porch on silent feet, he unclipped the holster on his Glock, planted his feet slightly apart, squared his shoulders and raised his hand to knock on the door. Ready to take on whatever came—

The door flung open and a goddess with brilliant green eyes and wild, fiery-red hair smacked straight into him.

Followed immediately by a bear cleverly disguised as a dog. A *growling* dog.

He stumbled back a step, grabbing the goddess's upper arms even as the bear—err, dog—slammed two paws roughly the size of the Opera House against his chest.

"Eep!" the goddess cried, and Jarrod's balls prickled in instant interest as the sexiest voice he'd ever heard caressed his ears for the second time that day.

Still struggling under the dog's massive force, he tightened his grip on her arms, his fingers telling him exactly what his mind had already decided. The goddess was smooth, warm and firm to the touch. Sex and sin and toned feminine strength in one incredible package. He could feel her triceps flex and coil beneath his hands, a realization that made his balls not just prickle with interest but rise up and grow heavy.

Fuck, he was in trouble.

The dog shoved him, teeth bared, muzzle wrinkled, and before his stupefied brain could process the situation, he fell backward, stumbling down the front porch steps, dog and goddess joining him—reluctantly, by the sounds of the dog's snarls and the goddess' surprised shout—in a very undignified free fall.

"Oof!"

The ground hit his ass, or more to the point, his ass hit the ground, at the exact moment the dog decided snarling just wouldn't cut it anymore and the goddess decided she needed to slam into him with her entire weight. Wicked teeth latched onto his shoulder just as a slender, curved knee rammed into his crotch, followed by a palm heel to the solar plexus.

Jarrod's groin and chest exploded in black stars of pain. He let out a shout that sounded like a croak, thanks in part to the strangled pain in his chest and the dog's canines threateningly latched to his shoulder.

Yep, definitely been in front of a computer for too long, Jarrod.

The surreal thought flittered through his reeling mind, seconds before another palm heel struck him in the jaw.

"Let go of me, dickhead," the husky voice growled, a dangerous caress. "Or I'll let my dog eat you."

"Wait, wait, wait!" Jarrod choked out, struggling under the massive dog's rather insistent attack. Thank God for his thick cotton shirt, otherwise his shoulder would look as if it'd been through a cheese grater. He gripped the goddess's arms tighter still, the base *male* part of his mind pointing out she reclined full stretch atop him now, her firm softness separated from his body by nothing more than two layers of clothing and a seriously protective mutt.

The thought sent a surge of eager blood through his veins, flooding his already semi-hard dick with wildly inappropriate intent. Unable to do anything else, Jarrod flipped the goddess and her hellhound, dislodging the dog's teeth in the process, and straddled them both. "Wait!" he panted, staring down into eyes the color of raw emeralds. With an abrupt shift in position, he pressed his knee—gently but forcefully—on the dog's neck, pinning the animal to the ground so the bloody thing couldn't take any more bites out of his hide, and then grabbed the goddess's wrists and pinned them to the ground beside her head.

"Get off me!" she snarled through clenched teeth, squirming beneath him. "Who the hell are you? Get off me, you prick."

She bucked again and Jarrod bit back a groan. With all her thrashing and writhing, there was no way she would have missed the growing bulge in his jeans. Damn it, his bloody erection kept poking her in the belly every time she moved, contained by his jeans or not.

Way too long in front of a computer, Jarrod. Way too long.

"Wait," he snapped one last time, and for a dizzying moment he wondered what the hell had happened to his vocabulary. Maybe he'd left it on the front porch along with his pride and professionalism.

The dog struggled to escape his weight. The goddess glared at him some more, her breasts heaving in furious contempt underneath the pristine white cotton of her t-shirt. "Wait? For what? You going to serenade me next? Get your knee off Jay Jay *now*!"

Jarrod sucked in a breath and the delicate scent of the woman trapped beneath him rushed into his being. Making his head spin. Bloody hell, she smelled so good.

"Get off me!" she roared. "*Get off me now!*"

Her voice cracked, the husky tones becoming raw. Throaty.

It was too much for Jarrod. Her voice, her eyes, the tousled insanity of her hair…hell, even the menacing worry for her dog. It was all too much. He couldn't help himself. Fuck, he couldn't *stop* himself.

Tightening his grip on her wrists, Jarrod St. James — once the poster boy for the NSW Police Force, now the poster boy for their geek squad, lowered his head to the woman imprisoned between his legs and kissed her.

Two seconds later, her bear disguised as a dog escaped his knee — most likely due to the fact his brain was focused entirely on the soft fullness of her lips — and sank its teeth into his shoulder. Again.

"Fuck!" he shouted, rolling off her and reaching for his gun.

What? You going to shoot the dog now?

"Jay Jay! Sit!"

Immediately, the dog dropped into a motionless sit, black stare locked on Jarrod's face.

Damn. Jarrod stayed equally still, his attention on the mutt, his shoulder throbbing. *That's impressive.*

"You have exactly twenty seconds to tell me who you are and what you want, young man," the goddess said, "before I let Jay Jay have you."

Jarrod jerked his attention back to the woman standing beside the part Doberman, part Wolfhound, part Kodiak bear.

Young man? How old did she think he was? Come to think of it, how old was *she?* The real Darci was forty, he knew, but this woman looked nothing like the photo on Ms. Whitlam's driver's license.

He ran his gaze over her form, taking her in from head to toe. She was short, no more than five-five at an educated guess, and had the kind of body he usually associated with gym junkies—all firm, toned limbs and smooth curves deliciously exposed to his inspection thanks to the short denim shorts and snug white t-shirt she wore. A body well looked after. Vibrant and fit with the right amount of flesh in the right places to grab.

But her direct green eyes, almost hidden by the wild tumble of red curls and edged by small creases he could only call laugh lines, spoke of a confidence and inner strength unusual for someone his own age. Hell, he'd rarely seen women in their thirties with such self-assured poise, let alone their twenties.

It was bloody sexy and his cock twitched in appreciation—even as he began to suspect he'd found the real Darci-Rae Whitlam after all. *Shit.*

"Five seconds, stud," she said in that sinfully husky voice, "and I'm calling the police."

The threat sent an unexpected shard of something thrilling into the pit of Jarrod's belly, and he laughed. "I *am* the police." He stood and reached into his back pocket, the muscles in his shoulder protesting as he withdrew his wallet. He was going to have a hell of a bruise there, thanks to her mutt. *Maybe she'll kiss it better?* "Detective Jarrod St. James," he said, showing her his I.D. "Cybercrime."

She blinked, her lips parting slightly, her right hand moving to rest on the top of her dog's head. "Cybercrime?"

He gave her an easy smile as he returned his wallet to his pocket. "Crimes involving illegal activity perpetrated via the use of computers and the internet."

Her eyes narrowed, an unreadable expression flickering in their depths. "I know what cybercrime is, young man. What I want to know is what a police officer *from* cybercrime is doing at my front door?"

There she goes with that "young" crap again. How old is she?

An insistent tightening stirred in his groin. *Who cares?*

"I have some questions for you," he said, shutting down the notion behind *that* thought. She may be the sexiest creature he'd ever seen, but he still had a job to do and at the moment, his job was telling him she might be a phone-sex worker possibly operating under a stolen identity. "Firstly, are you Darci-Rae Whitlam?"

Straight red eyebrows rose up her forehead and she stoked her dog's head. "Yes."

He studied her face. "Can you prove it?"

The mutt growled.

The goddess—damn, she really was beautiful—arched an eyebrow. "Would you like to see my last pay statement from the Department of Education?"

Jarrod shifted on his feet. The cop in him responded to her question—evidentiary proof? Real? Fake? The primitive male animal in him, however, responded to her strength. Everything about her turned him on. The sensual, sexy body, the unbelievable chaos of her flame-red hair, the laughter lines around her stunning eyes...even the steely challenge *in* those stunning eyes.

God, what would it be like to fuck her?

"Yes, please," he blurted out, the unexpected thought jolting him to the, well, to the groin.

She cocked her eyebrow again and turned away from him, presenting the round perfection of her ass. The denim of her shorts hugged the shapely curves and Jarrod had to bite back a moan.

Christ, he was in trouble.

She climbed the stairs, her ass cheeks bunching with each step, and nothing could drag his stare away. Not even a loaded gun pointed at his head and a threat to pull the trigger.

God, I fucking want her so badly.

Without pause or a backward glance, Darci-Rae Whitlam—or her imposter—disappeared inside the neat suburban house, the soft sound of the security screen hitting the doorjamb followed immediately by a low growl.

Jarrod blinked, jerking his gaze to Jay Jay.

The dog-bear-hellhound studied him, motionless.

"I won't bite," he muttered, remaining as still as the dog. "Wish I could say the same 'bout you."

Jay Jay bared long, sharp, pointed teeth.

"Hey." Jarrod assumed a wounded expression. "I'm the good guy here."

"That may be," the goddess spoke at his right, and he swung his head back to her, noticing the cell phone she held in her right hand. "But I rescued Jay Jay from a very abusive male owner when he was just a puppy. In his eyes, *all* men mean pain." She held out her left hand, an expectant look on her wonderfully mesmerizing face. "May I see your I.D. please?"

Jarrod frowned. "You don't trust me?"

For an answer, she laughed. A low, throaty chuckle, and Jarrod's groin tightened in immediate attention.

Flicking the silent Jay Jay a quick glance, he withdrew his wallet, slipped his credentials from their sleeve and handed them to her.

Their fingers brushed and for the first time in his life, Jarrod understood the concept of fate.

For whatever reason, he was *meant* to meet this woman. He just hoped to God it wasn't to arrest her, because frankly, he doubted he could do it. He'd more likely beg her to run away with him. To Melbourne, Prague...shit, Greenland would do. Just as long as she was with him and he got to bury himself in her —

"Hello, Sergeant Rylon? Yes, may I speak to someone in Cybercrime, please?"

Jarrod raised his eyebrows, the goddess's question once again throwing him for a loop.

She smiled at him, the action more than a little smug. "What?" she whispered, dropping the mouthpiece of the cell away from her lips a little. "You expected me to invite you in without checking who you were?"

Actually, he wanted to say, *I didn't expect you to invite me in at all.*

Not after the way he'd dragged her from the front porch, rolled her to the ground and kissed her, all within a minute of laying eyes on her. While wrestling with her dog, at that.

He opened his mouth to reply, his blood pumping through his body with excited anticipation. Christ, he was acting like a hormonally imbalanced schoolboy!

And doesn't it feel amazing? When was the last time you felt like this? Really?

"Can you confirm Detective Jarrod St. James, badge number 42-01-10, is, in fact, a cop?" She ran her gaze over him from head to toe, an inspection so thorough he felt his balls rise. His cock, already at half-mast, grew fatter in his jeans. He wanted her to look at him like that again while he was naked. Fuck, did he.

"Yes, I can see why he's called that." Her smile stretched wider. Cheekier. "Quite fitting, really. Thank you. You've been a big help."

She touched the screen of her cell and slipped the slim device into her back pocket, eyeing him again. He fought the urge to shuffle on his feet. And the urge to fold his hands in front of his crotch. There was no way she could fail to miss the sizeable bulge in his trousers. No way in hell.

Green eyes twinkled and she patted Jay Jay on the head once more. "Would you like to come inside, Detective St. James?"

Chapter Three

℅

What are you doing, Darci?

Darci walked through the foyer, heading for her living room. Jay Jay trotted beside her, completely at ease with the fact Detective St. James followed behind them.

That itself was worrying. Jay Jay rarely warmed to anyone. Vivian's husband, the benevolent Dr. Carmichael, CMO of the country's leading children's hospital and recipient of the Order of Australia, couldn't walk two steps into her home without Jay Jay growling up a storm.

So, is that why you've asked St. James in? Because Jay Jay's no longer trying to eat him? Or does it have to do with the way he looks? Like Sin and Sex got together and created your ultimate fantasy? Or maybe it has to do with the way the crotch of your knickers are sopping wet with a desire that borders on illegal? Or the fact the kiss he stole from you when you were pinned beneath him was truly the most wonderful, arousing thing you've ever experienced?

Is he the one? Have you targeted your cub already?

Darci pulled a face and entered her living room, all too aware of Jarrod St. James' presence. "Just let me get my pay slip," she said, crossing to the bureau under the far window.

St. James didn't answer and she turned, finding him standing before her framed *Rules of Attraction* movie poster hanging above Jay Jay's large day bed, his fingers massaging his shoulder where Jay Jay had bitten him.

She pulled in a silent breath, stealing a brief moment to study him. Tall and lean with broad shoulders and well-muscled arms, he wore his jeans and black polo shirt with the same casual confidence she'd admired in the new Phys. Ed.

teacher—a relaxed cockiness that said *I'd look this good in a hessian sack.*

Unlike Mr. Montgomery, however, Detective St. James seemed totally unaware of it.

No wonder they call him Calvin Klein at the cop shop. He could make a fortune as a model.

As if sensing her gaze, he turned from the movie poster and fixed his thousand-kilowatt blue eyes on her. "Copulating teddy bears?"

For a split second the reason for the controversial poster's existence in her house hovered on her lips—a present from her favorite senior class five years ago after she'd adamantly and unwisely declared there was *no way* teddy bears could be vulgar—and then, a shard of characteristic contrariness stabbed into her and she cocked an eyebrow. "Copulating teddy bears."

He regarded her silently, what looked like a small grin playing at the corners of his mouth.

Her own smile pulling at her lips, she turned back to her bureau, opened the top drawer and withdrew her latest pay slip from the Department of Education.

You're enjoying yourself, aren't you?

The thought whispered through her mind and her pulse quickened. *What kind of lunatic enjoys a visit from the police? Especially one questioning your identity?*

The kind who's not blind. Have you seen the way he —

"Have you recently purchased anything online using your credit card?"

St. James' question, spoken with such formal detachment, guttered the rising heat in Darci's core. Shame and self-disgust flooded through her and she pushed the drawer closed with aggressive force. A cop doing a cop's job. That's what she had to remember, no matter how sexy he was. A cop in her living room asking questions. Not a cub waiting to be seduced—or was that devoured—by a cougar.

"Yes," she answered, turning back to him. "A few things." She held out her pay slip, waiting for him to take it.

He didn't, his attention back on the film poster and its teddy bears in various sexual positions. "Was one of those purchases a U.S. visa waiver application?"

A lump formed in Darci's throat. "Yes."

His attention didn't move from the poster. "Why are you going to the U.S., Ms. Whitlam?"

"I'm going to the RomantiCon convention in—" She snapped her mouth shut, her cheeks filling with heat. *Oh, you idiot, Darci.*

That killer blue gaze returned to her. "RomantiCon?"

Darci fought the urge to fidget. What did she say? Make up some fictional convention? Give him a half explanation? Was omitting the full details to a cop wise?

She lifted her chin slightly, meeting his stare. "It's a convention for readers and writers of erotic romance."

St. James' unreadable expression didn't change. "Erotic romance."

Frustrated anger stabbed into Darci's chest and she met his stare. "Erotic romance." *Here we go again.* Someone casting judgment on her. He may be as gorgeous as all hell with the body of a sex god, but he seemed just as opinionated as Vivian. She let out a sharp sigh. So much for fulfilling her Cougar challenge with—

"Can you tell me what site you purchased your visa waiver from?"

Still a detached, professional tone. Darci suppressed the need to fidget again. Why did she feel guilty? Was this how her students felt when she interrogated them over missing homework?

"Ms. Whitlam?"

Darci ground her teeth, the ambivalent tone in St. James' voice putting her on edge. "I can show you," she said, crossing to the coffee table. She deposited her pay slip beside her closed laptop, angry and worried at once. "I have it bookmarked."

Her fingertips brushed the cool titanium of her computer just as Jay Jay whined, nudging her leg with his cold, wet nose. "Oh God, mate, I'm sorry." New guilt rolled through her. She'd totally forgotten he was still in the house. She scruffed his ears, shooting St. James a quick look. "We were on our way to the park when I opened the door and you..." She faltered a second, swallowing the words "grabbed me" before they could fall from her tongue. "Arrived."

The Sydney detective said nothing.

Patting Jay Jay again, she skirted the coffee table and headed toward the back of her house. "I'll just let him out and be right back."

St. James nodded once, still silent, and Darci hurried from the living room, a prickling sensation telling her that his stare was fixed firmly on her back. She should be excited. This was what she'd wanted, wasn't it? The undivided attention of a younger man? Isn't that really why she'd invited him in?

So why was she so...unsettled? Damn it, what was going on? She didn't like this feeling of...of... Damn it! She couldn't even find a word to define the feeling she felt! Argh!

Unbolting the back door, she pushed it wide, giving her small backyard a quick scan before turning to her dog. "Cop or not," she muttered, "if you hear me shout, come and bite his sexy ass off, okay?"

Jay Jay wagged his tail, its long length thumping against her leg in soft lashes. With a jovial *woof* and a goofy doggy grin, he trotted out the door, nose skimming the ground in search of the perfect place to pee.

Closing the door, she reached down and unlatched the dog flap then took a deep breath. She had to regain her calm. Her head was all over the place. She had to remember the young man standing in her living room wasn't just the embodiment of all her carnal, oversexed fantasies packaged into one delectable form. He was a cop. A detective, here to investigate a crime. Something was going on, and she got the feeling it wasn't good.

She took another steadying breath, dragged her hands through her hair, closed her eyes, counted to ten and walked back into her living room.

And stopped.

Detective Jarrod St. James sat on her sofa, his elbows resting on his bent knees, his blue, blue eyes taking in something on her laptop. Her *open* laptop.

"Rico seems a touch fond of spray tanning, don't you think?"

Darci frowned, his question making no sense to her.

And then it did.

Oh God. Her face flooded with heat. Tempt the bloody Cougar!

He lifted his head, an unreadable expression on his face. "Copulating teddy bears, erotic romance reading and now a blog dedicated to seducing younger men filled with images that borderline porn? A blog I see *you* have posted on. What kind of English teacher *are* you, Ms. Whitlam?"

Hot anger scorched away her shame. She stormed across the living room and slammed the laptop lid shut, glaring at him. "The best kind."

He stood. Slowly. Towering over her. His stare never leaving her face. "I wish you'd been *my* English teacher then," he murmured.

Darci narrowed her eyes. "And what does that mean?"

"This," he said, rounding the coffee table in a single step before snaking his arms around her waist, yanking her body to his and crushing her lips with his own.

His tongue delved into her mouth, urgent and hungry. The man kissed like a demon—wild and aggressive and dominating. It made her pussy weep with pleasure.

She'd wanted to kiss him the moment the last one ended on her front lawn. She'd never in a million years dreamed it would be this good, however.

His hands raked her back, cupping her ass cheeks in a squeezing grip. She whimpered, the surprised sound caught by his kiss as he tugged her harder to his body, pressing her hips to his.

His erection rammed into her belly, thick and hard and undeniable despite the denim of his jeans. A constricting pressure knotted in Darci's core at its insistence and she whimpered again, sliding her arms around his back to tangle her fingers in his hair. Goddamn it, why shouldn't she enjoy herself?

Wicked desire licked through her veins and she deepened the kiss, battling his tongue with fierce purpose, her knickers growing wetter with each tussling thrust and stroke. Her head spun and she held him tighter, lifting one leg and hooking it around his thigh. The change in position drew her sex closer to his cock. A low growl vibrating in his chest told her he was pleased with the new sensation. As did the less-than-gentle way he squeezed her butt again.

God, what are you doing, Darci?

She shut the question from her mind and rolled her hips, grinding her spread pussy against the bulge in his jeans with a purpose he could not misinterpret—*more.*

He obliged.

With another growl, he hauled her backward, surprising and delighting her when he dropped onto the sofa, dragging her with him. In a frantic jumble of arms and legs, he repositioned her astride his lap, her knees pressed on either side of his hips, his growing shaft nudging her pussy through their clothes.

Nudging? Damn, Darci. If you were both naked you'd be so impaled on his dick the neighbors would hear your screams.

Another wave of base pleasure crashed through her at the thought and she bowed her back, wanting *exactly* to be impaled on his shaft. Wanting it more than a rational woman in her forties should.

Oversexed.

She didn't have the chance to tell her sister's voice to fuck off. Jarrod tore his mouth from hers, dragged his lips down her neck, up again, dipped his tongue into her ear and returned to her mouth, pretty much destroying any chance of Vivian's righteousness sinking in.

Darci fisted her hands tighter in his hair, a part of her afraid he was going to remember he was kissing an older woman. She didn't want that. Not yet. Damn, not ever. Not when he made her almost come with just a kiss.

He groaned, thrusting his hips upward to stab his contained erection against her pussy. "Fuck, I want…"

His words—growled against her lips with raw lust—drenched her knickers again. He plunged his tongue into her mouth once more, each kiss growing harder, more demanding than the last. She'd never been kissed like this before—a sheer force of elemental, sexual urgency. He was dominating every second of the moment, taking from her, feeding on her mouth and lips and tongue. It was possessive, frightening. Christ, it was amazing.

With another groan, this one cut with something close to anger, he snatched at the hem of her t-shirt with one hand, shoving it up her rib cage. His fingers found her breast and he cupped its heavy shape, palming it, squeezing it through the thin satin of her bra.

Oh yes.

Concentrated pleasure shot through her. Spearing out from her breast, rippling through her body until her pussy flooded with wet need. She broke the kiss, throwing back her head to suck in breath after ragged breath.

And still he didn't ease his assault on her body. He shoved her shirt higher, yanking her closer to his hips, ramming his cock harder to her cunt even as he closed his mouth over the aching point of her nipple.

Oh yes!

The elated cry shot through her head. A second before he bit down on the rock-hard nub of sensitive flesh.

"Oh, fuck!"

She bucked against him, fresh pleasure sodding her knickers.

In answer, he snatched at the edge of her bra, tore it aside and claimed her exposed nipple with his mouth.

Oh, oh, oh.

Darci froze, every molecule in her body instantly on fire. She held on to him, fisted hands buried in his hair, her thighs gripping his hips. No one had sucked her breasts for a long time and she'd forgotten how amazing it felt. Or was that just the masterful work of St. James' mouth? Surely she'd have remembered something that felt like *this*? Ribbons of pleasure unfurled through her, sinking into the pit of her belly. Ribbons of pleasure threading through her existence, from her nipple down to her sex. She moaned, her head lolling backward, her eyes closed.

She hadn't forgotten. It had *never* felt like this.

His mouth and tongue and teeth still worshipping her left breast, St. James shoved the other side of her bra aside and closed his hand over her right. He captured its pebbled tip between his splayed fingers, pinching it between two knuckles. She bucked against his cock, the painful pleasure of the caress shooting through her, wetting her knickers more. "Damn, that feels so good."

"God, you've got the horniest voice," he groaned against her breast, his lips and teeth nipping her flesh on every word. "It's enough to give a bloke wet dreams."

The statement made Darci's pussy contract. She whimpered, rolling her hips back and forth so the rigid steel of his cock rubbed against her trapped clit. Damn, she was close to coming. So close.

Oh, you are an oversexed thing, aren't you? About to orgasm after just a little suck and grind.

St. James yanked her closer to his body, thrusting his cock upward as he squeezed her right breast again. "Say my name with your sexy voice."

Her sex constricted again at the demand.

He shoved his erection into the junction of her thighs again, the hand on her breast growing fiercer. "Say my name, Darci."

"St. James," she whispered, throat tight. Oh, she was going to come. How could she be ready to come? Wasn't she meant to be seducing *him*? Wasn't *he* the prey?

"No," he ground out through clenched teeth, his nostrils flaring. "My full name. Say, 'fuck me, Jarrod St. James'."

"Fuck me, Jarrod St. James!"

The words fell from Darci's lips before she could stop them. Jarrod's eyes widened. His nostrils flared again and in a single fluid move, he tore her t-shirt over her head and threw it away. His gaze raked her exposed upper body, an inspection so thorough and unhurried, Darci's heartbeat doubled. "You are the sexiest thing I've ever seen."

She chuckled, tugging his head closer to hers. "And you talk too much." She kissed him, silencing his own humored laugh. Their tongues battled again, a wild war she knew she was going to lose. She couldn't defend herself against the way he kissed. It was impossible. He fucked her mouth with his tongue, turning her into a creature of sheer sexual slavery. Her voice would give him wet dreams? His kisses would feed her fantasies for the rest of eternity.

His hands raked her back, charting wild paths over her skin, lingering at the dip at the base of her spine, skimming the angles of her shoulder blades until, with a dexterous skill that made her gasp, he unclipped her bra with one hand.

The satin cups fell away from her breasts, the cool air-conditioned air of her living room tickling her flesh immediately. Her already-hard nipples puckered harder and a soft moan escaped her, growing louder when Jarrod flattened his hand at the base of her neck, pushed her away from him a fraction and captured her right nipple with his lips.

He suckled, one hand splayed at the base of her spine, the other pressed to her chest, keeping her upright. As if he knew she was on the verge of crumpling into a melted puddle of screaming release.

So close, Darci.

"Fuck me, Jarrod St. James," she begged, her voice a raw breath.

With barely a break in skin-to-skin, mouth-to-breast contact, he rolled her beneath him, straddling her thighs, his knees taking all his weight. His hands fumbled at his fly, his mouth leaving her nipple to utter a short curse as his belt resisted his efforts to yank it open.

"Let me." Darci removed his hands and tugged at the length of leather threaded through the metal buckle.

He looked down into her face, a grin playing with his lips. "Yes, Miss."

His words should have insulted her. Or at the very least, disgusted her. She'd never played the teacher-student game with any of her past lovers, mostly because she hadn't wanted to. They'd been too boring. Jarrod, with his young, nubile body, seam-free face and cocky mirth, was far from boring, however.

She held his gaze, slowly pulling his belt through its buckle. *Oversexed, Darci. So oversexed.*

Jarrod's teeth flashed at her as his grin widened. "Maybe I should remove my jeans before we go any further. And my gun."

"Good idea." Darci nodded, a wanton part of her incensed at the idea. He had to climb off her to do so. Take his gorgeous, sexy body a few inches away from hers. She didn't like that idea. She wanted him so close an anthropologist would have difficulty figuring out where one ended and the other began.

Oh, for God's sake, Darci! Listen to yourself! You're a grown woman! What are you doing?

"Making out," she chuckled. "With the hottest cop I've ever seen."

Jarrod raised his eyebrows. "Thank you." He straightened. Slowly.

Darci squirmed on the sofa. He obviously knew he was driving her insane and by the glint in his eyes, he was enjoying it.

As was she.

His hands went to his gun holster first, unclipping the strap with a snap. He withdrew the weapon and bent sideways slightly, depositing it on the coffee table without removing his gaze from her face.

For a split second Darci wondered why a cop from Cybercrime would be armed, and then Jarrod's hands returned to his fly and her mind forgot about everything except the sound of his zipper lowering.

Oh, oh, this is really happening. You are about to have sex with a younger man. A bloody gorgeous younger man. Shit, what if he doesn't have a condom? What if —

Her phone rang.

Jarrod flicked the annoying device a less-than-impressed scowl. "Machine?"

Darci chuckled. "What do you think?"

"Heya, this is Darci-Rae. If this is one of my students, consider yourself on detention. Otherwise, leave a message after the beep."

Jarrod laughed. "You really *are* unlike any teacher I —"

133

"Hello, Darci-Rae. This is J.D. I want to spread your legs wide and fuck you with my —"

Darci's blood drained from her face. She stared up at Jarrod, her breath stuck in her throat. *Oh no. Nonono.*

"I want to tie you up and —"

She leapt from the sofa, crossing to the phone in two strides and snatching the handset from its cradle. "Goddamn it! I am *NOT* a phone-sex worker!" she yelled into the mouthpiece.

Silence followed. Absolute silence.

She slammed the phone down before the miscreant on the other end could recover, her pulse pounding in her ears.

"Damn it." The muttered curse scratched at her dry throat.

The sound of a zipper made her spin around and she found Jarrod buttoning his fly, his face expressionless. "Thank you, Ms. Whitlam, for your assistance." He retrieved his gun from the coffee table, sliding it back into its holster with decisive force. "If you'll excuse me, I have paperwork to complete."

"Jarrod…" she began.

He turned and walked from her living room without another word, the solid thud of the front door telling her he was really gone. The sound of the security screen slamming after it just a mocking exclamation point to the fact. She crossed back to the sofa and sank onto the cushioned seat, only a moment earlier occupied by St. James.

She stared at nothing, numb. What had happened?

What? You mean the fact you almost had sex with a complete stranger? Or the fact that the complete stranger abruptly left?

Her pussy throbbed, still waiting to be filled. Ready. Wanting.

Oversexed, Darci-Rae, Vivian's voice whispered in her head. *You should be ashamed of yourself.*

She let out a shaking breath and leaned forward, lifted the lid of her laptop. Opening iChat, she clicked on Rachel's Bugs Bunny avatar, uncaring that it was gray.

You will not believe what just happened, she typed. **I just made the biggest mistake of my life and had the most amazing experience while doing so.**

She hit send.

Almost immediately, Rachel replied.

Is it a younger guy? Ooooh, you *are* accepting the Cougar Challenge! Details! I want details!

Mouth dry, sex still pulsing, nipples still hard, Darci leaned forward again.

And her doorbell rang.

She jumped, her already-pounding heart slamming harder against her breastbone. Rising slowly to her feet, she walked toward the front door, pausing to collect her t-shirt from the floor where St. James had tossed it. She pulled it over her head, the sensation of the fine cotton rubbing over her nipples almost unbearable. When whoever was at the door left, she was going into her bedroom and firing up Mr. Tibbs. With this much sexual tension in her body, if she didn't do something she'd explode. Literally.

She opened the door.

"Darci-Rae Whitlam," Jarrod St. James said, stepping into her house. Towering over her as he drove her backward into the living room until her ass hit a wall, his hands pressed on either side of her head. "You're under arrest."

Chapter Four

℘

Her eyes grew wide, her lips parting in a soft gasp. "For what?"

Jarrod lowered his head to hers, the scent of her perfume—*jasmine?*—threading into his brain. "For being so fucking gorgeous I can hardly think straight."

She gasped again and he caught the sound with his mouth. Kissing her before she could say anything. He didn't want her to say a word for fear she'd tell him to get out of her house. *That* he couldn't do.

Not now.

And when will *you, Jarrod?*

He ignored the question, pressing his hips to Darci's until she was pinned to the wall behind her. It wasn't what he'd planned. He'd planned to apologize for his abrupt departure when she opened the door. He'd planned to ask her to dinner, maybe offer to drive her and her Kodiak bear to the park. But those plans went out the window when she stood before him again and all he could think about was having her. All of her. Starting with her mouth.

He kissed her, plunging his tongue past her lips. She moaned, a little hitching sound he liked a lot. Part frustration, part supplication, part invitation. He understood all too well.

Snatching one hand from the wall, he thrust it under the hem of her t-shirt, claiming her right breast. Her bare skin burned his palm, a branding as surely as it was a possession. He squeezed the heavy swell, pushing his erection to her belly as he did so. He'd never been so hard and he wanted her to know what she did to him.

She pushed her hips forward, rolling them upward until the junction of her thighs pressed against his groin. He groaned into her mouth, squeezed her breast harder. Pinched her nipple and cupped her breast again.

Now. He wanted to fuck her. Now.

He tore his mouth from hers, sucking in breath after gulping breath as he stared down into her face. "Jesus, I want you. So badly."

She swallowed, her hands brushing his collar, as if unsure what should happen next. "How old are you?"

He kissed her again, a brutal conquering of her mouth. "It doesn't matter. Consider me tempted beyond control."

She shook her head, fingers skimming his jaw. "I'm not what you think I am. I'm not—"

"I know what you are, Darci," he growled, lips scoring a line up to her ear. "You're a fucking sexy woman. I don't give a rat's ass how old you are, how old I am." He took her earlobe in his teeth and nipped gently, loving the way she whimpered when he did so. "I don't care one iota about our age difference."

She whimpered again, louder this time. That he was nibbling on her neck may have something to do with the increase in volume. Or the fact he was rolling her nipple between thumb and fingers. "But the phone call," she whispered, her hands slipping around his shoulders.

He smiled. She may be fighting with her head, but her body was doing its own thing. And he liked that thing. A lot. "I don't care about that either, Ms. Whitlam. Now let me make love to you before I embarrass myself and come in my jeans."

His utterly shameless statement made her whimper once more. Her arms wrapped completely around his neck, drawing him closer. She lifted one leg and hooked it around the back of his thigh, the action bringing her sex closer to his. "Okay."

The simple response was Jarrod's undoing. The trust in her voice—the voice of a sex goddess granting him access to heaven. He grabbed her shirt and yanked it over her head, throwing it aside. She stood before him, naked from the waist up. "Gorgeous." The adjective rumbled deep in his chest, more growl than word.

"Insane," she muttered, a wry smile on her lips.

Jarrod chuckled, stepping closer to her. "Insanely gorgeous, then."

He smoothed his hands down her rib cage, luxuriating in the satin warmth of her skin. There was nothing distracting his enjoyment—no bellybutton piercing, no tattoos of butterflies or Chinese peace symbols. Just beautiful skin and a flat stomach. The body of a woman comfortable with who she was.

"You have a thing for hyperbole."

Darci's low murmur made him smile. He moved his fingers to the waistband of her shorts. "Do I, Ms. Whitlam?" He popped the lone button of her fly.

She sucked in a swift breath. "'Insanely gorgeous, horniest voice, fucking sexy woman'."

Jarrod slowly lowered the zipper of her shorts. "Not hyperbole. Fact."

She laughed, the throaty sound making his balls grow heavier with want. "Yeah, right."

He grinned, enjoying their banter. He could talk to her all day. He *would* talk to her all day. After he did…this.

He shoved her shorts over her hips and down her thighs.

"Shit," Darci burst out.

Without a word he dropped to his knees, sliding the item of clothing farther down her legs until the denim bunched at her ankles. He skimmed his palms over the finely muscled shapes of her calves, up and down the long lengths of her thighs, his thumb stroking the lips of her pussy through the sodden material of the black knickers she wore. "*You* seem to have a thing for profanity."

Her eyelids fluttered nearly closed and she studied him through thick, dark lashes bereft of mascara, her breasts rising and falling with her rapid, shallow breaths. "Only since *you* walked through my door."

He leaned forward, brushing his lips over the exposed plane of her lower abdomen. "Then I best not waste it with idle chit-chat." He slid one hand down to her ankle, lifting her foot off the floor so he could free her of her flip-flops and shorts. He tossed them over his shoulder, cocking an eyebrow as he did so.

"Enjoying yourself?" she asked, the smile on her lips cheeky.

"Oh, you'd better believe it," he chuckled, smoothing his hand back up her leg and under her thigh, lifting it until it rested on his shoulder. "Now tell me, if I suck your clit through your panties, will you moan 'fuck'?"

Before she could answer, he pressed his mouth to her pussy—still covered by its shield of thin black cotton—and sucked on her drenched labia.

"Fuck!"

The word *was* a moan. A low, drawn-out moan that sent fresh desire surging to his cock. He flicked the tip of his tongue over the tiny button of her clit, her knickers so wet with her juices his head spun. The urge to rip those snug black undies from her body and bury himself up to the balls in her sweet cunt almost overwhelmed him. His cock ached, a physical pain he'd never experienced before. He licked at her pussy, stroking her clit with his tongue through the cotton of her panties even as his hands worked their way to the elastic band.

"Damn, that feels so good."

There was no surprise in her voice, only surrender and pleasure. "You *taste* so good," he answered, rising to his feet to gaze into her eyes. He brushed his lips over hers, tracing them with his tongue. "See?"

She stiffened a little, her mouth closed beneath his before, with a trembling breath, she parted her lips and touched her tongue to his.

A ripple of joy coursed through Jarrod. What he'd just done—let her taste her own juices, her own pleasure—was new to her, he could tell. Her hesitation and uncertainty spoke volumes. That she'd trusted him to be the first to let her experience such a beautiful thing filled him with inexplicable warmth. And made him hornier than ever.

Hooking his fingers under the elastic of her undies, he pulled his mouth away from hers. "You taste like liquid pleasure, Darci, and I so want to taste more."

Sinking to his knees, he pulled her underpants down, his breath catching at the sight of her neatly trimmed thatch of russet curls. *A real woman.* The disconnected thought floated through his head as he leaned close and touched his tongue to those soft curls, parting them until he found her clit.

"Oh!"

Darci's groan caressed his senses. Her fingers knotted in his hair, holding his head to her sex.

"Oh…"

He stabbed his tongue past her folds, tugging at one side of her bunched underpants until she lifted her leg and wrapped it around his shoulder.

Yes.

Her pussy opened to him, her cream slicking his lips as he lapped at her slit. She moaned above him, rolling her hips forward to meet his tongue's penetration, her hands tightening in his hair. "Oh!"

She moaned the little exclamation once again, louder. There was a truthfulness to the uninhibited sound that made his balls ache and his dick harder. Sliding his hands over her thighs, he stroked her nether lips with his fingertips before parting her folds farther still. He moved his mouth over her mons, sucking on her clit with gentle force. Her pussy grew wetter against his chin, the musky scent of her pleasure infusing every breath he took.

Darci pushed her hips forward, pulling his head closer to her sex with a subtle tightening of her leg. He fucked her with his tongue, rolling it over her clit in broad, flat strokes, stabbing into her folds with pointed penetrations, painting her clit again before sucking on it some more.

"Damn, that feels so good." The honesty of her earlier moans echoed in the panted statement. She thrust her cunt to his face, a low gasp escaping her when he slipped his thumb into her sodden pussy. "Even better," she murmured, tugging on his hair.

His chin grew wetter, her juices flowing from her with every wriggle of his thumb and caress of his tongue. He dragged one hand down her leg, reveling in the smooth curve of her calf before fumbling with his belt and fly. His cock was achingly rigid with desire. If he didn't feel something more than the inside of his jeans on the stretched skin, he'd go insane.

Shoving his hand past his open fly, he grabbed his erection and squeezed, the brutal pressure sending stars of painful pleasure through his groin. He wanted to sink its length into Darci's drenched cunt more than anything, but not until he'd made her come with his mouth. The raw rapture scalding through his veins was too intense for him to penetrate her now. If he did, he'd shoot his seed with the first thrust. He wanted her to orgasm before that happened. Only then would he allow himself release.

But holy fucking hell, he couldn't last much longer.

"Oh, oh, oh yes," she moaned, grinding her clit to his mouth. He licked her out, driving his thumb deeper into her pussy as he did so. Her clit dragged against his tongue—a pebbled knot of undeniable response. "Yes, yes."

Her leg tightened around his shoulders, her belly jerking with each hitching breath she took. She was close. He could feel it in the tension claiming her body. Taste it in the juices flowing from her cunt. With a twist of his wrist, he replaced his thumb's delving exploration with two fingers, scissoring them inside her tight passage as he nipped her clit with his teeth.

"Oh *yes!*" She bucked once, her grip on his hair turning painfully strong. "Yes! That feels so...so..."

He bit her clit again, plunging another finger into her sex, wriggling all three.

"Oh fuck, I'm going to...I'm going to..." She bucked again. "Oh, oh, oh, oh."

Her cries grew wilder. Rawer. Her pussy gushed with cream.

"Fuck yes, yes, yes!"

She came, her cries turning to whimpering mews, her hips thrashing in rhythmless thrusts.

Jarrod's cock jerked in his fist, his balls rising, the pit of his belly exploding with wet heat. He was going to fucking erupt. No matter how hard he choked his hard-on, he was going to come. Darci's release triggered his own and he couldn't stop it. He'd never had a woman respond so openly to his lovemaking. It was empowering. Awesome.

Overwhelming.

He tore his mouth from her cunt, stumbling back onto his haunches, eyes shut, face scrunched in agonizing pleasure. He squeezed his cock with brutal force. Fuck, he was going to come. Right here, right now. On her rug. Like a hormone-crazed teenage boy. How fucking embarrass—

A foot planted on his chest, shoving him backward. Hard. He fell on his ass, eyes snapping open to stare up at Darci as she straddled his splayed legs and dropped to her knees without a word.

"Darci," he began, voice choked, heart hammering.

She smiled at him, a wicked smile that turned the mounting pressure in his cock to a volcanic force, and reached for his erection with one steady, purposeful hand. Her fingers closed over his fist, her gaze holding his for a split second before she bent at the waist and closed her lips over the bulbous head of his cock.

He let out a groan that was more of a scream. Releasing his stranglehold on his dick, he fell backward onto the rug, whatever blood not already surging into his cock roaring in his ears. *Here it comes, here it...*

Darci's mouth plunged down his cock's turgid length, her lips sealed tight around its distended girth, her tongue lapping at its underside.

"Fuck!" he groaned, bolts of liquid electricity arcing through him. Radiating from Darci's sucking mouth. A violent spasm claimed him, followed by another. And another. He threw back his head, teeth grinding together, jaw clenched tight. Christ, no. He was coming. He couldn't stop it. He couldn't.

She took him deeper in her mouth, her lips pressing the hard rocks of pleasure his balls had become, her hands smoothing over his stomach.

"Fuck, Darci," he panted, staring sightlessly at the ceiling, the walls, the top of her head. "I can't hold back any longer. If you don't want me to come in your mouth you should st—"

She slid one hand between his thighs, cupped his balls in a firm grip and slowly sucked back up his cock, flicking her tongue along his length as she did so. And then plunged back down again. Fast. Hard.

Jarrod lost rational thought. His body convulsed, his cock jerked and his orgasm ripped through him like wildfire, scorching away any resistance to the elemental rapture of his release.

Taking him, possessing him. Draining him.

His seed pumped into Darci's mouth and she took it all, the back of her throat working over the head of his cock, her hands massaging his balls, her fingertips pressing at the puckered hole of his anus.

Jarrod let out a raw groan, hands grabbing at the rug, legs quivering, pulse pounding until, all control deserting him, he gave himself over to the pure pleasure of the blowjob and rode each cresting wave.

"Well," he muttered when the throbbing tension in his groin subsided somewhat. "That didn't exactly go to plan." His hands found their way to Darci's hair as she laid her head on his belly and he combed his fingers through the cool strands.

"What plan?" She settled herself between his spread legs, her breasts cupping his groin, her own fingers drawing lazy circles over his rib cage. "The one to arrest me?"

He laughed, shaking his head as he did so. "Well, that too, but that's not what I meant."

She lifted her head and studied him, eyebrows dipping a little. "You really were going to arrest me? Should I be calling my solicitor now?" She gave him a mischievous smirk. "You do realize what we just did could be considered entrapment, or accepting a bribe or something official sounding I'm sure they mention often on *Law & Order*."

Jarrod laughed again, the sound more at ease than any he'd heard himself make in a long time. "No, Ms. Whitlam. I'm not going to arrest you, although I have to admit the idea of putting you in handcuffs *has* crossed my mind an obscene number of times since I first saw you."

She cocked an eyebrow.

"I know you are who you say you are," he went on, his pulse kicking up a notch when her fingers played with his nipple. "What didn't go to plan was my utter and complete lack of control just now."

Darci studied him for a still moment, a smile pulling at the edges of her mouth. "I wouldn't berate yourself too much, Detective." She straightened to her feet and began to walk away from him, seemingly uncaring of her naked state. Jarrod watched her go, his cock growing heavy. It wasn't just refreshing to meet a woman so relaxed with her body, but a bloody turn-on. She flipped him a quick look over her shoulder. "A woman my age would consider what just happened the ultimate compliment."

Pushing himself up onto his elbows, he frowned at her before she disappeared through the doorway leading to the kitchen. "There you go with that 'my age' bullshit," he called, tucking his dick back into his jeans. "I *know* you've only just turned forty and you're talking as if you're checking yourself into a nursing home any day."

She came back into the living room before he could zip up his fly, a bottle of water in her hands. Her eyebrows rose up her forehead. "How do you know I've just turned forty?"

He gave her a pointed look. "I'm a cop investigating a crime, remember? I may not have known what Darci-Rae Whitlam looked like until the moment you slammed into me on your front porch, but I know your date of birth. Just out of interest, your driver's license photo looks nothing like you. When did you stop being a blonde with black horned-rimmed glasses?"

She snorted, the soft sound far sexier than it should have been. "When my sister told me to grow up."

Jarrod frowned, detecting an edge to her voice. What was that about? "Well," he said with a slow grin, wanting to see her relaxed and comfortable again, "I like the way you look now. A lot."

Lifting the bottle to her lips, she took a slow drink, her gaze never leaving his face. She still hadn't made any move to cover her nakedness and Jarrod's cock gave a little twitch. If she was standing any closer to him, he'd drag her back down to the floor and fuck her silly.

145

What are you waiting for then?

"And how old are *you*, Detective St. James?"

He grinned. "Young enough to qualify."

She narrowed her eyes. "Qualify?"

"Tempt the Cougar," he prodded, despite the uncertainty at his bravado. Why was it he could bust up a gang of Hells Angels without breaking a sweat, but the idea of suggesting what he *thought* he was suggesting, to a woman he'd known for all of seventy-four minutes, made him as nervous as all hell?

She turned and gave her closed laptop a long look, her expression neutral. Studied. "What crime are you investigating?"

The question took him by surprise. He bit back a curse, a sudden stab of professionalism making him start. "Stolen identity," he answered. "Someone has been using your personal information to establish a new identity."

Darci turned back to him, unreadable expression still on her face. "Would that identity have anything to do with being a phone-sex worker?"

Jarrod nodded. He was breaking so many rules right at this moment he could barely keep up. If the head of his division found out what he was doing he could face suspension, but he didn't care. Seriously, he'd just shared the most amazing act of fellatio with his key witness and was ready to do more. Telling her someone was using her name to operate an illegal phone-sex business was the least of his transgressions.

She let out a ragged sigh, crossing to where he still lay stretched out on her rug before dropping to her knees beside him. "That explains a lot then, doesn't it?" She took another sip of water, gaze fixed on the poster of the copulating teddies.

Jarrod looked at her, something indefinable stirring deep inside him. She looked so beautiful, so confident, and yet at the same time, vulnerable. The contradiction squeezed his chest and it was all he could do to not reach out and pull her down to his body and kiss her senseless.

Then do it!

"Based on the last phone call I heard," he said, struggling to keep his hands to himself, "I'd say yes."

She turned her attention from the poster and gave him a level look, her stare direct. A teacher's look if ever Jarrod had seen one. *Don't lie to me or there* will *be consequences.* "So," she said, tone calm but serious. "I have to ask—why did you run from the house earlier if you knew who I was?"

He swallowed, suppressing the urge to fidget. Not just because he didn't know how to answer her question, but because he was growing more and more aroused by the second. Every facet of Darci Whitlam's personality turned him on, from the quirky woman who talked to her dog as if he were a person to the sensual creature of assertive passion to the no-nonsense educator. *Oh man, you're sinking fast, Jarrod.*

"Two reasons," he answered, forcing his own voice to stay steady. "The phone call reminded me what I was here for. And made me realize what I was just about to do."

She studied him, teacher gaze unwavering. "So why did you come back?"

Swallowing again, he met her stare, throat—and other parts of his anatomy—thicker still. "I realized what I was just about to do."

His cryptic answer curled the corners of her mouth. "Hmmm."

She took another drink, her breasts moving slightly as she raised the water bottle to her lips. Jarrod pulled in a slow breath, enjoying the sight. He'd never known someone to be so at peace with her naked body. Every woman he'd ever fooled around with had so many hang-ups about the way they looked they'd scramble for the sheets or clothes the second he withdrew. Darci-Rae, however…

Fuck, she is sexy. Sexy and confident and gorgeous and…

His cock jerked, his balls growing swollen and hard.

I want her. Again. Now.

Unable to stop himself, he slid his hand up her thigh, skimming her hip before charting a slow path up to her left breast. She felt like sinful perfection and his cock flooded with eager heat.

Darci's eyes widened. She looked at him, her expression stunned, her body motionless.

A sinking sensation settled in the pit of Jarrod's gut. He froze, hand still on the heavy swell of her breast. *Oh fuck. You've read the signs all wrong, Detective. Get your hands off her, say you're sorry and get out of her house.*

"What?" she began, her stare sliding to his rising erection. It jutted from his open jeans like a bloody pole, thick and stiff and already purple with hungry desire.

Before he could grab the offending thing and shove it back into his trousers, however, Darci turned her gaze back to his face. "Already?" she asked, her smile hot enough to make Jarrod's head swim.

He snaked his arm up around her neck and buried his fingers in her hair, a wave of something very like bliss rolling through him. "One of the benefits of a younger man," he murmured with a grin, tugging her head down to his. "We're ready to go almost straight away." He brushed his mouth over hers, delighted when her tongue touched his bottom lip. An invitation.

With a growl, he yanked her against his body, capturing her laugh with his kiss. Capturing her breasts with his hands.

Fuck, if he was going to break the rules, he may as well do a damn good job of it.

Chapter Five

ဢ

He crushed her mouth with his, his tongue slipping past her lips to mate with hers. Darci kissed him back, the subtle taste of her sex lingering on his lips and breath turning her on more than it should. Damn, the *whole situation* was turning her on more than it should. She was rolling about on her living room floor with a man probably in his twenties, whom she'd known just over an hour, and the junction of her thighs was so wet with her juices she wondered why they both weren't floating.

This kind of thing didn't happen in real life. This kind of thing happened in the erotic romances she read, the ones she discussed with Rachel over the 'net. The ones Vivian scoffed at with such derision.

Jarrod's hand massaged her breast a little harder, nipping at her bottom lip as he did so, and she groaned in appreciative capitulation. Fiction or no, it *was* happening. To her. Right now. The hottest, sexiest guy she'd ever met was feeling her up and kissing her with such smoldering talent she could barely breathe. She was stark naked beneath him, her legs entangled with his, her pussy throbbing with a need she couldn't pass off as fantasy, her breasts crushed against his chest—and it was *real*.

Oh, wait until I tell Rachel.

The delighted thought flittered through her head. Seconds before Jarrod hauled himself backward and off her body.

She blinked, her chest constricting with shock as she watched him take a step away from her. "What...?"

He grinned, toeing off his boots. "I think it's a touch unfair you're the only naked one here, don't you?"

Darci laughed, her pussy throbbing harder when he unholstered his gun, tossed it onto the sofa and shoved his jeans completely down his hips.

His cock—longer and thicker than any she'd seen—stood proudly from the thatch of dark curls between his legs. She ran her gaze over it, her pulse quickening at the memory of its impressive length in her mouth. She'd never been one for giving head, but Jarrod's cock...

Jarrod in general, Darci. There's nothing about him you don't like.

It was true. So far, in their very short relationship, he'd pushed all the right buttons—both metaphorical and physical.

Her clit joined her pussy's eager throbbing, as if to prove the point. She watched him tug off his socks and discard them beside his jeans and gun, her sex growing tight when his shirt joined them.

Oh...

The inarticulate interjection whispered through her mind, the sight of Jarrod's naked body robbing her of intelligent thought.

Her mouth went dry. Her sex, wet.

Damn, he really was stunning. Long and lean, with muscles so divinely sublime they could only have been sculpted by a master artist. A mottled bruise marred his right shoulder—courtesy of Jay Jay's teeth no doubt—but the short stab of guilt sinking into Darci's belly got lost in her rising desire as she continued taking in the sight of his naked form. The smattering of dark hair across his chest only served to highlight the smooth strength of his pecs, and she followed its trailing descent down his six-pack stomach, past his shallow navel until it joined the curls from which his rigid cock jutted.

"I can see why they call you Calvin at the station," she blurted.

He chuckled, a faint pink tingeing his cheeks. "Don't believe them. I'm the ugly one of the unit."

She laughed at his obvious joke. She doubted the word "ugly" had ever been applied to Jarrod St. James. Nor that there was anyone alive better looking. It was impossible. "Don't believe you."

He ducked his head, running his hands up his stomach in an act she recognized as pure self-consciousness. Self-effacing. "You know us computer geeks. We're all sex gods underneath our clothes and pocket protectors."

Before she could respond, he stepped toward her, planting his bare feet on either side of her legs and extending one hand to her.

She took it without question, her trust in him not surprising her in the slightest.

He pulled her to her feet with fluid ease, the sight of his muscles flexing as he did so making Darci's impatient, licentious sex throb some more.

This is real, Darci. So very, very real.

"I'm going to fuck you now, Darci-Rae," he said, looking down into her face when they stood toe-to-toe. His lopsided grin returned, cocky and boyish at once. "I'm going to spend the rest of the day showing you just how much stamina I have." He slid one hand up her arm, over her shoulder to the back of her neck, a tender caress that made her shiver. Her nipples pinched into hard peaks and she swayed toward him, wanting nothing more at that very second than to feel them brushing against his hard chest.

A low, uneven moan rumbled in his throat as their bodies touched. "How much stamina *you* have," he murmured, nostrils flaring.

He snaked his other hand around her bare backside and yanked her hips to his, his lips brushing hers in a teasing kiss. "Bedroom," he whispered against her mouth. "Now."

The order sent a jolt of wet tension spearing into Darci's core. It wasn't the first time his sensual commands made her horny and she drew in a shaky breath. Surrendering control to someone else had never been her strong point. What did it mean that she wanted to do so with Jarrod?

Head buzzing, pulse pounding in her neck, she slipped from Jarrod's embrace and walked toward her bedroom. She'd read a few BDSM novels, Rachel having suggested more than one. They always aroused her, but she knew deep down she wasn't cut out to be a submissive.

So why did her sex constrict with wanton anticipation when St. James ordered her around?

Was there such as thing as lite-BDSM? BDSM sans the B? And S? And M? Or was his natural power and dominating personality—the kind she believed all good cops should possess—a turn-on for *her* specifically, a woman who spent every weekday being in control of the uncontrollable?

Or was it just Jarrod, full stop?

A man more suited to her than any of the ones she'd tried on before?

Connection. On a soul level?

She came to a halt in the doorway of her bedroom, suddenly unsure. What was she thinking? What did she *think* she was thinking? Connection? What the hell did that mean? Sex with a younger man? Trusting him when she knew almost nothing about him? This *was* real life, not a novel. She had to be out of her bloody mind if she thought anything apart from shame and regret could come from this.

Viv *was* right. She was oversexed. It was time to grow up.

Warm lips pressed to the side of her neck, Jarrod's hands skimming over her hips and up her rib cage. "I like the copulating teddies better."

She started, her heart racing, her stare jerking to the framed poster for the BBC's *Pride and Prejudice* hanging above her bed. "It's a classic," she murmured, her throat tight. She looked at the image of Colin Firth as Mr. Darcy, the epitome of the alpha romantic hero—handsome, arrogant, dominating, rent vulnerable by the one woman he fell in love with.

Arrogant. Dominating.

Handsome.

She closed her eyes, the image of the actor cast as her favorite fictional character replaced by an image of Jarrod St. James, his lopsided grin cocky, his eyes ablaze with undeniable desire.

Oh, Darci, what you're thinking is lunacy, you know that, don't you?

Jarrod's lips moved up the column of her neck with languid intent. "'In vain, have I struggled'," he whispered against the sensitive dip beneath her ear. "'It will not do'."

The breath left Darci in a groan, the words of Jane Austen's most famous hero flooding her sex with cream. No, it wasn't Mr. Darcy's quote that did it. It was Jarrod. Jarrod saying them, Jarrod knowing them, and knowing what they meant. Jarrod admitting what was between them wasn't expected nor deniable.

Jarrod touching her, kissing her, holding her.

Jarrod. Just Jarrod.

His lips moved to her ear, nibbling on her earlobe as he ran his hands up to her breasts. He took each one in a gentle grip, pinching her nipples between his fingers before sliding his hands farther up her chest to her throat.

She moaned, tilting her head to the side when his lips moved to her jawline. The way he kissed her now, unhurried, focused, made her breaths shallow. It was as if he had all the time in the world and wanted to spend every minute of it exploring her in great detail. Gone was the surprised hunger of their first kiss, gone the frantic lust of their second.

This was something unlike anything she'd experienced— a man in no rush, giving pleasure to the woman in his arms with just the innocent connection of his lips on her skin.

With tender force, he pulled her back against his body, his mouth nipping and sucking the bowed column of her neck before moving to her shoulder. His erection nudged the crevice between her butt cheeks, a long, thick rod she ached to feel buried in her sex.

"You have no idea how much I want you," he murmured against the curve of her shoulder. "I shouldn't be here. I should be on my way back to Sydney. I should be tracking down a crook, but you tempt me like…" He dragged one hand down her body, slipping the tips of his fingers between her closed thighs. "Fuck, I have no idea what you tempt me like, I just know I can't walk away from you. That's how sexy you are. That's how much I want you."

Darci rolled her hips, stroking his cock with the curves of her ass. How did someone so young know what to say to make her want to melt into a puddle of concentrated pleasure at his feet? She stroked her fingers down the length of his arm, pressing them to the backs of *his* fingers resting between her thighs. With gentle pressure, she pushed them harder against her drenched folds. "I'm beginning to get an idea," she answered on a low chuckle.

He groaned in her ear, taking over her unspoken suggestion and plunging his fingers into her pussy.

She gasped, arching her back into the sudden penetration. He cupped her right breast in his other hand, fucking her with two fingers as he did so. Slow, deep fucking, seeking out the sweetest spot within her sex, his lips still charting hot paths over her shoulder and throat.

"Tell me again why you shouldn't be here," she breathed, his kisses making her head swim. Or was that the determined stroking of Jarrod's fingers inside her sex? She didn't know. Didn't care. The swollen heat of her pussy throbbed and she felt the tops of her thighs grow slick.

"I haven't a fucking clue," he whispered. He withdrew his fingers from between her legs and turned her to face him, cupping her face in his hands and claiming her mouth with his.

The kiss was just as slow, just as languid as his earlier worship of her throat and shoulder. Thoroughly, and yet so very gently, his tongue traced the lines of her lips, slipping past them to take possession of her mouth completely. With each swirl and caress of his tongue, he took a step forward, guiding her deeper into her bedroom until the backs of her knees bumped against the edge of her bed.

She gasped, clinging to him as they both tumbled backward onto the mattress, the involuntary intake of breath turning into a laugh when Jarrod's cock nudged the folds of her pussy.

"Oh, you're laughing at me now, Ms. Whitlam?" He smiled against her lips, shifting until he had her pinned completely beneath his body. His cock head pressed at her sex again, with a little more assertion this time.

Darci shook her head, wrapping her arms around his shoulders to hold him closer to her still, letting him feel her answering grin with his lips. "Not at all, young man." She rolled her hips and his cock pressed slightly into her sodden slit. God, she so wanted to be impaled by it. Deeply and completely.

"Young man, young man." He growled, lifting his head enough to give her a smoldering glare. "Let's cut the 'young' and stick with just 'man', all right?" He shoved his hips forward, pressing his cock harder to her slick pussy. She was so wet she felt him slip past her outer lips easily, penetrating her a little more. Her head spun. She'd have to stop him soon. This whole thing was an act of sheer lunacy, but she wasn't *that* crazy. Before they went any further she'd need him to—

He nipped at her bottom lip with his teeth before kissing it with such thorough attention, she lost her train of thought and tightened her arms around his shoulders for fear she was about to be swept away by the flood of raw pleasure rolling through her.

"As I've pointed out before," he continued, lips scorching a path along her jaw, up to her temple, back down to her mouth again. "I don't give a rat's ass about your age or mine. Now shut up, stop laughing, stop pointing out the unimportant, stop doing *anything* except letting me fuck you until we're both covered in sex."

Darci's heart leapt into her throat. She arched her back, the branding contact of his mouth on her neck, working down her throat toward her aching, pleasure-swollen breasts, almost overwhelming her. "Don't you mean sweat?" she rasped, scrambling at his shoulders when he brushed the upper swell of her left breast with the tip of his tongue. *Oh...oh yes...*

He growled, the sound sending wicked vibrations through his body and into hers. "Right, that's it. You are so going to get it."

Before she could ask what "it" was, he closed his lips over her nipple and sucked. Hard.

She whimpered, awash with delicious bliss. She'd always known there was a reason she had breasts, until now she just hadn't known what it was. Now she knew—it was so Jarrod St. James had something to suck and bite and worship. What other reason could there be than the absolute—no, the *pure* ecstasy coursing through her?

She'd read more than one erotic novel in which the heroine came with just mouth-to-breast stimulation but until right at that very moment, she believed it a work of fiction. Now...

Jarrod moved his lips to her other breast, his fingers fondling the abandoned nipple with equal fervor. Twin ribbons of exquisite heat shot through her, sinking into the pit of her belly only to blossom into a mounting, pulsing tension. She moaned, rolling her head to the side, eyes closed. A distant, rational part of her mind recognized with relief that Jarrod's new position had removed his unsheathed cock from her cunt. A wanton, depraved part of her mind wept for the loss. She wanted him inside her. She couldn't deny that anymore, and it had nothing to do with the fact that he could quote Austen, looked like sin, was devoid of any wrinkles and gray hair and had the most impressive dick she'd ever seen in her life.

It was because, above all else, he wanted to make her feel pleasure. *Her* pleasure. He wanted to make her come. He wanted to give *her*, Ms. Darci-Rae Whitlam, something she'd hungered for her whole adult life. Complete and utter rapture.

And who was she to argue with a cop?

"Fuck, I love how your skin feels like velvet," he murmured against her breast, smoothing his hand over her rib cage, down over her belly to the tight curls of her pubic hair. "I could get off on just that alone."

She laughed. Or maybe she moaned. She didn't really know. Because at that moment, he replaced the hand on her mound with his mouth and her mind lost focus of anything else apart from the flicking pressure of his tongue on her clit.

He lapped at her sex, slow, firm strokes that made her want to weep. And still he explored her flesh with his hands, sliding his palms over her hips, up her rib cage, down her waist, over the tops of her thighs. They never stopped, his hands, touching her wherever they could reach. Never deserting his deliriously forceful occupation of her pussy with his teeth and tongue, he marked her flesh as his property.

Just when Darci knew she could hold on no longer, when she knew she was about to be washed away by her second orgasm of the day, he pulled away slightly, blowing a fine stream of cool air onto her hot, sodden folds.

She bucked, the unexpected contact of breath on feverish flesh sending a wicked chill up her spine. Her nipples pinched harder, her cunt constricted. "I don't know if I can—" she began.

"Of course you can," he cut her off, the conceit in his voice—muffled somewhat by the length of her thigh he was busily exploring with his lips—making her sex squeeze again.

As if to prove his point, he ran one hand down her leg, cupping the back of her knee to lift it from the bed. He raised it straight, stopping only when her toes pointed at the ceiling and resting her calf against the hard strength of his chest.

Blue eyes glinting with an emotion Darci swore was devilment, he gazed down at her. "Now this is what we are going to do, Ms. Whitlam." He skimmed one palm down the length of her thigh, his fingertips feathering the outer lips of her cream-slicked slit in a teasing stroke before snaking back up to her ankle. "I am going to kiss every part of your body starting with this unbelievably sexy leg until you beg me to do otherwise. When—and only when—you tell me you can't take any more, I will sink my very stiff cock into your very sweet pussy until you realize you can take a *whole lot* more." He grinned, that lopsided grin Darci bet could make any female on the planet wet with lust.

And that grin is all for you, Darci-Rae. How does that make you feel?

Amazing. Utterly amazing.

She gazed up at him as he towered over her, hugging her leg like a warrior holds his weapon when in a state of waiting repose, his stare fixed on her face, his cock pressing against the back of her thigh. "Is it wrong of me to be glad I'm a victim of crime?" she asked on a whispering breath.

His grin turned into a slow smile, softening the edges of his youthful bravado until Darci's heartbeat quickened. "Only if it's wrong of me to be glad of the same thing."

The silence stretched between them, heavy and pregnant with unspoken possibilities.

Say something. Anything.

She couldn't think of a word.

Smile fading, Jarrod studied her down the length of her extended leg, his Adam's apple jerking up and down his throat before, with a low groan she swore was a curse, he closed his eyes and pressed his lips to the side of her ankle.

She sucked in a swift breath, closing her own eyes. If she didn't, she would die of sensory overload. The touch of Jarrod's lips on her ankle—a part of her body she never would have labeled an erogenous zone—was almost too much to bear. How would she survive *watching* him kiss her there? How would she withstand the sight of his naked body pressed against her leg, knowing his cock hovered but a hairsbreadth from her hungry cunt?

She bit at her bottom lip. Sensory overload. Sight and touch. God help her if she started to catalogue the way he smelled, the lingering taste of his sweat on her lips, the sound of his ragged breath drawn with tenuous control through flaring nostrils...

"Oh, Jarrod..."

Her groan fell from her, her nails driving into her palms as he ran a slow path of hot kisses down her calf to the sensitive hollow at the back of her knee.

Her pussy constricted again. Harder. The tension in her core grew thicker.

He kissed the back of her knee with total adoration, running his hands up and down her leg as he did so. With each caress of her thigh, his fingers brushed her drenched folds. Again, again. Again.

Darci began to moan, lifting her hips to his downward stroke, the need to be filled with his strength growing more compelling. "Jarrod," she groaned, pushing her hips upward. "Jarrod...please..."

And still he kissed the back of her knee. Tiny, nipping kisses, tiny flicks of his tongue on her skin. She whimpered, the pressure between her thighs building. Her clit throbbed, a world of concentrated want. Swollen need. "Please," she moaned again. "I can't..."

He slid his mouth down to her cunt in one long, dragging kiss and plunged his tongue into her wetness.

Shards of tension shot through her. "Jarrod!" she cried, shoving her hips upward.

Her climax rushed at her. She could feel it coming. She couldn't stop it. She couldn't. And she wanted Jarrod inside her more than she wanted breath. "Please…"

He tore his mouth from her sex. "Condom."

The word was a growl. Low and raw.

She waved her hand at the bedside drawer. Head spinning. Pulse racing. Eyes closed.

The mattress dipped and bounced beneath her, the sound of wood sliding against wood filled her ears and then he was back. Where he should be. Between her legs, his flesh sliding over hers, his hands owning her body. Her pleasure.

"Can you take any more, Darci?" he asked, his breath as shaky as her own.

She shook her head.

His fingers closed around her ankle and he lifted her leg off the bed again, extending it straight up. "Yes," he murmured, sliding his arms around her calf as he shifted on the mattress. "You can."

With one sudden, fluid thrust, he sank his cock into her sex.

Her cry burst from her throat, her back arched. She grabbed at the duvet beneath her, needing something to hold onto. Oh lordy, he felt—

"Jesus, Darci, you are so tight!"

Jarrod's proclamation, ground out from between clenched teeth, sent electrifying shards of wet tension straight into her center. She closed her eyes, her body, her *mind*, so aware of the stretching thickness of his length filling her completely, her breath caught in her throat. Of his heavy balls pressing to her ass cheeks every time he thrust into her. Of his warm fingers circling her ankle, his strong arms holding her leg to his even stronger chest.

"So tight," Jarrod moaned, his lips on the instep of her foot. "So amazingly tight."

She wanted to say something witty, something loaded with innuendo, but the words were lost. Stolen by the intense pleasure roaring through her. She closed her eyes, her teeth catching her bottom lip. With every stroke of Jarrod's length inside her, her ability to function on a higher level—to articulate, rationalize, vocalize—was stolen by pleasure until she was left with just thrumming, indescribable need and want. A woman barely capable of expressing how amazing Jarrod made her feel. "Oh," she breathed, "yes!"

Jarrod answered with a drawn-out groan, ravishing the sole of her foot with his mouth as he plunged deeper into her sex.

"Yes," she whispered again. "Oh yes."

"You have the sexiest fucking foot," Jarrod stated against her sole, his hands sliding over her calf.

For some reason, the absurd claim made her heart quicken. "Thank you."

He laughed, the sound vibrating through his chest and into her leg. He pressed his lips to her foot's arch and thrust harder into her sex, each stroke growing quicker. The base of her spine tingled, her orgasm rushing at her with such alacrity her head spun. She drew her fists closer to her body, dragging the duvet with her, afraid of being swept away. As ludicrous as it sounded, if he kissed her foot again, she might very well erupt.

How was it she'd had lovers before, orgasms before, but she'd never felt like…like *this* before?

"Sexiest fucking foot." Jarrod's fingers moved back to her ankle, his lips skimming a line down to her calf. "Sexiest fucking calf." He tugged her leg a little higher, the action lifting her backside off the bed a fraction, just enough to cause his cock to sink deeper into her sodden sex. She ground her teeth, her breaths shallow. Rapid. "Sexiest fucking knee." He kissed the back of her knee again, exploring the very place he'd only so recently charted as if he'd never been there before, all the while thrusting into her deeper and deeper, faster and faster, his balls slapping her butt.

"Sexiest fucking *everything.*"

That was it. Jarrod's proclamation, uttered in a low growl, was it. Darci's climax ignited, surging through her body like a firestorm of exquisite tension. She rammed her hips higher, taking him into her even deeper still. Wanting all of him. "Oh God," she cried, fingers scrambling at the tousled duvet, palms slapping it. She pushed into Jarrod's penetrations and, just when she knew she was about to die in the inferno engulfing her, when she couldn't take any more—she couldn't, *she couldn't*—Jarrod's rhythm turned wild and he slammed into her harder yet, his arms imprisoning her leg to his chest, his fingers digging into her flesh.

And then he threw back his head and let out a choked roar, his cock jerking inside her sex, his orgasm claiming *his* body as surely as he'd claimed hers.

Chapter Six

ℬ

Something very wet and very cold touched Jarrod on the cheek. He jerked fully awake, his semi-dozing state evaporating in an instant, his hand snatching for the spare Glock he kept under his pillow.

Not your pillow...not your house...

The confusing thought barely registered in his brain before his sleep-fogged eyes focused on the massive creature sitting motionless but a foot away from his head.

Jay Jay.

He stared at Darci's dog, remaining flat on his belly. "Hey, mate."

The dog thumped its long tail. Once.

With slow, obvious actions, Jarrod rolled his head to the other side, expecting to find Darci grinning at him.

Nope. The other side of the bed was empty. He was on his own. The only evidence he'd just spent the last two hours fucking the most amazing woman he'd ever known were the rumpled sheets and three empty condom packets on the bedside lamp table.

And a slightly tender pecker already growing stiff at the untimely memory of said fucking.

He swallowed, rolling his head to look at Jay Jay again. "Where's Darci, mate?"

The dog thumped its tail again, but still didn't move.

Which meant Jarrod didn't know if *he* should either.

He'd never owned a dog. Being the computer-nerd-slash-bully-victim he was growing up, he'd kept pets less likely to take him away from the computer or be used against him by the local thugs. A blue-tongue lizard residing in a fully decked-out terrarium beside his desk in his room was not only practical, the creature could never be attacked and hurt by Wilson "Billy" Laylor down the road. All well and good while growing up, but of no help to him now. If he tried to climb out of the bed and go to Darci—something he very much wanted to do right at that moment—would the dog leap at him?

He gave Jay Jay a lopsided smile. "I'm going to sit up, mate. Is that okay?"

Jay Jay's tail thumped one more time, his tongue lolling from his mouth.

"I'll take that as a yes," Jarrod muttered, pushing himself slowly into a sitting position on the mattress.

Jay Jay straightened to all fours instantly, stare fixed on Jarrod's face.

"If I climb out of this bed, will you try to eat me?"

The dog cocked its head to the side, ears pricked, and then, without so much as a woof goodbye, turned and trotted out of the room.

Jarrod let out a rather embarrassed chuckle. He'd faced down dogs before when he was working homicide. Why the hell did *this* dog unnerve him so much?

Are you kidding? He's Darci's dog. Isn't that reason enough? He almost gnawed your shoulder off when you first met him. Anything that reminds you of Darci unnerves you. Bloody hell, the woman herself unnerves you. And turns you on.

The straining pole of his cock, jutting up from his groin, illustrated that quite clearly.

Ignoring his erection *and* still tender shoulder, he looked around the room. Where was Darci? They'd had quite a bit of fun in the last two hours. Enough to feed his fantasies and make his dreams wet for many, many months to come. Trouble was, he wasn't inclined to leave. In fact, the thought of driving back to Sydney, of walking away from Ms. Whitlam and her acerbic wit, sexy-assed body and throaty voice, made his chest ache.

Planting his bare feet firmly on the floor, he straightened from the bed. The unexpected physical response to ending this…*thing* with Darci unsettled him. What he needed right now was some hard, fast, loud sex to ease his mind.

His cock twitched in approval and he left the bedroom, casting a parting glance at Colin Firth hanging above her bed. "Still like the copulating teddies better."

He walked through Darci's quiet house, the cop part of his mind wondering why it was so quiet, where Darci was. Another side—a side he'd rarely allowed out to play—enjoying the act of just being in a comfortable environment. He had no clothes on, he was horny, there was a bloody big dog-slash-bear living in the house but he felt…at home.

He grinned, scruffing his hair as he entered Darci's living room. He'd never felt at home anywhere apart from behind a computer or chasing down a crook. Who'da thought it?

Padding across the small, neat room, he paused at Darci's partially open laptop, giving the glowing apple on its lid a contemplative look. If he quickly checked out the fraudulent site from which she'd obtained her U.S. visa, they'd have more time for fooling around before he had to head back to Sydney.

His chest squeezed again at the unwelcome thought. He didn't want to head back to Sydney. Two hours south was two hours too far from Darci. How could he see her smile anytime he wanted if he was two hours south?

Uh-oh. Are you hooked already?

Pulling a face, he dropped his naked butt onto the sofa and pushed the laptop's lid completely open.

He noticed two things immediately.

One, the Tempt the Cougar blog was still open. And two, Darci had recently been iChatting with someone called Rachel.

Are you serious? OMG, girl. That is fan-freaking-tastic! You know we're gonna want to know alllll the details, don't you?

He read Rachel's last line of communication again. His fingers itched to scroll the session back so he could read whatever Darci had said beforehand. He shifted on the cushion, his dick growing harder still. Why he was getting even more turned-on over the idea of Darci talking about him as a conquest, he didn't know — but boy, was he.

Welcome to Tempt the Cougar, my lucky Australian soul sister, Rachel suddenly typed, and Jarrod started, jerking back a little from the laptop. **Can't *wait* to hear what Vivian has to say about this. God, she's going to freak! Wish I was there to see her reaction.**

The phone rang. Loudly.

Jarrod jolted to his feet, completely, inexplicably flustered, his stare locked on the noisy, inconvenient device.

"Heya, this is Darci-Rae. If this is one of my students, consider yourself on detention. Otherwise, leave a message after the beep."

"Hello, Darci-Rae," a thin, somehow crude male voice crooned over the connection. Jarrod's gut rolled, a deep sense of rage surging through him. "Fancy my surprise when I found your name and number on hotcalls.com.au. You know what I want to do to you, don't you? I want to bend you over your desk and —"

In a whirlwind of naked flesh and wet hair, Darci ran into the living room. She bolted past Jarrod without a second glance, snatching up the phone handset and slamming it to her ear. "Terry Cahill, I know it's you!" she snapped, her voice like cracking ice. "When you get to school on Monday you better be prepared for a —"

Before Jarrod even knew what he was doing, he crossed the room and jerked the handset from Darci's white-knuckled grip. "Terry Cahill," he all but snarled, the disgust in his gut threading through an unexpected, overwhelming need to protect Darci. "This is Detective Jarrod St. James of the Sydney metro police department. The number you are calling is being monitored and I am tracking your location as we speak. I will be there within the hour to collect you." He paused. For a second. "Better be telling your parents they need to contact their solicitor."

The other line fell silent. For two seconds. Then, "It was a joke!" the less-crude, far more thin and wavering voice squeaked, the teenage boy's terror flooding through the connection like an erupting wail. "I didn't mean, I didn't mean to—"

Jarrod cut him dead. "I suggest, then, you think twice about harassing my girlfriend in such a way," he snarled. "Or we'll be having a nice little chat in the interrogation room. Do you understand?"

The phone clicked, the connection killed.

"Oh my God!" Darci burst out laughing beside him, sliding her arms around his waist and pressing her very naked body against him. "I don't believe you *did* that!"

Jarrod looked at the phone in his hand, the pulse in his neck thumping. He gave Darci a grin, fully aware it was a little stunned. Even more aware his erection was trapped between their bodies—its length pressing against her belly with unabashed intention. "Neither do I."

She shook her head, her smile so happy and open his head swam. "Girlfriend? Considering what we've just been doing it may sound a little odd to say this, but isn't *girlfriend* rushing it a bit?"

No.

The absolute certainty of the word filled his giddy head, catching him off guard. Frowning, he gazed down into her face. It *wasn't* rushing. Fuck it. He'd only known her a few hours but he wanted to know her for longer. Much longer. He slid his hand down to her wet ass and tugged her closer to his body. "I think there're distinct possibilities here, don't you?"

Darci's smile faded. A slow desertion of her happiness. She stiffened in his arms, her expression becoming guarded. Closed. "I need to finish my shower and get dressed." She pushed at his chest, and it was all he could do not to tighten his arms around her back and refuse to let her slip away from him.

But he did, and she walked away, the tension in her body obvious.

Jarrod frowned again. What had just happened?

Gut knotting, he followed her, breaking into a half-trot to catch up. "Hey," he said, snaring her wrist as she walked through her small kitchen. "What's going on?"

She pulled at his hold, refusing to meet his eyes. "Nothing. I've just got things to do, and I'm sure you have to get back to Sydney."

"Err, no." This time he refused to let her go, curling his fingers more firmly around her wrist, forcing her to stop walking. "I don't have to go back to Sydney. Not yet. And you have nothing to do except explain to me what's going on. Why the cold front all of a sudden?"

Direct green eyes lifted to his. "I'm forty, Jarrod. I'm past the age for meeting parents and necking in the movies." Her jaw bunched and she pulled at his grip on her wrist again. "I'm past the age of being a *girlfriend*. Especially to a man almost half my age."

A heavy beat thumped in Jarrod's temple. He narrowed his eyes, stepping closer to her. "'Why the hell can't a woman in her forties have the best sex of her life with a man in his twenties?'" he said, keeping his stare locked on hers as he quoted her own words from the Temp the Cougar blog. "'Why the hell do I feel guilty when I flirt with a younger man? Enough, I say. I want what society has long said I can't have, dammit'. Was that a lie? Just a frivolous blog entry designed to make people believe you have convictions, that you actually want what society says you shouldn't?"

She tilted her chin, the anger stirring in his chest clearly echoed in her level gaze. "Wow, you really did take a good look at that blog, didn't you? See anything else that interested you?"

"I'm not interested in the blog, Darci." He stepped closer, the heat from her body warming his own naked flesh. "I'm interested in *you*."

She stared at him, the little pulse in her neck beating so wildly he could see it. "Don't do that, Jarrod." She shook her head, trying to pull her wrist free once more. "Don't pretend you're going to be here for breakfast in the morning."

He closed the miniscule distance left between them, pressing his body to hers as he slid his free hand up her neck, over that wildly beating pulse to cup her face in his palm. "I'm not pretending, Darci." He dipped his head, almost—*almost*—brushing her lips with his. "How do you like your eggs?"

Before she could answer, before she presented some other lame arguments against the amazing *thing* they'd discovered, he kissed her, dipping his tongue into her mouth with hungry force.

She hesitated. For exactly two-point-five seconds.

With a low groan, she kissed him back, her tongue mating with his, just as hungry, just as forceful. He pushed her backward, moving her across the room until her ass hit the kitchen counter. The gentle impact jolted her hips forward, mashing the curve of her sex to his groin, and his cock erupted in pleasurable pain. Oh Christ, he wanted her. So badly.

He knew the argument wasn't over. He knew, despite her bravado on the cougar blog and her own self-assuredness, there was *something* stopping her from giving herself over, heart, soul *and* mind, to the possibilities he felt between them. He'd get to the bottom of that something later. After he showed her just how amazing she was—*they* were. Together.

Releasing her wrist, he grabbed at the backs of her thighs and yanked her legs upward, lifting her off the floor and onto the low counter. The height was perfect. Her backside rested on the edge of the smooth wood, his cock nudged the folds of her pussy. "See?" he murmured against her lips, raking his hands up and down the backs of her thighs. "Even the kitchen gods know we fit."

She didn't answer. Not with her usual sardonic wit, at least. She moaned, her head dropping back to bow her neck, her hands burying in his hair, her legs wrapping around his hips. The underside of his cock pressed against the velvet lips of her sex, parting them ever so slightly, and he let out a raw groan. He hadn't thought this through. He wanted to sink his dick into Darci's sweet cunt so much it hurt, but her dwindling supply of condoms was back in her bedroom. He didn't think he had the strength or control to leave her long enough to get them.

"Fuck, woman." He groaned again, dragging his lips up to her ear. "You're driving me insane."

She laughed that low, throaty chuckle he loved so much. "I think the feeling's entirely mutual."

Pulling back from her a little, he gave her a stern glare. "Don't move. Don't even breathe. If you're off this counter when I get back, I'm giving your ass a damn good smack."

She cocked an eyebrow at him. "Isn't that all the more reason *to* move?"

Jarrod's heart skipped a beat at her question, a thick spasm jerking his cock harder. An image of Darci bent over the kitchen counter flashed through his head, her tight, firm backside stuck up in the air, waiting for his palm to—

He shook his head, smoothing his hands up her thighs until he could squeeze her hips. "Oh, Ms. Whitlam, don't tease me like that."

She leaned forward, tracing the tip of her tongue over his bottom lip. "Hurry up. Before *this* old lady smacks *you*."

He ran to her bedroom. Stark naked, hornier than ever, his stiff dick whacking his stomach, his aching balls slapping his thighs. He didn't care how ridiculous he must look. He didn't care about anything except the promise in Darci's eyes and the happiness in her voice.

Thirty seconds later, he ran into the kitchen again, both delighted and downright disappointed to see her sitting in the exact same position he'd left her.

She watched him stalk toward her, her full breasts rising and falling quickly, her tongue darting out to wet her lips.

Without a word, he stepped between her thighs, shoving them apart. Grabbing her hips, he yanked her to him, her gasp filling his already engorged cock with new hunger. He explored her body with skimming hands, traveling over the curves of her hips, the dip of her waist, up her rib cage to her breasts. He cupped each swell in his palms, captured her nipples between his fingers. "Lift your arms and grab the cupboard handle," he ordered, flicking his gaze above her head for a split second.

She did as he bid her, holding his stare as she raised her arms and closed her fingers around the wooden knob on the cupboard door.

He sucked in a deep breath, the feel of her breasts lifting and stretching in his hands almost undoing him. "Don't move," he ordered, his voice scratchy.

She nodded, remaining silent as he began to massage each breast in slow, circular caresses. He lowered his stare to his handiwork, the sight of her bountiful flesh over-spilling his hands sending fresh blood into his already-throbbing cock. They were magnificent. Lush and full and ripe. Later, he would fuck her breasts. He would press them around his cock and pump into their perfection. Now, however...

He lowered his head and took one rock-hard nipple into his mouth, rolling his tongue over its distended form until he heard her moan. Dragging his mouth to the other nipple, he did the same, his balls rising when that raw whimper vibrated in her chest again. He closed his teeth on the nub—a sharp little bite that made her hiss and buck harder into his cock.

"Oh!" she cried.

He straightened, rubbing his thumbs over her nipples as he stared down into her face. "Have you ever had someone make you come just by sucking your breasts, Darci?"

She shook her head, her breath shallow.

"Would you like me to do that now?"

Her lips parted, her breaths coming faster.

"Say, 'suck my breasts until I come, Jarrod'."

"Suck my breasts until I come, Jarrod."

Her voice was barely more than a whisper, and yet her absolute desire reverberated in every syllable.

He returned his mouth to her breast, sucking on the erect nipple of her left first. Soft, gentle sucks, giving way to harder, stronger pulls. She squirmed, shoving her hips forward. Her cream-slicked folds ground against the base of his cock and the top of his sac and for a sheer second of torture, he thought he was going to come himself. How could he not, when his mouth and hands were full of her lush flesh, her musky pleasure filled his every breath and her wet desire drenched his groin?

Forcing the building tension in his sex to abate—a little— he dragged his mouth to her other breast, flicking his tongue at its nipple in a quick series of stabs before sucking it sharply.

"Oh," Darci cried, bucking against his cock again. "Oh…"

He increased his torment of her nipple, stroking her breasts with his fingers, squeezing them, pushing them together and stroking them once more, all the while suckling on her nipple until he felt the muscles in her legs and belly begin to tighten.

And still he continued to adore her breasts, rolling her nipple between his teeth, nipping gently, biting harder. He pinched her other nipple with his fingers, echoing the rhythm of his mouth, drawing from her another cry. "Jarrod," she gasped, shoving her pussy at his swollen cock. "I'm going to…"

He rolled his tongue over her nipple, bit it once and then sucked it better, his hands cupping and squeezing, squeezing and cupping.

"Oh, oh." She writhed against him. "Oh, just…just…just…"

She cried out, hips bucking, her orgasm flooding from her pussy, painting his dick and balls with cream.

It was almost too much. He almost came himself there and then.

Almost.

Snatching at one of the condom packets he'd grabbed from the bedroom, he dropped to his knees. Tearing the foil square open with his teeth, he slipped the condom out and placed it over the tip of his cock. With one hand he slid the sheath down his length, with his other he parted Darci's folds until he exposed her clit, its pink beauty slicked with the product of her climax. As his fist pumped his own cock, he leaned closer, stabbing his tongue at her clit, again and again and again. Milking her of her orgasm.

"Oh fuck, Jarrod." Shocked disbelief rang through her cry. Her thighs began to quiver. She cried out again, a keening sound that made Jarrod's cock throb to an almost unbearable steel. "Oh God, again?" she gasped, her cunt pushing against his mouth as another climax took her. "*Again?*"

Her cream filled his mouth, coated his tongue. He drank her pleasure, lapped at it, his own fist pumping his cock, torturing himself even as he readied for what came next.

"Yes. Oh yes, yes…" Darci continued, each cry louder than the last, each word ringing with astonishment.

His head spun and he knew he couldn't hold back any longer.

Snapping to his feet, he grabbed Darci's backside and slammed his cock into her cunt. Burying himself up to the balls in her tight heat.

Just as his own orgasm began to shear through his very soul.

Chapter Seven

೮ಾ

Jarrod's nails dug into the cheeks of her ass, his hands gripping her hard as he pumped his cock into her sex. He stretched her to the limit, his size and length filling her completely.

Her third orgasm detonated deep in her core and she threw back her head, beyond caring how clichéd the action was. Holy God, she felt as if she were exploding. The soles of her feet tingled, arcs of pleasured electricity shot up her spine. Her sex constricted, squeezing Jarrod's thrusting cock, the force of her climaxes shuddering through her.

She cried out again, the sound echoed by Jarrod's own. His rhythm grew erratic, his pounding penetrations faster, wilder. She held him for dear life, sure she was about to be swept away by the blazing release claiming them both.

Oh God, how did she survive this? How did she —

Jarrod roared again, a long, drawn-out cry that sounded as if it were being torn from his body. His fingers drove harder into her butt cheeks, and suddenly he was holding her motionless, his nostrils flaring, his eyes squeezed shut, the muscles in his shoulders and jaw bunched. And yet, deep in her sex, his cock jerked, powerful spasms she felt in her core.

"Fuck," he groaned, slamming into her one last time, his hands turning gentle, his lips finding her neck. "Fuck, Darci, I didn't..." His lips moved over her throat, across her shoulder, his hands and arms smoothing up her back to hold her in an embrace she could only describe as reverent. He pressed his forehead to the curve of her shoulder, a slight tremble in his body. "I never..."

The words stumbled to silence and she closed her eyes. He didn't need to finish. She knew what he was thinking, what was going through his mind. She'd never experienced anything like this either. Nor expected it. This was something more than just fucking. She could feel it. In her heart, her soul. In whatever mysterious part of herself that governed all her base, elemental behavior and thoughts.

Something had changed from the lust-driven frenzy of their earlier sex. Something she couldn't fathom. Or believe.

"Christ, Darci," Jarrod murmured against her jaw, his fingertips stroking small patterns across her upper back. His cock, still buried deep within her pussy, pulsed once more, and Darci bit back a moan. He felt so right inside her. *She* felt so right. She'd never felt…righter.

Righter? There goes your vocabulary again, Darci-Rae. Along with your dignity and sense of shame.

The scoffing interjection whispered through her head and her stomach rolled. She let out a sigh, fighting like hell against the warmth of Jarrod's arms, the gentle pleasure of his kisses on her neck and jaw. Without uttering a word, she leaned back a little and pressed her palms to his chest, pushing him away.

His shaft slipped from her pussy, an overwhelming sense of emptiness taking its place inside her. Not looking at him, she lowered herself to the floor and left the kitchen, scooping up his discarded polo shirt from the back of the sofa in the living room as she made her way to the back door.

She pulled the item of clothing over her head, Jarrod's distinct scent—sandalwood and subtle aftershave lotion— taunting her with each breath she took. Opening the back door, she stepped out onto the small deck and dropped onto the edge. The warm wood kissed her naked butt and she closed her eyes for a moment, her folds still tender with the memory of Jarrod's thrusts.

Oh Darci, what have you done?

A cold, wet nose nudged at her hand and she opened her eyes to find Jay Jay standing before her, tail wagging, a big doggy grin on his furry face. She rubbed his ears with both hands, pressing her forehead and nose to the top of his head. "I don't think this has gone the way I thought it would, mate."

Jay Jay twisted his head to the side and licked at her cheek. She straightened with a small smile, swiping at his loyal kiss with the back of her hand.

"Not the way I thought it would at all," she muttered, gazing at the rambling native shrubs and trees lining her back fence.

A quick fuck to prove I could. Tempt the Cougar. Power to the old broads. That's what this was meant to be. How could it have gotten so...so...complicated so damn quickly?

She pulled in a slow breath, Jarrod's scent permeating her body as she did so. God, what would Vivian say if she turned up at the next family dinner with Jarrod in tow? What would her sister say if Jarrod accompanied her to the next black-tie charity event? Or award ceremony? What would the media say? The Australian press would have a field day! She could see the headline in the *Sydney Morning Herald* already.

Sister of famous author Vivian Carmichael drags infant lover to auspicious event. Family appalled. Students shocked. Parents disgusted.

She swallowed, her mouth dry, her throat thick.

Jay Jay's friendly woof alerted her to Jarrod's arrival and she tensed, the sight of his jean-clad legs appearing in her peripheral vision telling her he'd plunked himself down beside her.

Jay Jay woofed again, tail wagging. He nudged Jarrod's knee with his nose and the Sydney detective laughed, the wry sound making Darci's throat thicker still. "At least *you've* accepted me, mutt." He scratched at Jay Jay's ears and, despite keeping her gaze locked firmly on the back garden, Darci

177

couldn't help but notice his arms were bare. Which meant his chest was too.

Oh, Darc...stop it! Of course he is. You're wearing his shirt now.

Suppressing an exasperated groan, Darci turned and gave Jarrod a level look. "Jay Jay also licks his own butt and eats the neighbor's cat litter. What does that say about his tastes?"

Jarrod laughed again, his eyes crinkling. "That they are eclectic, individual and unpredictable. A lot like his mistress, really."

Heart trying to leap into her tight throat, Darci turned back to her garden, staring at the empty birdbath nestled amongst the grevilleas and bottle brush trees. "I think it's time you left, Detective. I'm pretty certain you've gotten everything you need from me for your case."

Jarrod didn't answer her.

She sat motionless, wishing he would just go. It was easier that way. Maybe she could order Jay Jay to bite him...

"Actually," Jarrod said, and Darci's pulse thumped harder in her neck, "I still have a few questions. To start with, is Vivian your sister?"

The breath burst from Darci in a sharp gasp. She looked at him, not hiding the surprise in her face. "How do you know that?"

Jarrod's expression remained neutral. Cop-like. "Your friend, Rachel, said she couldn't wait to see what Vivian said about this—'this' being you and me, I'm assuming."

"So? How did you make the leap to her being my sister?"

"You mentioned your sister earlier. When I asked you about your hair." He looked as if he wanted to do something then, the muscles in his shoulders flexing a little before he shook his head. "I sensed a certain...edge to your voice. Being the amazing cop I am, I put the two together."

"We don't always see eye to eye, Vivian and I." She frowned, her pulse not only thumping harder, but faster. "Why do you ask me about my sister, anyway?"

He raised his eyebrows, his forehead barely wrinkling. "There's gotta be *someone's* voice in that stubborn head of yours, telling you what's happening between us is a dumb idea. I figured it was hers."

Damn, Darci, he's perceptive.

And right. How can he be so right about her so quickly?

Because he's right for you?

The thought made her chest clench and she licked her lips, her mouth suddenly so dry she wondered when she'd swallowed a glass full of dust.

"Vivian's voice is the voice in *everyone's* head in this country," she said, returning her stare to the birdbath. "She's Australia's most revered author."

Jarrod straightened, his hands grabbing at his knees with such ferocity Darci started. "Vivian's *that* Vivian? Vivian Carmichael?" He rolled his eyes, shaking his head in melodramatic awe. "Why didn't you tell me earlier? Well in *that* case she's completely right. I don't know *what* I was thinking, hanging around with an old hag like you."

"Hey!" Darci glared at him, indignation hitting her hard. No, not just indignation. Pain. And rejection. "You've just been fucking this *old hag* and having a bloody good time while you were at it."

Jarrod burst out laughing, his eyes twinkling with that same devilish mirth she'd first seen on her front lawn about a lifetime ago. "Ah, you see? It's not Vivian's voice in your head now, is it? It's your own. Telling you that what Vivian thinks is a load of bullshit. Reminding you how good we are together." He grinned. "How *right* we are."

The wind left Darci in a grunt, as if someone had smacked her square in the chest. She stared at him, unable to find the words to tell him he was wrong.

Perceptive bloody bastard, isn't he?

"Y'know," he went on, his grin pulling at one side of his mouth. "I've read some of Vivian Carmichael's books." He leaned toward her, his expression growing surreptitious, as if he was about to share a great secret. "She's no Jane Austen."

The snort escaped Darci before she could stop it and she gave him a wry smile, even as her heart started beating faster. "She's won more awards than you could poke a stick at."

He shook his head. "She's a bit of a prude, in my opinion."

"My father doesn't think so."

Jarrod cocked his head. "J.R. Whitlam? The Prime Minister's Literary Award for Excellence winner? The 'voice of a nation', I think he was called back in the sixties, correct?"

Darci nodded, Jarrod's literary knowledge leaving her more than impressed. A tight tingle began in her belly and she grabbed at her bottom lip with her teeth. What other books had he read? What other genres? Horror? Did he read Stephen King? Koontz?

Dammit, Darc. No. Stop it. Now.

"If I remember correctly," Jarrod commented, the offhanded tone in his voice undermined by the pointed gleam in his eyes, "your father is responsible for the first book ever to be banned by the Federal public education system for being too…" He pulled a contemplative expression. "Raunchy."

Darci narrowed her eyes, her gaze never leaving Jarrod's face. "How do you know all this?"

His lopsided grin widened. "Geek, remember? What else does a computer nerd do when trying to avoid the school bully but hide out in the library?"

Darci shook her head, her eyebrows pulling into a frown. "You are—"

"Amazing?" Jarrod cut her off. "Thank you. No more than you, Ms. Whitlam." He leaned toward her again, this time so close his lips almost brushed hers. "I think your sister needs to worry about herself and your father only needs his youngest daughter to show him what he's forgotten."

"And what's that?" Darci whispered, her throat so tight she could barely breathe. Oh God, he was so close, so funny, so sexy, so goddamn...*right*.

His smile crinkled the corners of his eyes. "How to live."

"And how do I do that?"

He chuckled, one hand coming up to cup her face. "For a smart, educated, witty, sarcastic, stubborn woman, you really ask some silly questions, you know that?" Before she could respond, he brushed his lips against hers. "By living *your* life, Darci-Rae. Any fucking way you want."

He kissed her. A deep kiss that reached all the way to her soul.

She moaned into his mouth, sliding her arms around his shoulders and pulling herself against his chest. His tongue delved into her mouth, dominating, demanding, and she gave everything back, loving the way it felt sliding over hers. Loving the way Jarrod yanked her even closer to his body, his hands tangling in her hair, his heart beating beside hers.

They both came up for air, gasping, staring at each other, Jarrod's eyes blazing with an undeniable need that Darci felt in the pit of her stomach. "What do we do now?" she wondered, still in shock.

He ran his thumb over her bottom lip. "First, we go inside."

She smiled, letting her eyelids become heavy. "Hmmm."

"Then, we cancel your credit cards."

She blanched, giving him a puzzled look. That wasn't what she'd expected him to say.

"There's still someone out there pretending to be you, Darci." He traced her bottom lip with his thumb again, dipping it into her mouth this time to skim the edge of her bottom teeth. "I don't want them bankrupting you before you get the chance to buy your cub something totally expensive. Like a personalized collar or some such thing."

She cocked an eyebrow, an exquisite tension blossoming between her thighs. A happy little throb she knew was on its way to being a big, demanding throb. "My cub?"

"Then," he continued, ignoring her question, his hand slipping from her lips to skim the column of her neck, the swell of her breasts. "You jump online and post a blog entry at Tempt the Cougar. I'm pretty certain Rachel is waiting with bated breath for The Details."

Darci laughed, enjoying not only Jarrod's cheeky words but his hands on her body. "The Details," she repeated, leaning into his cupping caress of her breast, her nipple pinching tight as he rolled his thumb over its tip.

"And then," he murmured, smoothing his hand down her body far enough to slip it under the loose hem of his shirt and capture her bare breast beneath, his fingers gently but firmly massaging its pleasure-swollen weight, "we give Jay Jay a really big bone, promise to take him to the beach later and set about making all sorts of new details to share with Rachel. Long, hard details. Hot, sweaty details." He brushed her lips with his again, the tip of his tongue touching hers with teasing cockiness. "Details deserving of an erotic romance novel. How does that sound?"

"Like the perfect afternoon," she murmured against his mouth.

"Oh." He pulled back a little, his expression puzzled. "Just one more thing. How *do* you like your eggs?"

She grinned, a slow, dirty grin she knew would disgust her sister. "Scrambled. With toast and bacon, please."

"Always gotta be bacon," Jarrod mumbled, the words almost lost to his kiss. He plunged his tongue back into her mouth, squeezing her breast in one hand as he fisted his other in the hair at her nape. He held her motionless, plundering her mouth, worshipping her body — and she let him.

"Ah, fuck it." His breath fanned her lips as he pulled away ever so slightly. "Who wants to go inside on a day like today?" With fluid grace, he scooped her up in his arms, capturing her little squeal of delight with his mouth before crossing her lawn to the outside dining table sitting under the blanketing shade of an ancient wattle tree. He laid her out on its worn, wooden surface, standing between her spread thighs, his eyes ablaze with a hunger she felt all too well in the rigid length of the erection pressed to her pussy. The throb in her core increased. Grew warmer. Damper. She pulled in a shaking breath, the smell of summer in her backyard lost to the musky potency of her desire.

His hands working their way beneath her shirt, he inched the cotton higher up her torso, the tips of his fingers kissing the under swell of her breasts as he pushed his denim-trapped cock harder to her cunt. "If I make love to you here, right now, on this table," he murmured, dancing his fingers over the straining tips of her nipple, "will Jay Jay bite my naked ass?"

The squirming heat in Darci's sex constricted and she lifted her hips a little, desperate to have Jarrod's long, thick cock inside her. "Not if I tell him to go inside," she replied.

Jarrod pressed his upper body to hers, nuzzling her neck, his hands cupping her breasts. "Tell him to go inside, Ms. Whitlam."

"Jay Jay," she croaked, struggling to raise her voice past a panted rasp. "Inside, mate. On your bed."

She heard her dog's nails scramble over the deck floor, the soft thud of the dog door banging shut, and then Jarrod grabbed at the hem of his shirt, tugged it over her body and she was naked. Wonderfully, gloriously, totally naked. Outside. In her backyard.

About to be made love to by a sinfully gorgeous younger man.

"Oversexed, Darci," she chuckled, closing her eyes at the sound of Jarrod lowering the zipper of his fly. "And loving every minute of it."

"Nothing oversexed about you, babe." His voice was rough. Raw. "Just absolutely sexy."

She smiled, sucking in a swift breath through her nose when she heard the distinct crinkle of a little foil packet being torn open. Oh, how she'd grown to love that sound in the last few hours. Almost as much as she'd grown to love—

Jarrod's cock sank between her spread folds, sinking so deep she felt as if he'd pierced her very core and all train of thought derailed.

He thrust into her in long, slow strokes, each one driving deeper, each withdrawal almost driving her mad with pleasure. His mouth moved over her throat, her shoulders, down to her breasts and up to her lips. His hands worshipped her breasts, her nipples, the flat plane of her belly and finally, her clit. He pumped into her, rolling his fingers over the swollen button of flesh, two perfectly harmonized assaults on her sex.

She moaned, arching into his penetrations, uncaring if her neighbors heard the unmistakable sounds of pleasure. Uncaring if the *world* heard.

"Darci-Rae Whitlam," Jarrod growled, plunging his cock into her pussy with rising speed. "You are under arrest for making me fall in love with you so fucking quickly."

Darci's heart slammed into her throat and she opened her eyes, staring into his burning blue ones. "And my punishment?"

His nostrils flared, fine beads of sweat glistening on his smooth forehead, his cock sliding almost out of her sex before plunging back in again. "Life sentence. No chance of parole."

She bit back a whimper, both of pleasure and sheer rapture. "What if I talk dirty to you? I've been told I have a great voice for phone sex."

Jarrod chuckled, withdrawing ever so slowly, ever so slightly, until the bulbous head of his cock stretched the lips of her pussy. He pinched her clit, once, twice, his lips curling into a wide smile as she cried out, the shudders of her orgasm beginning deep in the pit of her belly. "Not even then," he murmured.

And sank his cock back into her sex.

* * * * *

Australians never waste time when a challenge has been thrown down.

Well, who would have thought I'd post so quickly after only just joining? What has it been? Seven hours? Wow. Umm, what can I say? I came, I saw, I cougared?

Apparently, and unbeknownst to me, I was the victim of identity theft. The site I went to in order to arrange my American visa waiver for my upcoming trip to RomantiCon (pause for excited squee *squeeeeee*) was a fraudulent one. The bastards got my name, address, passport number, phone number and credit card details! Can you believe it! (I have since discovered "I've" bought close to five thousand dollars worth of sex toys from a shop called Plug and Play. Wow, I didn't know I was that sexually ferocious. Actually, yes I did. *grin*)

Anyway, to cut a long story short (although not that long, it *has* only been seven hours), a very, very, *very* fine young police officer from Sydney's cybercrime division arrived at my front door to investigate the situation and, well, to put it bluntly—I cougarized him.

Okay, admittedly, he probably helped cougarize *me*, but can I say, this is the first time in my life I'm more than happy to be a victim of crime? I'd like to take this moment to say a big thank you to the rotten sod who stole my identity and used it to establish an illegal phone-sex business. If you hadn't been so hideously horrible, Detective St. James never would have arrived at my door.

To the ladies of Tempt the Cougar...I can't wait to meet you all in person at RomantiCon (note to self, Darci. Organize a new passport ASAP). I have lots and lots of details to share. And a story idea bubbling in the back of my head. One about a high-school English teacher in her forties who has her identity stolen online and meets a very sexy, young detective trying to track down the bad guys... What do you think? Sounds too unrealistic? LOL

To Rachel, my friend who knows me better than my family. Guess who I've invited around for breakfast tomorrow? Yep, Vivian. It's been too long since my sister and I had a chat. Oh, and guess who is cooking said breakfast? Detective St. James tells me he makes a mean plate of scrambled eggs. With bacon, of course.

Now, if you will excuse me, I need to get back to what I was doing. I have a young cop handcuffed to my bed and I really think he needs tending to. *wink*

Comments

Rissa: Actually, the story idea sounds very plausible. I'm an about-to-be-forty elementary teacher anxious to be cougared. Way to go on your quick conquering of the challenge. Umm...but if he's cuffed to the bed, why the heck are you on the computer?

Edie: Things happen, don't they? Once you let the possibility of a younger man into your life, there he is, and in the most unexpected way! But you go for it, girl, and have mucho fun!

Monica: And we have a winner!!! Fastest cougar out of the gate goes to Darci. ::BG::

Lynn: Darci, you work fast! A woman after my own heart. Did I ever tell you how my "cub" and I met? We were getting it on in the back of his limo within two hours. There's something about sex with a near stranger. Yum. And, when it turns into something more... Well, it's the best of both worlds, I say. :)

Welcome to the club. Can't wait to meet you in person at RomantiCon! Actually, my man and I might be in your neck of the woods sometime soon. We've been traveling in Asia and I've always wanted to go down under. Maybe we can meet up for a double date! So...where would one find the Plug and Play?

What? A girl can never have too many toys!

Autumn: OMG! I nearly spit my coffee on my keyboard. And now Mitch is behind me, nibbling my ear and saying, "About those handcuffs. Do they only have them in Australia or can two more play that game?"

Lori: Handcuffed to your bed??? Hell, woman! What are you doing talking to US??? Go get him and we can't wait to meet you at RomantiCon.

Rachel: OMG! Call me later. I need deets!

SUMMER OF THE COUGAR

Nicole Austin

ഊ

Dedication

ഇ

To all the readers who love my characters and stories as much as I do. Thank you for your support, which allows me to continue on this amazing thrill ride.

Acknowledgements

ഇ

My sincere thanks to Ciana Stone for creating yet another fabulous series premise and inviting me to join the fun.

And a special thank you to all the ladies of the cougar club. I am awed and inspired by your incredible talent, humbled by your generosity and honored by your friendship.

Author Note

ഇ

You'll find the women of Cougar Challenge and the Tempt the Cougar blog at
www.temptthecougar.blogspot.com

Trademarks Acknowledgement

෬

The author acknowledges the trademarked status and trademark owners of the following wordmarks mentioned in this work of fiction:

Ben Wa: Ben Wa Novelty Corporation

Cinderella: Disney Enterprises, Inc.

CNN: Cable News Network LP, LLLP

Jaws of Life: Hurst Performance, Inc.

Chapter One

℘

Tempt the Cougar Blog:

Today is the first official day of summer break and the start of my new life. No more rambunctious fifth graders, classrooms or papers to grade. Robby is off to college for a special summer program and I'm living alone for the first time in my life. Talk about scary!

Sold the house, bought and decorated my new condo, packed up my "teacher" clothes and shopped for a sexy new wardrobe, traded the minivan for a cherry red convertible and got tattooed. I now have a colorful butterfly on my right hip—just above my bikini line—to symbolize my metamorphosis from Army widow and soccer mom to cougar on the prowl. Rawr!

There's just one thing left on my list—the cougar challenge. Hopefully this will be a summer full of hot lovin' with younger men! I've got eight glorious weeks to play, although I'm not sure how to get started or where to find and stalk my prey. Maybe I'll head to the beach, sip a couple of margaritas and check out the scenery.

Wish me luck, ladies.

Rissa

Larissa Cross cruised along the coast with the top down, a warm breeze rushing through her hair. She plugged her MP3 player into the stereo and cranked up the volume as Steven Tyler's signature scream blasted from the speakers. There wasn't a cloud in the bright blue sky and the weather forecasters had rated the day as a ten on the suntan scale.

A picture-postcard-perfect Florida day and a great way to kick off her new life.

Well, her new summertime life anyway. In the fall it would be back to "Miss Cross" and the comfortable routine of teaching elementary school. She tried not to think about all the changes she'd made in the past year because when you put them together it added up to a rather frightening conclusion—midlife crisis.

Where the hell did all those years go?

Next month she would hit the big four-oh. Pretty sad she'd waited this long to finally rediscover herself. "Better late than never though."

The changes had all started with the first erotic romance book she'd read. Then her friend Cam had introduced her to the cougars, a group of woman with one primary thing in common—lust for younger men. The original seven cougars met at RomantiCon, an erotic romance conference put on by their favorite publisher. Monica had been the one to throw down the gauntlet, challenging them all to find a younger lover. Rissa highly anticipated meeting everyone in person at the next conference.

She grinned, absorbing the thrill of competition. Nothing appealed to her more than the prospect of conquering a challenge. The cougar challenge was perfect for her and had arrived at just the right time in her life. She couldn't wait to try some of the erotic acts that had gotten her so hot and horny when she read all those steamy books.

A truck full of young guys honked and whistled at her. Hmm...maybe the challenge wouldn't be too difficult. These boys looked way too young but their appreciation still made her smile and gave her confidence a boost.

With a wave to the boys, she turned into the jam-packed parking lot for the public beach. As she claimed one of few available spaces at the back of the lot, her car sputtered, coughed and gave a loud hiss before the engine stalled.

"Oh great!"

Rissa knew next to nothing about cars, yet even she realized the smoke billowing out from under the hood meant bad news. She jumped out and raced to the front, intending to pop the hood. That's when she noticed the flames.

Thankfully the pickup had pulled in behind her. The teenage boys who piled out to help were on the ball, whipping out cell phones and calling for reinforcements while warning others in the immediate area to stay back.

In the few agonizingly long minutes it took for the cavalry to arrive, Rissa convinced the boys to salvage the contents of her trunk. Once they had her lawn chair, overstuffed beach bag, umbrella, towels, cooler and her precious e-book reader on the side of the road it looked like someone was having a yard sale. Or more apropos—a fire sale.

"Miss Cross?" one of the boys tentatively inquired.

Oh no. He must be one of her former students. Didn't that just make her day. "Yes." She lowered her dark sunglasses and peered over the tortoiseshell frame at him.

"Remember me? Tyler James. I was in your class?"

Prior students always failed to realize how much they'd changed or how many kids she taught and expected her to remember them. She played along to make him feel better. "Oh my gosh. You sure have grown up, Tyler. How's high school treating you?"

Once the others learned she was an elementary school teacher they became a band of protective alpha-males-in-training and stayed by her side, assisting her through the crisis.

In a flurry of flashing lights and blaring sirens, a fire truck, ambulance and police cruiser arrived. The firemen quickly set to work and extinguished the flames while the medics checked for anyone with injuries and the police wrote reports. By the time the firemen were done, her crispy car appeared ready for the junkyard.

What now, Miss Smarty-pants?

Should she call a tow truck? How the hell would she get back home? Anyone she could ask for a ride lived over the bridge, at least a half hour away. She was in no mood to sit and wait that long.

There would be so much to work out now. Thank goodness she had insurance. She'd have to get in touch with the agent to file a claim. Damn, she really loved that car. Her first non-family car in two decades. Now she'd have to shop for another and get a rental in the meantime.

Rissa plopped down on top of the cooler with a heavy sigh as her wonderful plans for the summer disintegrated. In need of some emotional support, she longed to call one of the cougars.

What would they do in this situation?

A wicked grin tugged at her lips. The cougars would tell her to check out the emergency workers and if possible get pictures. They'd also tell Rissa to flirt her ass off and get one of those hot young studs to take her home.

"Who owns the car?"

She looked up as one of the firemen headed in her direction while scribbling information on a battered clipboard.

"Uh...me. I do."

Oh yeah, I do. Please and thank you!

Damn, the man was gorgeous. Better than any of the pictures the girls posted on their *Tempt the Cougar* blog.

He was tall, at least six-one, and had a shaved head. A bit of dark stubble covered his scalp, ran along his square jawline and above his mouth. A very sexy mouth. He had to be in his early twenties by her estimation. Not too young or old. Perfect age for cougar prey.

"Name?"

Yes, what is your name, hot stuff? Please tell me.

Broad shoulders blocked out the sun as he moved to stand before her. What she wouldn't give to have him strip off the fire gear and let her see his body. From his solid build she guessed he had lots of yummy muscles. Maybe even a six-pack. She easily pictured running her fingers over his tanned skin, feeling the sinew ripple beneath her fingertips.

"That's Miss Cross," Tyler, her proud protector, stated. "She's a teacher in Tampa. Elementary school."

What a wonderful, helpful boy.

The fire god nodded toward the police officer ready to ticket the boys' pickup. "If that's your truck, you might want to move it."

"Aw crap," one of the boys groaned. The group loped off, leaving Rissa alone with the hunk whose sharp focus all of a sudden made her nervous and fidgety.

He might have been preoccupied earlier but now she had his undivided attention. Coal black eyes took a slow journey from the top of her head down her see-through cover-up, pausing at breasts nearly spilling out of tiny bright blue triangles before dipping down to linger on her tattoo then stroke her legs. And boy did his gaze ever have the impact of a physical caress. Everywhere his eyes touched her skin tightened and long-ignored nerve endings tingled.

If he can do that with a look, imagine what he'd be able to do with those big, strong hands.

That thought notched up the temperature by a good ten degrees and had sweat trickling between breasts that felt swollen. Her body hummed with sexual need and her nipples were standing at attention, clearly visible beneath the thin material of her bikini top.

"Hi. I'm JD Harmon."

He extended a hand and she slid her fingers into his firm grip, biting back a gasp as lightning bolts raced up her arm and headed straight for her core. All those erotic stories she'd been reading had left her ready for some action. And JD the fireman was looking like a prime candidate.

"They're going to send a wrecker for your car. Insurance company will probably total it since the entire electrical system is toast."

Rissa held on to his hand as if it was a lifeline and stared up at those mesmerizing dark eyes. She knew he was talking to her but the words didn't penetrate the haze of lust that had swallowed her whole.

"Miss Cross?"

"Rissa," she absently mumbled. He let go of her hand and a wave of disappointment crashed over her. But then he turned and bumped her hip with his, making a space to sit down. Right next to her on the narrow cooler. Close enough she caught a whiff of sandalwood cologne and clean, masculine sweat. Mmm...he smelled wonderful. Hot and spicy. The right side of his body pressing against her from shoulder to ankle felt even better and gave her a rush of positive vibes.

I am cougar, hear me roar!

"Do you have a way home?"

"I...home?" Her voice once again disappeared, along with the original question.

Good idea. Your place or mine?

"We'll make sure Miss Cross gets home," Tyler said as the boys reappeared. A couple of his friends groaned and he silenced them with a hard look. "We live across the bridge in Tampa," he informed the fireman.

Rissa saw her chance to make a move on the hunk slipping away.

"You're still over by the school, right?" Tyler asked.

Damn interfering kids! Didn't they have anything better to do?

Then the wonderful JD took her hand, helping Rissa to her feet, and she forgot all about the teenagers. They walked a few steps away and he got close. Real close. *Oh yeah!* His head lowered toward hers and her heart slammed against her ribs as she leaned toward him, praying he'd kiss her.

"Are you okay with the kids taking you home?"

"I-uh...sure."

Dammitdammitdammit.

"Okay. The guys are waiting and I've got to get back to work. But...umm, I have your number. Would it be all right if I call you? We could see a movie or go out to dinner — "

"Yes!" Her breathless, eager reply made her cringe but what the hell. Rissa didn't care. She'd never been asked out by a younger man, certainly never by a man half as handsome. She wasn't about to let this chance pass her by.

"Oh. Hey, that's great! Listen, I'll call you later. You know," he nodded toward the boys, "make sure the kids got you home safe and sound. Okay?"

Good lord, did the man not know the power of his appeal? How could he act tentative and unsure about her, an old, widowed soccer mom?

No, she silently reprimanded. *You're a desirable, single, available woman. He'd be crazy not to ask you out.*

"That would be nice. Thank you, JD."

His entire face lit up when she said his name.

"Great. I'll talk to you later, Rissa."

The cougars were going to freak. First time out and she'd scored. Or she would score once they got together. She'd already started composing her next blog post in her head.

They'll want pictures.

Rissa dug in her bag, grabbed her phone and snapped a photo of JD in profile as he climbed into the truck. Didn't turn out great or do him justice since she was too far away. The girls were going to love it regardless. She hit the text button and sent the picture on its way, winging through cyberspace.

In less than a minute, replies demanding details and offering congratulations started pouring in. She put them off and made her friends wait, letting their anticipation build. Besides, she hated trying to text on the phone. She waited until the boys got her home and logged on to instant message.

Rissa: I'll try to make this long story short.

Cam: Details. Need details!

Lynn: The juicier the better :D

Rissa: Drove to the beach and my POS new car caught fire. But lucky me, JD was one of the yummy firemen who came to my rescue.

Rachel: The pic was grainy. Describe him?

Rissa: I'm estimating twenty-four, at least six-one, couldn't tell much about his body with the fire gear on but he's got the most amazing eyes, big capable hands and he smells delicious.

Monica: Well all right. Go for it girl!

Stevie: Please tell me you got his digits.

Rissa: No but JD got mine. Said he'd call and we could go see a movie and have dinner.

Cam: Yeehaw! Saddle up and ride 'em.

Rissa: Umm…yeah. But what if he doesn't call? I'm sitting here next to the damn phone like some angsty teen. How pathetic is that?

Autumn: Get this straight, Rissa. You are not pathetic. Of course you're going to be nervous on your first time out.

Lee: He'll call! I know he will.

Rissa: I sure hope so!

When she turned out the lights and finally climbed into bed it was after midnight. She'd had calls from the insurance agent, the salvage yard and the car salesman. Each time the phone rang, excitement and anticipation surged only to be let down when it wasn't JD.

What had she been thinking? Why would a buff young guy want her? Yes, she worked out, watched her diet and stayed in shape. Still, time to face reality. She had two grown children and was getting older. She would be lucky to get a man her own age in bed. She didn't stand much chance with a twenty-something fireman.

From an early age she'd known that she wanted to be a teacher. Right out of high school she married her sweetheart and went to college while Tim joined the Army. They had not planned on having children early but these things don't often happen according to schedule. Mariah came along when the ink on Rissa's college diploma was still wet and Robby had been born eighteen months later. Then Tim died in a stupid accident one month before Robby's first birthday.

Nineteen years and no serious relationships. There had been a couple of brief affairs but sex hadn't been important to her. She'd been too busy with the kids to truly miss it. Not until she found erotic romances. She'd never experienced many of the titillating things she read about. Now her body hummed with sexual need and she actually owned several adult toys.

She had hoped JD would reintroduce her to pleasures of the flesh. *His loss!* This wasn't a race, although she felt the familiar drive of competition. She had all summer and lots of young studs to choose from. She vowed that the next one to pique her interest would earn her cougar status.

Like her friends, many of whom were now in fulfilling relationships, she'd be bold, daring and confident. Maybe she'd even be scandalously naughty and get two younger men in her bed — at the same time — focused on giving her one hell of an amazing night.

Stevie raved about her experience with multiple partners. Monica, Autumn, Lynn and Loralee all had tried out ménages.

Why shouldn't she find out what all the fuss was about and experience that ultimate pleasure?

Ha, take that, JD!

Chapter Two

ॐ

"Damn, I'm tired."

"That was one crazy shift."

"I'm going to veg in front of the TV all day."

"Dream on, Doug. Tracey will never let you get away with that."

The guys all laughed. JD didn't hang around to chat. He had better things to do this morning. Like grovel and beg for forgiveness from one very sexy lady. Real hardship that.

No sooner had they gotten back to the house after he'd met Rissa than they'd raced off to battle an apartment fire. That had been a bad one. And the calls had just kept coming, one after another. By the time he'd had a chance to pick up the phone it had been after midnight and he hadn't wanted to wake her. Hopefully she would understand.

"Hey, where's he off to so fast?"

"Yo, JD. You got a hot date?"

"Oooh, maybe with the sexy Latin schoolteacher whose car burned up. There were some definite sparks flying from her."

"None of your business." JD didn't slow down. He knew if he did he wouldn't make it out of there for at least an hour, and he definitely had something better in mind than hanging out with the guys.

It was still early but he was done waiting. JD closed his truck door and dialed Rissa's number before pulling out of the parking lot.

"Hello?"

She had such a great voice. It reached right through the phone to tug at his cock, which came to instant attention. "Mornin', gorgeous."

Her response was several long seconds in coming. "Who's this?"

His brow furrowed. How many men had she been expecting calls from? "JD...the firefighter." Nothing. "We met yesterday...at the beach. You know, when your car was on fire."

He couldn't be that *damn forgettable.*

"And?"

Fuck! The chill carried in that one word traveled down the length of his spine and every muscle tensed.

"Sorry I didn't get to call you yesterday. God, I was dying to hear your voice. But we stayed busy 'til after midnight. I have to admit, I was very tempted to call you then just to find out how your voice sounds when you're sleepy. I figured you'd had a rough day, though, and I didn't want to disturb your sleep."

"Oh, that's all right." The ice cracked and started to melt. "Your job is very important."

Work was the last thing he wanted to talk about. "Hey, listen. My shift's over now and I'm starving. Have you eaten yet?"

"Not yet."

"Great. Can I take you out for breakfast? It's rush hour so it will take me about an hour to drive over to your place."

"No."

His heart dropped. Shit, he'd really screwed up by not calling her last night.

"Forget going out. I'll cook."

Yes! JD punched his fist in the air. He couldn't remember the last time a woman other than his mother had cooked for him. And a homemade meal would be nicer than a restaurant. More intimate.

"Awesome. I'll be there quick as I can." He couldn't wait to see her again.

"Don't you dare rush. Drive carefully." She probably used that stern tone to tame unruly students. He wasn't immune to its power, which had his stomach flip-flopping.

"Okay, I will."

"See you soon, JD."

He disconnected on a groan. God, he loved hearing his name roll over her tongue. Rissa had a low and very sensual voice—perfect for dirty talk and phone sex. A man wouldn't mind hearing that voice whisper in his ear every morning. Like luxurious silk, it clung to him, molding to his body—warm, tantalizing and intimate.

Rissa Cross was one sultry woman. He'd bet his paycheck she'd also be fiery. Damn sure she was the most beautiful woman he'd ever seen outside the pages of a magazine. Her naturally dark-toned skin looked even softer than her thick mass of long brown hair. She smelled sweeter than honeysuckle. And that body. If he'd had a teacher that looked half as good he would have never learned a damn thing. All he would have studied was her.

Miss Cross kept herself in excellent shape. Hourglass shape—full breasts, narrow waist and curvy hips. The bright butterfly tattooed on the side of her belly was both sexy and elegant. But her lips—images of her wide mouth and pouty, glossed lips would haunt his dreams. Oh, the things he imagined her doing with those lips. Meeting his own hungry kiss, tasting his skin and stretching around his cock as she sucked him down her throat.

He shifted, adjusting his erection to a less painful position in his shorts. His mind filled with seductive images of all the ways their bodies would fit together.

JD couldn't help but press harder on the gas pedal.

* * * * *

Only a few hours after sunrise and the temperatures were already in the mid-eighties. Rissa considered putting on a nice outfit and fixing her hair after her morning run then quickly discarded the idea. Comfort won out over vanity. It was simply too hot for excess clothing. Besides, either JD wanted her or he didn't. No amount of primping would change his desires. And why get all dressed up when she intended to be naked before long.

She settled on a yellow eyelet camisole and denim shorts, skipping undergarments entirely. The top fell somewhere in the gray area between decency and blatant invitation, revealing a flirty glimpse of cleavage. After running a brush through her hair she pulled the heavy mass into a ponytail. A quick swipe of gloss across her lips was her one concession to makeup.

Now for breakfast. Her *abuela* swore the fastest way to catch a man was to cook for him. Rissa didn't want his heart, but hoped the meal she prepared would get her in JD's pants.

The spicy scent of chorizo and onions grilling in the skillet had her stomach growling. She scrambled in some eggs and raisins then the completed dish went into the warm oven along with a plate of fresh tortillas. Earlier she'd made salsa and set the table. But she was hungry for more than food. Rissa had every intention of getting JD on the menu.

She headed for her laptop to check email when someone knocked on the door. Glancing at the clock she noted how fast he'd made the drive. She started talking as she opened the door. "Wow, you made good ti—"

The sight of JD waiting on her doorstep, smiling at her broadly, had the words dying in her dry throat as Rissa nearly swallowed her tongue. She'd imagined how he'd look out of the uniform. Her imagination had nothing on reality.

Washed so many times the material was nearly threadbare, his blue T-shirt bore the fire department emblem and lovingly conformed to his chiseled torso. Intricate lines of a black tattoo that accentuated his huge biceps disappeared under his left sleeve. She longed to trace all those twisting, twirling lines with the tip of her tongue, and contemplated how much skin they covered.

He'd tucked the shirt into a faded pair of low-riding shorts that failed to disguise the thick bulge that extended all the way to his left hip. Saliva flooded her mouth and she wondered how he'd taste. Her breasts felt swollen and heavy, and with each ragged breath her rock-hard nipples rasped against her top. Shifting her weight from one foot to the other, Rissa realized more than her mouth had gotten wet.

"Damn, honey. You're even more beautiful than I remembered."

He lifted his right hand and held out a red fire extinguisher bearing a festive streamer of multicolored ribbons. How had she failed to notice the large red cylinder dangling from his fist? "I brought you a present."

"Um...thanks." Rather unique gift.

"When you get another car, I want you to put that in the trunk so I'll know you're safe."

Awww!

The sweet gesture left her speechless. For several long moments she stared into his dark eyes. Reflected in their depths she saw the potential for a future. A long-lasting relationship.

Rissa shook her head to dispel the rather disturbing idea. She wanted to live, have fun, sample all the different flavors she'd never tasted—not tie herself to one man. No matter how sweet and sexy and thoughtful he might be.

Breakfast. They were supposed to be having breakfast.

"Come on in." Stepping back from the door, she allowed him to enter her home. Not sure what else to do with it, she put his gift in the hall closet. Turning back toward him, she said, "I hope you're hungry. I cooked—"

The breath rushed from her lungs as her back came up against the wall. Warmth and JD's masculine scent enveloped her as his hard body fitted against her soft curves. It was a glorious fit. His body caged hers and his fingers bracketed her face, holding her in place.

"I'm starved." His voice rumbled close to her ear. "For you." Then his lips, soft yet firm, brushed along her jaw, moving slowly toward her mouth. She could have ducked or turned her head away. Longing for his kiss, she did neither. At the first touch of his lips to hers, Rissa spontaneously combusted. Fire raced across her skin and her blood turned to molten lava. From head to toe she burned and her toes curled into the carpet.

Dios, she might need that fire extinguisher to put out the flames.

He claimed her mouth in a scorching hot kiss and her lips opened wide, inviting him inside. JD accepted her summons. His tongue thrust into her mouth, slid against hers and she moaned as his bold and sweet taste washed over her like warm, delicious honey. Without conscious thought, she wrapped her arms around his neck and clung to him.

JD took over, exploring her mouth with his tongue, drinking down her needy moans and whimpers. Her breasts were crushed against his chest and everywhere they touched, from shoulder to knee, his body heat left a wake of desire licking at her skin.

She had never been so thoroughly and completely kissed. And if the shudders that shook his body were any indication, she wasn't alone. Their kiss had the same potent effect on him.

The heady mating of their mouths ended way too soon. Resting his forehead against hers, JD stared into her eyes as they both struggled to find solid footing. Her body hummed with desire, aching and ready for more. She wanted so much more.

"Damn, baby," he panted. "You're burning me alive."

Burning him? He's the one who started the inferno. He damn well needed to do something other than stare at her. Preferably something involving the long, thick erection that had left its impression branded over her abdomen.

"Now that we have the first kiss out of the way, we can relax and enjoy breakfast."

Breakfast? Her brain short-circuited. How could he think about food when she was primed and ready for sex? She wanted nothing more than to rip their clothes off and get lost in his amazing body. To hell with the food, they could eat each other.

A vivid image filled her mind. JD stretched out on the bed naked, her on top of him. Their bodies locked together in a sixty-nine, hungrily devouring each other. She could almost taste the tang of his semen on her tongue, feel it sliding down her throat.

Lust slammed into Rissa, melting bone and muscle. She would have dropped to the floor if not for his strong arms holding her tight.

"Come on, baby. Let's eat. We can work off the calories later."

Damn right they would. Perhaps on top of the kitchen table, getting all hot and sweaty then taking a shower together. She'd wanted to have shower sex since one of the cougars had raved about the wet and slippery glide of soapy hands over damp skin. Taken from behind, bent over in the shower with the spray sluicing over their bodies.

Oh yeah! She had a lot of ideas for how they could work off breakfast.

Chapter Three

Rissa could barely see to place the last of the silverware in the dishwasher. She laughed to the point tears streamed down her cheeks as JD told her hilarious stories about the bizarre calls the fire department routinely received.

"This one tops all the rest. It will go down in history. We got a call for an assist from the medics. Patient was inside the house but unable to come open the door. No big deal, happens sometimes."

The wicked grin drawing up the corners of his sensual mouth told her the call had been anything other than ordinary and likely involved sex. Many of his stories did.

"We busted open the door and hung around to make sure the medics didn't need anything else. Brian and Sean are two very serious dudes, but they came out of that house wearing big cheesy grins. They had a sheet covering one hell of a huge mass on the stretcher and we knew something weird was going on. We didn't see what until they turned at the end of the driveway."

He paused for effect and the anticipation got the better of her. "What? What was on the stretcher?"

"A couple."

"A couple of what?"

"Not what, who. Two people, a man and woman. They were naked under the sheet. The woman was on top, facing the man underneath her."

"Why would they put two patients on the same stretcher?"

"Couldn't separate them."

The sparkle in his dark eyes told her the sexual punch line to his story would be shocking.

"They were joined at the hip—literally. Stuck together. When the woman orgasmed, her vaginal muscles clamped down on the guy's already swollen cock and stayed that way."

Rissa scratched her head as she considered his words. Sure, it had been a long time since she'd had sex. She still didn't see how what he described was possible.

"You know, like when someone gets lockjaw."

Her confused expression prompted further explanation.

"Lockjaw happens when a sustained spasm of the jaw muscles causes the mouth to clamp shut. Only in this case..." His grin grew impossibly wider. The rest came out in fits and starts punctuated with robust laughter. "This was a case of l-lock pussy. The m-muscle spasms...of her orgasm...d-didn't stop. The pressure...oh god. The pressure around the base of his cock made...him swell. Like a really tight cock r-ring. Same effect."

"No way."

"Yes way. Had to take them to the hospital. The doc had to shoot her up with muscle relaxers before she finally let go of the poor guy."

Rissa narrowed her gaze on him. Something told her there was more to the story. "You went to the hospital, didn't you."

It had been more statement than question. JD nodded anyway. "Had to. They might have ne-needed the Jaws of Life to save that poor guy."

Her mouth dropped open and for several long seconds she fought a valiant battle not to laugh. She didn't want to laugh, no matter how funny. But snapping her mouth shut tight to bite her tongue just reminded her of the woman clamping down on the man.

Unable to hold back any longer, she slapped a hand over her eyes and turned her face in to her shoulder. He knew though. She might be able to hide her expression but nothing would quiet her sobbed laughs or the violent shaking of her body.

JD loved making Rissa laugh. The way her face and eyes lit up gave him a warm sensation different from the blinding, all-consuming sexual heat she generated. She lived totally in the moment and he got the distinct impression it hadn't always been that way. Almost as if she was making up for lost time. Yet whenever he hit on a personal subject or question, she quickly changed the topic or tried to distract him, which only piqued his interest in knowing more.

He knew he'd surprised her by not falling in with her plans of heading straight for her bed after breakfast. Not that he hadn't been tempted. The painfully hard erection filling out the front of his shorts was testament to how badly he wanted her. But he wanted more than a casual tangle in the sheets.

Her distraction worked in his favor. She laughed the whole way out to his truck and they were on the road before she tensed up.

"Hey, where are we going again?" Her arms crossed defiantly over her chest and she muttered something in Spanish he didn't catch. Probably nothing good. "I don't remember agreeing to go anywhere."

That fiery temper—damn, it did funny things to him. All that heady passion bottled up and ready to explode turned him on. He wanted her to open up and unleash all that heated energy, let it pour all over him.

He let her stew for a few moments before answering. "My friend's place on the Hillsborough River."

"And why are we going there?"

"It's a surprise."

"I hate surprises."

Yeah right. That's why excitement radiated from every pore of her luscious body. He wasn't fooled by her adamant denial.

"How much farther?"

Her foot tapped an impatient rhythm against the floorboard. After making the turn onto the dirt drive, JD squeezed her knee. "Relax." He pointed to the ranch house about five hundred feet away. "We're here."

He parked close to the detached garage and moved around the truck to help her down from the elevated cab. The confused look on her face when he opened the garage and lifted the two-seater kayak from a set of hooks was priceless.

He found it hard to believe he was delaying what they both wanted. But he couldn't deny the strong need to delve deeper and get to know the intriguing woman first. He'd learned enough about her to know that if given an inch she'd launch a strenuous protest to his plans. JD didn't give her the chance. He had the kayak in the water and Rissa settled in the forward seat before she could voice her frustration. Using the edge of his paddle, he pushed off from shore.

They'd remained quiet other than his instructions for navigating, but once comfortable with the slow and easy glide of the kayak, Rissa visibly relaxed, allowing her inquisitive mind and adventurous nature to take over.

"The river seems endless. How long is it?"

"More than fifty miles. Runs all the way from Pasco County to Tampa Bay."

"It's rather...swampy."

He chuckled over her scrunched-up expression of distaste. "The river starts in the Green Swamp."

"Oh." Flat and unenthusiastic.

As they floated along, he pointed out bald cypresses and longleaf pines as well as various wildlife. Considering her wary reactions, he decided not to point out the water snake weaving its way around her paddle. He had no interest in going swimming if she panicked and rocked the boat.

"That's a strange-looking log."

They floated closer and JD bit his tongue to remain quiet. Several turtles and a mature, eight-foot-long gator sunned themselves on the log Rissa had her gaze locked on. When she realized why the log appeared odd her entire body tensed and she let out a sharp whimper.

"There's no need to get upset. He's just enjoying the nice sunny day, same as everyone else."

"Y-you didn't tell me there are alligators in here."

"How long have you lived in Florida?" He didn't wait for her answer. "There are gators in almost every body of fresh water, honey."

Rissa's wild gaze shot around, taking in the other people calmly maneuvering their small boats along the waterway. With the sound of her heart pounding in her ears, she made a conscious effort to regulate her erratic breathing. No one else looked alarmed by the presence of a huge, prehistoric reptile and its mouth full of bone-crushing teeth. And JD projected a relaxed confidence that should be reassuring.

Yeah but how long have you known him?

A little over twenty-four hours. She barely knew the hunky man. He could be a deranged murderer who lured women out to this deceptively peaceful river to chop them up and feed the pieces to the gators, effectively disposing of any evidence. Hadn't people thought infamous serial killer Jeffrey Dahmer to be handsome, intelligent and charming? At least until police discovered his gruesome propensity for rape, torture, dismemberment, necrophilia and cannibalism.

A sharp peal of humorless laughter burst from her lips. Damn, she hated when her overactive imagination broke free.

"Rissa? Are you okay? If you're not up to this or are too afraid, we can turn around and head back."

Oh hell no! The challenge was on now. No way would she tell him to turn back. If JD and all these other idiots were able to conquer the big, bad swamp-river with all its creepy wildlife then so would she.

"Nope." Squaring her shoulders, she paddled with new determination and drive. "I'm fine."

The more she thought about it, the more she questioned his sanity and motives. She'd made it clear she wanted to fuck and instead he'd brought her kayaking. What red-blooded man passed up an easy lay?

"So how long have you been a teacher?"

And what was with all the personal questions? JD insisted on complicating things, which boggled her mind. Countless female friends had complained their men didn't want to talk or get involved in their lives. She'd thought most young men would give their left nut to find a non-clingy woman who wanted to have no-strings, casual sex with them. Apparently, JD wasn't one of them.

"Forever." She glanced over her shoulder and considered him. "Are you gay?"

When he recovered from a choking fit, she felt him glare a hole in the back of her head. "Why the hell would you ask that?"

"I all but gave you an engraved invitation to take me to bed. Instead you bring me out here." She shrugged. "You're hot as hell, muscular, young and sexy. In a word—perfect. All the perfect ones are either married or gay."

A sickening knot formed in her stomach. Rissa would *not* sleep with a cheater. "Please tell me you're not married."

"Nope. Not married, divorced or gay. Don't have any kids. Haven't been in a committed relationship in some time."

She sighed in relief.

"What about you?"

Great, they'd come full circle to the serious personal relationship questions she'd tried to avoid. Fine. She'd give him the same rapid emotionless response. "Widowed, two kids, both off to college. No lesbian tendencies—not that there's anything wrong with that. Not committed to anyone." She turned again to meet his intense stare. "Not interested in serious entanglements so you can relax, I won't be trying to drag you to the altar."

She turned back around in time to notice a snake dangling from a tree branch way too close for comfort. With a pronounced shudder, she paddled faster.

"What *are* you looking for, Rissa?"

Not much. Success in the cougar challenge and a good time.

This one question she actually appreciated. Recognizing the opportunity, she didn't sugarcoat or evade answering. By making her intentions clear they'd avoid any uncomfortable misunderstandings or messy emotional stuff.

"I just want to have fun."

Calling on every ounce of his self-control, JD still almost laughed right in her face. She had herself convinced but he didn't buy the detached attitude for a second. He'd been hit on by enough good-time girls that he could spot one a mile away.

The more time he spent with her, the more apparent the truth became. They were out on the river for several hours. He listened carefully, picked up her silent cues and read between the lines. Rissa Cross wasn't hard to figure out, and regardless of what she wanted him to believe, she was far from a casual fuck.

All the clues were there. She refused to share personal information, hoping it would keep emotional distance between them. But she'd messed up when she left discussing his life an open and acceptable topic though. Rissa greedily devoured all the details he shared. Getting to know him she started to genuinely like him, which made her interested in knowing more.

Her emotions were already involved whether she admitted it to herself or not. Each one was easy to see in her expressive features and soulful eyes. Not that he'd been able to watch her expression in the kayak but he hoped she'd listened as he talked about himself. He would play along, for now, let her believe she was safe from the deeper connection between them.

As he locked up the garage after their ride, she rubbed against him and gave an enticing feline purr.

"What do you say, stud? Want to come back to my place?"

The intimacy of sex would bring them even closer and strengthen the emotional bonds. Getting naked with this confident, vibrant and sexy woman had been on his mind since he'd first seen her. And yet, JD didn't want to rush it. Everything he knew about Rissa had alarm bells ringing long and loud.

Up until the past few months a casual fuck was exactly what he'd wanted. Not anymore. He was ready for a woman to share his life with. Rissa very well could be that woman. Making sure they had more than one night would be up to him.

He wasn't about to back down from the challenge of capturing Rissa Cross' heart. She didn't know it yet, but she was as good as his.

* * * * * *

A vivid rush of violent curses spoken in Spanish was punctuated by the loud bang of the front door slamming shut. Her entire body shook with rage and dissatisfaction. Rissa went straight to her computer and started a group instant message with all the cougars currently online.

Rissa: Leave it to me to find a hot yet defective younger guy.

Cam: Oh crap. Is he impotent?

Lori: Defective how?

Monica: What's wrong with your hunky fireman?

Lynn: CAM! Don't even think that. How horrible. He's not, is he?

Rissa: Not impotent. I felt a very big, hard bulge when he kissed me. And I left no room for doubt. Told JD exactly what I wanted, mainly his fine ass in my bed. He didn't go for it and I'm still not a cougar.

Rachel: Maybe he wants more than an easy lay.

Cam: Yup, definitely impotent. Or gay.

Edie: Plenty of fish in the sea. Get your hook into a different one.

Rissa: He took me kayaking on a swampy river full of snakes and gators.

Lynn: What happened after that?

Monica: Please tell me he at least set up another date.

Rachel: There has to be more to this story. Spill!

Rissa: He called this morning and I invited him over for breakfast. Everything was going good. JD has an amazing sense of humor. I invited him to bed and he took me kayaking then dropped me off at home. Didn't even come inside. He starts a 24-hour shift in the morning. Said he'd call me when he gets off.

Rachel: What did you say?

Lynn: Yeah, tell us the rest.

Rissa: I told him we could both get off if he came inside. He laughed, said there's no rush then offered to take me car shopping. Ugh!

Cam: Hopefully he's a good negotiator.

Monica: I hate car shopping.

Edie: Maybe one of the salesmen will be a hot young stud.

Rissa: What the hell am I supposed to do now?

Her friends were full of advice. Some of it actually sounded good too. So JD had turned out to be a dud. There were plenty of available younger guys out there. She just had to find one...or more.

"To hell with sitting at home alone."

Rissa took a shower, put on her sexiest come-fuck-me dress and went on the hunt. A few hours later, in a hip nightclub, she pushed melting ice around with a straw in the margarita she'd been nursing.

"Darlin', it pains me to see such a pretty lady all down in the dumps." The blond bartender leaned his elbows on the counter separating them. "Want to talk about it? I'm a great listener."

"Isn't that rather cliché?" Rissa gave him a thorough once-over, taking note of his wavy hair, deep tan, muscular build and vivid green eyes. Definitely younger, she figured mid-twenties. A total hunk.

One big problem—no spark. Not even a mild tingle.

Same as every other hot young guy in the place, he left her feeling cold. Her damn libido had picked the one it wanted and as far as her body was concerned, there was no substitute.

Her only solace came in the fervent hope that wherever JD may be tonight, he also suffered.

"Whoever he is, I hope the bastard knows how lucky he is."

The bartender's comment brought a reluctant smile to her lips. "He could have been lucky but left me high and dry."

219

"Ouch! His loss, beautiful. With the number of guys in here checking you out and offering to buy you drinks, I don't think you'll have any problem finding a replacement."

She sighed heavily.

"Ah. You don't want a replacement. Damn, that's tough. You could always use someone else to make him jealous, spur him into action." His broad grin flashed a row of perfect white teeth. "My shift ends in an hour. I'd be happy to help you out."

His heated gaze lowered and blatantly traveled over her upper body before once again meeting her eyes.

"Thanks, umm…" Rissa realized she didn't even know the blond Adonis' name. And why the hell couldn't she want him? Oh wait, that's right. He was available and interested and she wanted the unattainable fireman. She bit her lip to stifle a groan.

"Spence—but you—you're welcome to call me yours."

God how she wanted to take Spence up on his offer. Spend the night with his hard young body pumping into hers. If only his arms were beefier, his eyes coal black instead of bright green, and that mop of blond hair had been shaved off.

"Thanks, Spence. That's a very tempting offer but I've got a date with BOB."

"Aww, darlin'. Why settle for a cheap imitation when you could have the real thing?"

She merely smiled, handed him an extravagant tip then headed home to an empty bed and cold sheets, not even bothering with her vibrator. Spence had been right. A cheap imitation wouldn't suffice when her body knew what it wanted.

Chapter Four

∞

A few hard taps with a hammer had a hook secured in the wall. With tender care and a great deal of reverence, JD hung the heavy frame. He stared in awe, seeing his own satisfied grin reflected back in the glass. The frame held a mere bit of paper and ink, nothing special, yet it represented the culmination of all his hard work and determination.

In smaller frames next to the diploma hung official documents issued by the state of Florida — his firefighter credentials and brand-new teaching certificate.

He would always crave the adrenaline rush of fighting fires, the heady thrill of saving a life. Still, he wasn't getting any younger and was ready to start a regular career. In less than two months he would be a teacher — elementary school. If that didn't scare the shit out of him nothing else could.

As often happened, his thoughts turned to his favorite teacher. Perhaps the beautiful Latin spitfire would offer some words of wisdom on handling a classroom full of rowdy kids. Not that he'd have too much trouble. JD's love of children was the driving force behind his new career choice. Next month he would serve his last stint as a weekend warrior in the Guard and hang up his fire gear, although not for good. He still planned to spend part of his summer breaks working for the fire department.

Anxious to share his news, JD pulled out his cell and hit the speed-dial button. Rissa answered on the second ring. Her sensual voice had the immediate effect of making his cock twitch in interest.

"Hey, baby. Damn I've missed you. It's been a crazy couple of days."

"JD?" Her incredulous tone turned his anticipation to irritation.

"Yeah, it's me. Listen, I talked to my buddy at the dealership. He has a couple of cars for us to check out this afternoon if you're ready to shop." She hadn't forgotten his promise to help with the car shopping, had she?

"I...uh— You still want to take me car shopping?"

"Of course I do. And this time I'm going to make sure you don't end up with a fire hazard." The idea of her being in danger shredded his nerves.

"Oh, okay. Do you want me to meet you there?"

"No, I'll swing by and pick you up. The dealership is over there in Tampa. Two o'clock work for you?"

"Sure. And JD?"

"Yeah, baby."

"Thank you."

A few hours later when he knocked on her door, Rissa showed her thanks with a thorough, hot, wet, full-body contact kiss that took him from flaccid to rock-hard in under two seconds. All conscious thought flew right out of his head.

There was nothing gentle about her kiss. Her teeth nipped at his lower lip then her tongue thrust into his mouth, teasing and tasting. Exploring. Staking a bold claim. Days of pent-up need exploded and rained down over him. JD greedily took it all, demanded more. Their lips finally parted out of necessity and they both sucked air into oxygen-deprived lungs.

"You missed me." The idea stoked his male ego.

Rissa panted in his ear, her hot breath washing over his neck. "You will not leave me wanting again. I don't care what else happens today, buy a car or not, when it's all said and done, you *will* fuck me."

Her sexual demands had JD ready to forget their appointment and drag Rissa straight to bed. Instead he asked,

"Is that my homework, teach? Because I've always been an overachiever and I have the next three days off."

He let the implication of how he'd spend those days hang in the air as she locked the door. Once settled in the cab of his truck, JD contemplated satisfying her demands right then and there but thought better. An arrest for public indecency would end his new occupation before it got started.

The woman had kissed him so good he'd completely forgotten to share his exciting news. "I don't plan on being a lifer in the fire department. I've been going to school. Graduated last month."

"That's good."

Her unenthusiastic comment while digging for something in her purse put a damper on his mood. He glanced between the road and Rissa as she slicked gloss across her luscious mouth then fluffed her hair.

"I got my —"

"So did you tell your friend I want a convertible? I don't care what kind as long as it makes me look good."

Dammit! She changed the subject or tuned him out almost every time he tried to talk about his personal life or ask questions about hers. What the hell would it take for her to let him into her life?

"Yeah, I did. He has three cars to show us."

Rissa blew out a relieved breath when JD went along with the change in topic. She liked him but had no interest in getting more involved than they already were.

She glanced over and the sight of his crestfallen expression created a sharp pain in her chest. From the moment she'd opened the door it had been obvious something big had happened and he was dying to share. The kiss had proven to be only a temporary distraction. Now she wished that she'd let him tell her whatever it was because he looked like she'd just kicked his puppy and she felt lower than dirt.

He remained silent for the rest of the drive then treated her as a casual friend. Their appointment turned out to be with the dealership manager, JD's uncle Emilio. Rissa tried to ignore the conversation while the two men caught up but certain information filtered through. She learned that JD had a big family. Two brothers, a sister, tons of aunts, uncles and cousins. Most of them lived in Florida although one brother was overseas with the Air Force.

She would have gone insane with worry if Robby had followed in his father's footsteps and joined the Army. Rissa suppressed a shiver and interrupted the happy reunion. "So, what have you got to show us, Emilio?"

* * * * *

The thrill of driving home in her new car and the adrenaline rush from the amazing deal JD's uncle had given her had Rissa jacked up. Yet neither could touch her anticipation of what would happen when they got home.

She found staying within the speed limit to be one of the hardest things she'd ever done. At each stoplight they made eye contact in the rearview mirror, increasing the need humming through her. Rissa had never wanted a man half as much as she hungered for JD. She could almost taste their combined lust in the humid summer air.

Pulling into her assigned parking space with a squeal of tires, she jumped from the car and raced up the stairs. She left the front door open, dropped her purse in the entryway and started to strip, leaving a trail of clothes in her wake.

With a hard kick, one shoe flew into the living room. Not missing a step, the next landed in the hallway. The peach blouse she yanked off now hung from a wall sconce. She had no idea where her chocolate brown skirt or panties had landed, but on the way into her bedroom she looped the strap of her pink lace bra over the doorknob.

Crawling onto the center of her four-poster bed, Rissa lay on her side facing the doorway. She bent one arm and propped her chin in her hand. The other arm followed along her curves, fingers trailing down to tangle in the soft curls covering her mound.

She'd decorated her bedroom in rich, warm colors and sensual materials for just such a moment. The lighting, although dim, was enough to see everything that mattered. Her skin felt stretched tight and her heart pounded in her ears as she impatiently waited.

JD stepped into the doorway, still fully dressed, her panties dangling from his fingertips. He leaned against the doorframe, lifted the material to his face and took a deep breath. He looked so damn sexy. And for the night, he was hers.

Every muscle tensed and Rissa swore she felt his hard exhaled breath against the throbbing flesh between her thighs. She trembled in expectation as he leaned casually in the doorway, his gaze leisurely traveling over every inch of bare skin. How the hell did he remain so calm and collected when she felt like a tightly wound coil ready to snap?

Without a word, he straightened and took a slow step forward. The heat of his dark gaze never left her as he moved closer. Fisting his shirt, he tugged the material free of his jeans and dragged it up his body. Mesmerized by his movements, not even a bomb blast would have drawn her attention from the tanned flesh revealed inch by torturously slow inch.

Chiseled muscles rippled over his washboard abdomen. Her gaze followed the solid planes and angles as his torso broadened into a magnificent chest with solid pecs and flat, dark nipples she hungered to touch, to taste. Mmm...she'd love to lick every swirling line of that sexy tattoo covering the beefy muscles of his left arm. A light dusting of dark hair on his chest narrowed to a thin line disappearing beneath the waistband of his jeans.

God, the worn denim had driven her to distraction all afternoon. Faded blue, almost white near his groin, slung low on trim hips and cupping his muscular thighs to perfection.

He stayed still as she looked him over. As their eyes met, Rissa became lost in the intense fires burning in the dark pools. No man had ever looked at her with such undiluted longing. It did funny things to her insides. Thousands of butterflies took flight in her belly and her heart felt stretched, swollen with a barrage of emotions.

His hands slid over his abdomen and her gaze dropped to watch dexterous fingers work the fastener and draw down the zipper. JD leaned over, blocking her view as he pulled the denim toward his bare feet. Shoes she hadn't noticed him kick off lay on the floor near the doorway.

Tossing his pants to the side, JD rose to his full height and Rissa nearly swallowed her tongue. Sweet Jesus! She may have taken on more than she could handle. But what a damn good time she'd have giving it her all.

His thick, ruddy shaft hung heavily between his widespread legs. Roped with plump veins and capped with a broad crown, a bead of fluid glistened at the slit. But what drove her crazy was the gold, open hoop with small balls capping each end that pierced his crown.

Rissa's mouth went dry for a moment before flooding with saliva as she imagined taking his beautiful cock in her mouth. And her pussy—Christ! Her pussy clenched and hot cream slid over sensitive tissues to coat her inner thighs as she contemplated the wonderful friction of her body stretching to accommodate that big cock. Before the night was over she intended to know how that piercing felt thrusting into her aching body.

Long fingers fisted his shaft, tugging upward and giving her a glimpse of the hefty sac drawn up close to his body.

"JD," she pleaded, unable to lift her gaze from the solid fist squeezing and gliding over his cock. Thankfully he understood and took the last few steps bringing him to the edge of the mattress.

Rissa couldn't remain still or wait any longer. She'd waited too long for this. Her body took over, moving before the conscious thought formed in her head. His hand dropped away as her fingers slid over the hot, silken skin, her fingertips learning his shape, tracing pulsing veins. Over the super-smooth head, around the thick ridge, against a spot on the underside where the hoop disappeared. A spot that made the thick flesh jerk within her grasp.

Her fingers barely met around the shaft beneath his crown. As she slid her hand farther her fist was forced wider, fingertips losing contact at the substantial base. She leaned in closer, closed her eyes and took a deep breath, drinking in his heady scent. He smelled hot and masculine, like long steamy nights.

Opening her eyes, she met his heavy-lidded gaze as she stuck out her tongue and captured the fluid dripping from his slit. He cursed as she hummed in appreciation of his salty male flavor then lightly tugged his piercing. One small taste wasn't enough. She wanted — needed more.

Rissa held his gaze as her tongue circled the head, quickly becoming addicted to the invigorating taste of JD, spice and pure sin. She knelt on the bed before him, breathless, holding the hard length in her hand, drawing the large head into her mouth. A riot of energy surged through her, making her feel more alive than she had in years — wild, feminine, powerful. She moaned, sucked at his crest and flicked her tongue on the sensitive spot underneath. The sharp hiss she drew from him sent excited shivers racing along her spine.

JD's fingers bunched in her hair, flexed, tightened. The slight bite of pain made her scalp tingle and she sucked harder.

"Rissa." His voice had turned rough, raspy. The command in his tone had her gaze snapping to his face. "Stop."

Stop? She didn't want to stop. Her mouth watered to suck him deeper. She swallowed hard, hungering for the hot wash of his cum in the back of her throat.

"Lay back on the bed and spread your legs, baby."

Oh, okay. That sounded promising.

Small spasms shimmered along the walls of her sex and she scrambled to follow his command. She glanced at him and shivered. JD stood tall and confident, the embodiment of pure masculine power and carnal need. One hundred percent alpha and sexier than hell.

On quivering limbs, she moved to the center of the bed, overwhelmed with lust, restlessly rubbing her thighs together.

He growled her name and she trembled as heat spread from the soles of her feet to the top of her head. Dominant men irritated the hell out of her. She'd contemplate why in this situation, this man taking control turned her on...later. For the time being she planned on living in the moment and drowning in the pleasure gathering within her core.

"Spread those gorgeous legs and let me see how wet you are for me."

Testing his control, she moved with slow deliberation, bending her knees and sliding her feet toward her bottom. Anticipation and hunger flickered in his eyes as she let her knees fall to the bed, spreading her wide.

"Use your fingers. Spread those pouty lips."

JD fisted his hands at his sides in an effort to hold himself in check when everything in him screamed to be greedy, grab Rissa and take what he wanted. There had been a brief moment she'd bristled over his taking control but there was no hiding her body's heated response. Her nipples tightened into hard pebbles and thick cream glistened on the flushed folds she bared for him. He'd sensed her need to give up that iron-fisted control. To let someone else take responsibility, allowing her to simply feel.

Her internal struggle had played out on her expressive face, from the crinkling of her forehead with deep thought to the white teeth gnawing on her plump lower lip and the shiver of anticipation when Rissa surrendered to her desire.

When her lips had parted and she'd drawn his cock head into the damp heat of her mouth, his balls had clenched and he'd almost come from the unbearable pleasure of her teasing tongue. He wasn't selfish enough to let it happen. The vital drive to ensure this amazing woman reached satisfaction first pulled him back from the edge of climax. He intended to watch her orgasm several times before indulging his own needs.

Unashamed of her nakedness or vulnerability, Rissa's fingers circled her clit, stroked her wet slit and two plunged into her pussy. Glazed eyes watched him from beneath dark lashes as her hips thrust, riding her hand.

While he enjoyed observing, JD wanted to deliver her pleasure. He took her wrist in a loose fist and drew her fingers from her body, pinning her with his hungry stare as he brought the wet digits to his lips. She moaned as he sucked her fingers into his mouth, noisily slurping up her bold, musky essence. In that moment, he knew her taste would be the ultimate addiction, one he'd never manage to get enough of or completely satisfy his craving for.

He released her wrist and climbed onto the bed between her legs, right where he'd longed to be since the first time he saw Rissa sitting on a cooler in that tiny blue bikini.

Taking her hands, he guided them to her slick folds, positioning her fingers holding back her wet, flushed flesh. "Keep your hands there, spreading that pussy wide for me. And keep those eyes on me, baby."

Chapter Five

ဢ

After placing a sweet kiss on her butterfly tattoo, JD moved between her legs, his broad shoulders wedging her thighs so far apart the muscles strained. The man was sin incarnate—from the top of his shaved head to his tattooed biceps and pierced cock. And his naughty grin. Lord, that wide smile melted Rissa faster than chocolate in the Florida sun.

The incandescent heat of his dark gaze sizzled across her bare skin and held her captive as his head lowered. She needed his tongue on her clit with a vicious desperation. The warm brush of his breath over her heated flesh had Rissa crying out with incoherent mumblings. Her eyes slammed shut and her head thrashed from side to side. Time and place lost all meaning as she held her breath, waiting for the first touch, knowing in her heightened state of arousal it wouldn't take much to push her over the edge.

"No, open your eyes."

At his command her eyes opened but he made her wait. Finally, after what could have been seconds or hours, his tongue glided up her slit then grazed over her quivering clit. The hot, wet caress filled every muscle with tension.

"Damn, you taste sweet."

His words echoed in her ears as his lips closed around her clit. She clutched at his head, fingers slipping over the smooth skin until landing on his ears, which she held to keep his wicked mouth right there on her pussy where she so desperately needed him.

"Uh-uh," he chastised. "Put those fingers back where I told you to keep them."

She rushed to comply, eager for more. Once her hands were back in position, he sucked her engorged nub and lashed it with his tongue. That was all it took to send her flying. She screamed his name as a powerful orgasm detonated in her core and shot out to every sensitized nerve ending.

He lapped at her liquid response, refusing to let the tension ebb. Stiffening his tongue, he circled her clit before moving lower to fuck her opening. The walls of her channel pulsed as he tongued her, fast and energetic. One orgasm blended into another in an endless succession as Rissa soared and dipped, flying higher and higher.

He never stopped, barely paused, mercilessly driving her from one shattering peak to another, again and again, not staying in any one spot too long. Her thighs trembled weakly, yet she kept her legs spread wide, numb fingers holding her open for him. He thrust three fingers into her pussy, stroked her G-spot with a come-hither motion that drove her crazy. He didn't ease back until she no longer had any strength to hold on and collapsed into a heap.

Her breasts were swollen, achy. Rissa lifted her hands from the mattress and cupped them, plucking at her pebbled nipples. Heat rose through her body as JD paid close attention to how she handled her breasts.

"That's so hot, baby." He lifted to his knees and moved up her body until he straddled her torso and his heavy cock bobbed above her hands. "Press them nice and close so I can fuck those beautiful breasts."

She loosened her grip, made a channel for his cock between the full globes then molded her breasts around him. JD's hands covered hers on her breasts then his hips rocked forward. As the crown pushed past her cleavage, Rissa tucked her chin and licked the silken knob, rewarded by his deep moan. On the next pass she sucked the head into her mouth and tugged at his piercing with her tongue.

JD's head fell back between his shoulders with a mumbled curse. His cock slid back and forth, her saliva creating a slippery path to ease his way. He rolled her nipples between his fingers and thumbs, Rissa moaned and her hips bucked.

She'd read about this in some of her books but never thought it would be enjoyable for the woman. She'd been so wrong. The eroticism of sucking at the head of his cock while it thrust between her breasts and both their hands pleasured the mounds was a huge turn-on. The proof of her arousal soaked into the sheets beneath her.

JD continued to fuck her breasts and she experimented, gently scraping her teeth over his crown and tugging harder on his piercing. He gasped, thrust faster but then pulled back and with an agonized expression, squeezed the base of his shaft tight. "Not yet. I want to be in you when I come."

He climbed from the bed then quickly returned, rolling a condom over his rock-hard cock. He knelt between her legs, lifted her hips and placed two pillows under her bottom. Leaning down, he latched on to one puckered red nipple and sucked it against the roof of his mouth. She moaned and pumped her hips.

"Look at me, Rissa." Lost in the moment, she didn't immediately respond. JD pressed the tip of his cock against her fluttering entrance.

"I want you to see who's making love to you."

Making love? Her eyes sprang open wide and she met his intense stare.

No. Her heart slammed against her breastbone. This wasn't love. It was just sex. She whimpered, struggled to suppress the emotions trying to break free but did as he asked, keeping her eyes trained on him.

JD stared into her eyes as he pressed into her body, stretching her to accommodate his thick girth. His piercing rolled over highly sensitive tissues, creating stunning sensations that had her walls tightening on him. She thought it impossible for there to be more, yet he continued to push into her until his balls rested snug to her ass and his crown nestled against her cervix.

"You're so tight...hot...wet," JD praised.

He held still, allowing her to adjust, savoring the moment. Rissa had other ideas and wiggled beneath him, rolling her hips, enticing him to thrust. After several erratic heartbeats, he pulled back until only the crest remained within her. Her legs shot around his hips, locking them together. He chuckled. As if he could leave the snug grasp of her hot pussy.

No, now that he'd discovered paradise in Rissa's arms he wouldn't be going anywhere.

He wanted all of her, was dying for the taste of her. Their lips met, joined in a soft and tender kiss. She opened and as his tongue took her mouth, he thrust his hips in counterpoint. They moved together, Rissa meeting him with matching fervor. The passion built, escalating along with the force of his thrusts. His head swam, intoxicated by how readily she responded to his every touch.

JD was getting close. Too close. The skin covering his balls stretched taut and the telltale tingling gathered at the base of his spine. Wanting to make their first time together last, he reluctantly pulled from the tight clench of her pussy.

"Nooo!" Rissa cried and made a mad grab for him. He moved faster, grasped her hips and turned her onto her stomach.

"Relax. We're far from finished."

The tension in her body eased marginally with his reassurance. She'd surprised him earlier with her eager submission. He decided to push her a bit more to discover how much she'd be willing to surrender and how deeply it would affect her.

"On your knees," he ordered. "Shoulders on the mattress."

She scrambled to comply and JD's lips stretched into a goofy grin. Oh yeah, she was primed and anxious to give up control, which worked for him. He loved when a woman entrusted him to provide for both their pleasure.

Her knees were spread wide, her luscious ass thrust proudly upward, presenting a temptation he refused to ignore. His palm landed with a resounding smack that jiggled her right cheek and surprised a squeak out of Rissa. He waited, gave the warmth a few seconds to kick in and sure enough, she lifted her ass higher, seeking more. He spanked her left cheek twice before returning to the right, delighted by her sultry moan.

"Fuck, Rissa! You're perfect."

He rubbed her pinkened cheeks, spreading the heat, leaned forward and nibbled on one fleshy, rounded globe. He had to get back inside her, buried balls-deep, their skin slapping together with each hard thrust.

"Reach back and spread that beautiful ass for me. Show me how wet and ready you are." When she hesitated he dropped his voice, adding a note of authority to his tone. "If you want my cock, you'll do as I say...now!"

Rissa gasped but hurried to satisfy his demands and put herself in the embarrassing position. Knees shoulder-width apart, ass in the air. Her fingers slipped, scrambled for purchase on her slick skin, and pulled the cheeks apart. She was on display for JD. Vulnerable. Yet she didn't feel weak or exposed. Rissa felt sensual and seductive. Primed and ready. Energized.

"Beautiful."

The word, spoken in a low, raspy tone filled with need, went straight to her head. She'd never given a man control over any aspect of her life. With JD, this incredible younger man, doing so came naturally. His erotic demands amplified her arousal for him. No other man had such a profound effect on her.

His hands grasped her hips, held her in place as his broad crown probed her opening, made a shallow thrust. One hand moved inward, skated over her tight pucker then circled. "I'm going to fuck this ass, baby." It wasn't a question but a promise. "Later. First I want this tight pussy."

Rissa shivered and her pussy spasmed. She was curious about anal sex, wondered if the reality was half as exciting as the erotic novels described. She had a hunch that with JD it would be even better than what she'd read. Hell, he'd made her crave the heated slap of his palm spanking her ass. He'd likely make her crazy to take him in her untried bottom.

"Oh, you like that idea."

She didn't have the breath to speak. He circled her nerve-rich anus again and his thumb exerted gentle pressure. "Breathe, Rissa. Nice and easy."

She took slow breaths and fought to relax. His thumb slid past her opening and she gasped as a riot of sensations flooded her body.

JD drilled his thick, hard cock into her pussy, filling her so good. He didn't pause or go slow. Her breasts swung, nipples scraping on the sheet with each pounding thrust. He took her hard and fast, stimulating her everywhere at once. His balls thudded against her clit as his cock stretched her, the piercing creating wonderful friction over her G-spot. And that thumb in her ass moved in the same tempo. Sweet Jesus. There was no holding back. Her orgasm detonated in her engorged clit, spread to her pussy, which clamped down hard on his shaft, and fluttered through her spasming ass. Her entire body tightened and then spiraled in a spectacular freefall.

She floated, dipped, soared out of control with only JD keeping her from flying away. The pillow absorbed her ecstatic tears. He grounded her, fucked her through the orgasm. As her strength ebbed, Rissa collapsed in a sweaty heap, facedown on the bed, tremors still rocketing through her. JD stayed with her, his cock still deep within her pussy, his muscular body blanketing her back. Then his muscles tensed, his cock swelled and his hips bucked wildly as heat blasted her right through the latex barrier.

Neither moved nor spoke as they panted, sucking air into oxygen-depleted lungs.

* * * * *

Warmth covered her back and one breast. Groggy, Rissa reached out to tug the duvet over her. Only her hand didn't find crinkly, feather-stuffed cotton, landing instead on a wall of solid muscle. She blinked rapidly and everything came to her in a rush.

There was a man…in her bed. All night long. Wow! That hadn't happened since Tim died. She didn't bring her flings home. Not before JD. But then JD was turning out to be the exception to many of her rules.

Her body ached in some pretty interesting places, but considering the mattress gymnastics she'd performed with JD that was understandable.

She had no regrets. Far from it. It had been an incredible night. There wasn't a surface in the bedroom that hadn't seen action. She had to hand it to the young stud. He had some creative and inventive ideas. And stamina to spare. Holy crap. How had she managed to keep up with him?

She saw just one problem. He'd stayed the night. What the hell was she supposed to do now? Hand him his clothes and push him out the door? She was hungry and in desperate need of a shower.

Her thoughts bounced around in different directions but it finally hit her. *Oh. My. God.* She was a cougar. Wait until she told her friends. They were going to want lots of explicit details but she intended to be selfish and hoard those for herself.

Yup, time to get rid of the hunk. Maybe if she fed him breakfast he'd go.

A memory surfaced of the lost puppy she'd made the mistake of allowing Mariah to feed. Damn moocher had settled in and never left until Mariah got a place of her own and took him home.

On second thought, she wouldn't offer JD breakfast.

She peeled his fingers from her breast and rolled out of bed. A cup of coffee and a shower would clear her head and she'd send the fireman on his way. Plans made, Rissa slipped on a robe and stumbled into the kitchen.

She filled the coffeemaker with several heaping scoops of Colombian and breathed in deeply. The rich aroma perked her up, adding pep to her step. But when she walked through the bedroom and spotted JD sprawled out on her bed, she stumbled over her own feet, nearly falling flat on her face.

He slept on his stomach, gloriously naked, one arm stretched out across the bed. Miles of tanned skin stretched taut over sculpted muscles that were impressive even when relaxed. Her gaze followed the indentation of his spine from shoulder to the rise of his drool-worthy ass and down the crease to thick thighs. One knee was bent, leg drawn up. His balls stood out in stark contrast to the white sheet they rested on. She absently noted that, unlike the rest of his body, his legs were hairy.

Her mouth went dry and she wondered why rushing him out the door had seemed like such a good idea when all she could think about was running her tongue down his back and licking that magnificent ass.

Giving herself a mental shake, Rissa hurried into the bathroom before she acted on the desires her crazy hormones urged her to indulge. Unfortunately, getting him out of sight did not get him out of her mind.

She cranked on the shower and slipped out of her robe, studying her body in the mirror while she waited for the water to heat. There were a few tiny wrinkles next to her eyes but overall her skin remained smooth and supple. She palmed her breasts, lifted slightly. Not quite as high, yet they were firm and even. The touch of her hands made her rosy nipples stiffen and turn a deeper shade of red. Releasing her breasts, she trailed her hands over her flat stomach and flared hips. Her legs were toned thanks to years of exercise.

Looking good!

Hell, she'd managed to catch the eye of the young hunk stretched out on her bed.

Why the hell am I not in bed with him? Oh yeah, temporary fling, Rissa reminded herself and wondered how long she'd be able to keep JD at a distance.

Steam rose around her as she opened the shower door and stepped inside. The hot water eased tired muscles but did nothing for her arousal.

Really, what would it hurt to crawl back into bed with JD?

She closed her eyes as visions of all the wonderful ways she could wake him up raced through her head. Squirting some shower gel into a mesh poufy sponge, she worked up a thick lather then started washing her arms. As she dragged the sponge between her breasts she remembered the sensation of JD's cock sliding through her cleavage. Her heartbeat sped up as her breasts became achy.

Big hands wrapped around her and she was pulled back against a warm, very masculine body.

"Here, let me do that for you, baby."

Any thought of resisting vanished as his fingers closed around her breasts and brushed over her nipples. Her muscles liquefied and she melted against him, surrendering to the addictive pleasure of wet skin gliding against wet skin.

JD thoroughly washed and stimulated every inch of her body. When his soapy fingers stroked between her legs and separated her tender folds she turned to face him. Rissa knew what she wanted and it wasn't his fingers. The man had a gift for oral sex and she wanted to put that talented mouth to good use.

"Think of me like those little chocolate candies. I melt in your mouth, not in your hands."

Chapter Six

ဢ

Sneakers pounded on the path in tempo with the high-energy music blasting into her ears through tiny speakers connected to the MP3 player strapped to her arm. Perspiration dotted her skin and soaked her sports bra. Sore muscles protested the movement but Rissa pressed on.

Only two miles into her normal five and she was feeling the burn. She had missed her daily runs a lot over the past few weeks. Not that she'd been sitting on the couch eating bonbons. No, she'd been getting lots of physical activity putting JD through his paces.

Good lord, did he have stamina. They'd christened every solid surface in her condo, including the balcony. Just thinking about that night sent shards of pleasure splintering through her exhausted body.

When he wasn't working, JD barely gave her time to breathe. A few nights ago she'd snuck out on the balcony to get some time alone. With a short, silky robe covering her, she had leaned against the railing and stared out at the water spraying from a lighted fountain in the courtyard.

Before long, JD had found her and taken advantage of her position. He fucked her from behind, right there on the balcony. Her fingers stiffened with the remembered ache of holding the railing in a death grip. She'd drawn blood from biting her lip to keep quiet.

She'd never had sex in public. Now she longed to do it again. It was sexy and naughty and so fucking good. JD had flipped her robe over her hips, exposing her ass and wet pussy to the light evening breeze. He'd taken her hard and fast with minimal foreplay, talking dirty the entire time. The inherent danger of someone seeing or hearing them had made it that much better. Made her that much hotter.

Rissa wasn't surprised when a large masculine form appeared at her side and kept pace with her. She didn't have to glance over to know it was JD. Her entire body had gone on high alert, tingling with sensual awareness the moment she sensed his arrival.

She wasn't sure how or when it had happened, but JD had slipped under her radar and insinuated himself into her life.

On his days off he'd started showing up on her runs. Out of the blue one day he'd knocked on her door and taken her out shopping because he wanted a woman's opinion. And then there were the phone calls, several times a day, just to talk or to say goodnight if he was working.

Some of his personal things had made it into her condo too. His toothbrush resided on the bathroom counter, there was masculine soap in her shower and beer in the fridge. When she had done laundry yesterday the basket contained more of his clothes than hers.

Regardless of her stance on relationships, Rissa had to admit that having him around was nice. Comfortable—like roommates except with benefits. There was no pressure and he'd backed off with the personal subjects. They'd formed a relaxed, easy partnership of sorts.

Neither felt the need to fill the silence with random chatter. They walked the last two blocks to her condo where they shared the shower and their bodies.

Shower sex had become her favorite way to connect with JD. Wet skin sliding against wet skin, the sensual caress of sudsy hands. Warm water pelting her and the cool tiles against her back. She wound up clean and refreshed instead of sweaty and tired.

They dressed and headed into the kitchen, working together on breakfast, neither having to ask how the other took their coffee or preferred their eggs.

"Wanna go to a barbeque tonight? Nothing major," JD clarified. "Just the guys from the station. We'll toss some burgers and dogs on the grill, have a few beers."

"Sure," Rissa readily agreed. She had no plans and it sounded like a nice way to spend the evening. "We can walk over to the farmers' market and pick up some fruit for a salad."

The phone rang and since her hands were full JD answered with a cheery greeting. His expression soured as he listened. "Sure. Just a second. I'll get her."

He handed her the phone and a sense of dread tightened her chest. She tucked the cordless between her ear and shoulder and continued to whisk the eggs. "Hello?"

"Mother, it's not even eight a.m.," Mariah screeched. "Why is there a man there? What the hell is going on? He sounds young."

Aw shit. There went her good mood. Busted by her daughter. How embarrassing. She set down the bowl and refused to meet JD's gaze before rushing down the hall to her bedroom. Rissa hadn't dated while the kids lived at home, so a man answering her phone must have been a major shock for her daughter. Mariah's barrage of questions continued unabated. Rissa plopped down on the bed and struggled to get a word in.

"Calm down, honey."

"Calm down? *Calm down?*" Her voice got higher as she repeated the words. "How am I supposed to calm down? Is he some pervert? Were you having sex?"

"Mariah," she snapped. "Shut up!" Her daughter instantly went quiet and Rissa breathed a sigh of relief. "He's a friend and what he's doing here is none of your business."

"You didn't deny having sex with him," Mariah squealed dramatically. "I'll take that as a yes. *Dios*, Robby is going to freak."

"Watch your mouth, young lady. And bite your tongue. Whether I'm having sex or not isn't a subject you will be discussing with your brother."

"I can't come home right now so Robby's going to have to get down there and kick some ass."

"He most certainly will not! I am a grown woman and more than capable of handling my own affairs." No sooner had the word left her mouth than she knew it had been the wrong one to use.

"Affair? You're having an affair. Daddy's probably rolling over in his grave." Mariah let loose with a steady stream of curses in Spanish.

"Don't make me come to that school and wash your mouth out with soap, Mariah." She took a few deep breaths in an attempt to calm down. Losing her cool with her daughter would not help. "I am a single adult woman in my prime. Your father would not have wanted me to stop living when he died. He'd want me to enjoy my life." She knew it was the truth. Tim would have been upset over all the years she'd spent alone.

"I'm getting on a plane. You get that man out—"

"You will do no such thing!" Her heart raced as JD strolled into the room, bare-chested, devious grin on those lush lips. Rissa did her best to ignore the sexy ripple of muscles over his torso as he moved, and focus on her daughter.

"What you are going to do is hang up this phone, calm down and go to class. You will not call your brother and get him all wound up."

JD went down on his knees and pushed her thighs apart then moved into the space.

No, she frantically mouthed.

He ignored her silent protest. His hands wrapped around her ankles and slowly moved upward. Rissa gasped as calloused fingers swept along her inner thighs. She covered the mouthpiece with her hand and hissed at him. "Stop it."

"Uh-uh," he mumbled. "Tell her about me."

"Are you crazy?"

"Mom? What did you say?"

"Nothing. I have to go now." Blunt fingertips eased under the edge of her shorts and panties, pulled them to the side then glided along her hot, wet slit. She clamped her jaw down hard enough to crack teeth.

"He's with you right now, isn't he?"

"You're always so hot and wet for me," JD praised. Two fingers parted her folds then zeroed in on her pulsing clit. His warm breath washed over her and Rissa wasn't able to keep her hips from pumping toward him.

"Oh my god, he is. I can hear him."

"I-I'll call you later." Rissa's voice was unnaturally high. "After you've calmed down."

"You mean after he fucks you."

Two thick fingers thrust into her and pleasure rocked her, turning Rissa's breathing choppy. JD kissed her clit and hummed, the vibration of his lips almost pushing her into orgasm.

"Goodbye, Mariah," she panted, her voice shaky. "I'll talk to you later."

Her daughter was still ranting when Rissa pressed the power button. The phone dropped from numb fingers and she fell back on the mattress. "Jesus, JD. I was talking to my daughter."

"Mmm…" he purred then his tongue lashed her clit. "But I'm hungry."

Was it possible to overdose on oral sex? If so, it would be one hell of a way to go.

All thought disintegrated as JD's fingertips stroked that amazing spot on the upper wall of her pussy and his lips closed around her clit. His rough, hot tongue flicked rapidly over her clit and Rissa came hard, pussy clenching on his fingers.

He brought her down from the intense waves of pleasure with gentle touches and kisses. Her body went limp and he shifted her clothes back in place. The bed dipped as he leaned over her for a hot kiss flavored with her essence. She didn't shy away from tasting herself.

He stood and held out a hand to pull her onto her feet. "Come on. I want breakfast now."

"But you didn't—"

A quick kiss silenced her protest. "Later. I'm going to feed you first."

Rissa was stunned. She'd never known a lover, or any man for that matter, to be so selfless. While JD finished making breakfast she headed straight for the computer and hastily wrote a blog post.

Tempt the Cougar Blog:

Help! I need serious cougar reinforcement and advice.

After my husband died I didn't date and the few affairs I had were conducted away from my kids. Well, my daughter called this morning while JD and I were making breakfast and he answered the phone

To say Mariah freaked out would be putting it lightly. That darn kid is too smart for her own good. She could tell from his voice that he's younger than me and she connected the dots with relative ease. You have no idea how embarrassing it is to be confronted by your child about your sex life. She threatened to come home or send her brother home to "kick some ass".

I took the cordless phone into the bedroom, JD followed and proceeded to...um, distract me. Mariah knew something was going on. I told her that I'm single and in my prime, and that her father would have wanted me to enjoy life. JD wanted me to tell her about him and proceeded to do wicked things to me with his tongue. I had to end the call before I was moaning into the phone.

It's my own fault for putting this part of my life on hold and never letting the kids see me around men other than family. They just aren't prepared for the reality of mom being human and having sex. Oh Lord, what a mess! The last thing I need is my kids racing home to confront my much younger lover. Yikes! What the heck do I do now? How do I handle this?

Lori: Oh boy, this is tough, honey. Listen up! First, settle down a little bit and when you are good and calm, have a heart-to-heart with her. Tell her what you just told us. You are a woman in your prime and your life isn't over. Why shouldn't you have love and happiness and all the good things? Assure her that your relationship with them won't change. You love them but why shouldn't you have your own happily ever after?

Stevie: Yeah, well, when they show up and find you two naked and draped across the couch, they'll get used to it fast enough! LOL Live your life for you not them. You've done that already.

Elizabeth: Rissa! First, you sit yourself down and repeat after me. "I deserve to have a sex life. I am woman, hear me roar!" Next, sit your daughter down and gently but firmly draw the line. This is something I had to do with my girls, too. Turns out what they were really looking for was reassurance that my relationship with them wasn't going to change, and that I really did know what I was doing with Kevin. Then sit JD down and reassure him that your relationship with your daughter is not going to dictate how you feel about him. Rissa, I may be delving too deep here, but it sounds like JD used the only option you left open for him to get his point across. Your refusal to tell Mariah about him probably hurt. You've got a good thing going here. Don't let anyone but you and JD dictate where this relationship goes.

Her friends used scary words. Happily ever after, relationship. Yikes!

They were right about talking to Mariah though. Rissa would prefer to do so in person but might have to settle for a phone call considering the geographical distance between them.

But Elizabeth's reply made her pulse beat frantically. Could her friend be right? Had she hurt JD's feelings by refusing to tell Mariah about him? In that moment all she'd wanted was to end the conversation not draw it out. She had no problem with telling her daughter about him, but not on the phone while he pleasured her.

She made a mental note to reassure JD she wasn't embarrassed to be sleeping with him.

* * * * *

After breakfast they headed to the market then went to see the latest action flick critics had been raving about. The movie didn't have much plot, just lots of shooting, things blowing up, fast cars and beautiful women. JD loved it. Rissa had remained lost to her worries over whether she should say something about what happened earlier or not.

She leaned against a tall wooden fence and took in her surroundings. Children raced around oak trees, laughing and carefree. Adults congregated in intimate groupings, discussing a wide variety of topics. The teenagers all stayed inside to play video games. A large dog sat next to a smoking barbeque grill, begging for a taste of the sizzling burgers. She seemed to be the only one who noticed the magnificent pink blush highlighting puffy clouds as day faded into night.

How the hell did I wind up here?

"Didn't you come with JD?"

Oh great! She hadn't intended to actually ask that question out loud. Biting her lip, she tried to remember the name of the petite blonde seated at the nearby picnic bench giving her a concerned glance. Was it Trisha? Tracey? She'd been introduced to so many people that she wasn't sure but thought Tracey was right.

"Sorry, just thinking out loud."

Tracey laughed. "JD does tend to have that effect on women. Not that he's ever brought one around before."

Interesting. Tracey seemed to have the down and dirty on JD. Rissa sat on the bench. After helping the toddler seated between them with his cup, her attention returned to his mother. "So he's a player? Not that there's anything wrong with that," she rushed to add.

Tracey considered for a moment before responding. "I wouldn't necessarily call him a player. JD just had not found what he's looking for." Bright blue eyes sparkled as she flashed a knowing grin. "Not until recently."

"What makes you think that?" Rissa scoffed.

"I've known JD for a long time. I've never seen him so aware of a woman before. He may appear to be engrossed in whatever the guys are saying, but no more than a minute or two goes by before his eyes are on you. Plus, Doug told me they're all sick of hearing about you. He's talked about nothing else for the past few weeks."

And how had *her one-night stand turned into weeks?*

"He's special to you too."

Rissa's gaze snapped to Tracey's. "What? What gave you that impression?"

"You're not hard to read and every time you look at him there's a dreamy longing. When your eyes lock with his the desire rolls off the two of you in waves everyone feels."

She groaned and before she could stop herself, she was searching him out through the crowd. The corner of her lip twitched as she watched him lift a small girl high above his head and spin her around. The girl squealed in delight. Another child, a boy, wrapped himself around JD's leg and he reached down to ruffle the head of dark hair.

He'd be a great dad.

A sharp pang sliced through her chest and killed her train of thought. She had to keep this real or one of them — probably both — would get hurt.

"Lust," she mumbled. "A summer fling. There's no future for us. JD's young, a thrill seeker. One day he'll want to start a family. I've already raised my children, seen them off to college." She wasn't capable of giving him that even if she wanted to.

"Maybe," Tracey conceded. "Maybe not. Have you discussed any of this with him?"

Rissa shrugged. "No. JD's a good time. There's nothing serious between us."

As if on cue, JD's dark eyes found her, stroking over her skin, heating her blood. Her nipples hardened and her panties got wet.

"If you say so but I don't buy it, Rissa. Looks like serious intent written all over his face to me."

She shook her head in denial but her heart pounded harder in agreement. And just what was she supposed to do with these growing emotions? Their time together had an expiration date. In August, like Cinderella at the stroke of midnight, she'd turn back into "Miss Cross". Go back to her normal life. A life that had no place in it for a summer lover.

And yet the thought of not having JD in her life made it hard for her to breathe.

What a colossal mess!

* * * * *

The dreamy look on Rissa's face made his heart ache and fill with hope. He'd achieved a great feat this morning getting her to say yes to the barbeque, then lost ground when she refused to tell her daughter about him. The woman drove him nuts with her insistence on keeping distance between them. Personal subjects were forbidden and she'd refused every previous invite to meet his friends and family. Her daughter's phone call confirmed his suspicion that her kids had no idea she was seeing someone.

He was happy to see her start talking with Tracey. Maybe now that the ice had been broken and she'd met his friends from the station Rissa would be comfortable enough to let him into her life. He'd love to meet some of the people who were important to her, especially her kids.

"You might not want to leave her alone with Tracey for too long," Doug cautioned. "There's no telling what my wife will tell her."

JD laughed. "I don't have any secrets."

"Yeah, right," Doug scoffed. "That's why you've told her how hard you worked to earn your degree. I bet you didn't even tell her about the new job."

He sighed and rubbed his scalp. Feeling stubble rasp against his fingers, he made a mental note to shave in the morning. "It's complicated."

"Hell, everything about women is complicated." Jordan Moore, B shift's captain, took a long pull on his beer then pointed the bottle at JD. "It's your job to figure out how to make it simple."

All of the guys within hearing range laughed, a few commenting on the impossibility of reaching such a lofty goal.

"Hey," Jordan griped. "Once I laid down the law with Mary life got a lot easier."

Sam Lang, B shift's lieutenant, choked on his beer. "You are full of shit, Jordan. Mary's the one who laid down the law. It wasn't until you learned to obey that the two of you stopped fighting all the damn time."

Running from her brother, Kyle's daughter, Jillian, launched herself into his arms. JD lifted her up high and spun the girl until she screeched. Her brother, Evan, tried to tackle him, only managing to hug his leg and attempt to climb up and reach his sister. Absently, JD mussed the boy's unruly hair, imagining how much he was going to enjoy being a teacher.

He loved kids, babysitting his nieces and nephews had shown him how much. When he realized how good he was with them he'd started thinking about teaching. Taking charge of school field trips at the station only reinforced his desire to work with children. In another month his dream would become reality. JD couldn't wait.

He was dying to get some pointers and ideas from Rissa but every time he tried to talk about his new job she'd shut him down. Finally he'd stopped trying. Maybe tonight would change that.

JD glanced over at her again and his heart beat faster. She was so damn beautiful, smart and funny. Everything he'd ever wanted. He had a lot riding on his hopes and dreams for the future. With Rissa at his side, he just might have a chance of seeing them come true.

Chapter Seven

ഇ

Warm air skated over his cock, which jerked, snapping to attention. JD reveled in the exquisite dream. The tip of a damp tongue circled his crown before dipping into the slit to lap up a salty drop of pre-cum. A hum vibrated through his flesh and the skin covering his balls grew taut. Tight, wet heat engulfed the tip of his cock, taking him from sultry dream to waking reality.

Opening his eyes, he looked down his torso. In the dim light of her bedroom, he drank in the heady sight of Rissa curled up over his groin as she devoured him with her desire-filled gaze. Her plump red lips were stretched wide around his cock and the dark mass of her silken hair fanned out to blanket his lower body. He knew the image would haunt him for the rest of his life.

God, she was so fucking beautiful. And he was totally and completely in love.

Pressure squeezed his chest, pushing his heart up into his throat, and lightning jolted his sternum. His heart stopped beating and he tensed for several long moments. Then just as suddenly his mind and body eased as he slowly came to terms with his fate. He was head over heels in love with a woman who wanted him for nothing more than sex.

Unaffected by his inner turmoil, Rissa continued her sensual assault, twirling her tongue around the ridge of his crown before taking him to the back of her throat, strong muscles swallowing around him, milking his cock. At the sound of his guttural moan she redoubled her efforts, sucking with hard pulls, tonguing him with new enthusiasm.

Needing to touch her, without conscious direction, JD's hands cradled her head, fingers spearing into her dark hair, flexing against her scalp. "Damn, baby. So good."

Mind-blowing good.

He'd been tired from his last shift at the station but sleep was highly overrated compared to the sexual hungers of his fiery lover.

Her lips released him and her tongue trailed the length of his shaft, sliding lower, down to his scrotum. Gently she took first one then the other globe into her mouth, suckling and swirling her tongue insatiably.

JD became lost in the sensation of having Rissa pleasuring him with her mouth. She shifted, one hand gliding over sleek curves and moving between her legs. Two slender fingers disappeared with a wet slurp that drove him wild.

Sexy as it was to watch Rissa fuck her fingers, JD was dying for a taste of her sweet cream. "Come here," he demanded.

Rissa shuddered and he couldn't suppress a satisfied grin. The strong-willed, confident woman loved surrendering to his command in the bedroom.

Releasing her hair, he patted his chest. "Straddle me, baby. Give me that delicious pussy. I'm hungry."

She refused to let go, stroking his shaft as she swiftly moved to assume the position he wanted. With her knees bracketing his shoulders, she knelt over him, palming his balls, her ravenous lips closing around him once again.

JD stretched out the moment, forcing both of them to wait as he blew a hot stream of air over her drenched pink folds. He swirled a finger in the fluids gathered along her slit, drawing the lubrication back over the shallow groove all the way to her tight pucker. His fingertip pressed past the ring of muscle, stimulating her hidden nerve endings.

Rissa sucked in a hard breath around the cock filling her mouth. While he had hinted at his desire for anal sex, JD had only ever gone so far as fingering the forbidden channel. It was the only thing they had not yet explored together. There was no denying that his finger shafting into her ass felt incredible. Still, the idea of trying to take his huge cock in the tiny orifice filled her with anxiety, fear and excitement.

Would he be content to finger her ass or would this be the time he went further? She realized that JD was the one man she trusted not to hurt her. The one man she could relax and enjoy a new experience with.

So focused on the shallow thrust of his finger stroking the sensitive tissues just inside her bottom, Rissa faltered and his engorged shaft slid from her slack mouth. The wonderful friction immediately ceased.

"You want more, Rissa?"

"Oh god, yes. Please, JD. Don't stop."

His teeth nipped at the juncture of her thigh and shudders tore through her body.

"Then keep going, baby. You stop and I stop."

She eagerly took him back into her mouth, sucking on his turgid flesh, twirling her tongue around him. Whatever he wanted, she'd do it as long as he continued to pleasure her.

JD stayed still for a drawn-out moment but his finger began to move again, making small circles, stretching her narrow channel. He pressed a hot kiss against the susceptible spot on the outer curve of her ass that always drove her wild. He licked a hot path along the fold where her thigh and bottom joined, all the way to the crease of her ass, then slowly inched toward her empty, aching pussy.

As his tongue thrust past her trembling entrance, his finger drove deeper into her ass. Rissa groaned and scraped her teeth gently over his length. JD's moan vibrated through her pussy and his hips bucked.

He licked and sucked at her swollen tissues, that talented tongue searching out all her most sensitive areas and tormenting them with earth-shattering bliss. A second finger joined the first in her ass, moving in conjunction with the two slamming into her pussy and reaching that wonderful bundle of nerves high on her upper wall. At the same time his lips closed around her clit and his tongue flicked it rapidly.

A powerful orgasm crashed over her, crushing her under a wave of debilitating ecstasy. She couldn't breathe or move as intense spasms blasted through her from head to toe. JD murmured encouragement against her overstimulated flesh, keeping her climax going until the pleasure became almost painful.

She collapsed on top of him, gasping for air, and his touch gentled, bringing her softly back down until his palm landed a jarring swat to her ass.

"Don't you dare fall asleep now that you've got me wide awake. We're far from finished."

"Damn," she panted. "I love…your enthusiasm."

Every muscle cushioning her body stiffened and Rissa cringed as her choice of words filtered through her mind. Crap, she'd messed up again. Now he'd think she was getting all touchy-feely and be freaked out.

"Give me a second." Rissa rolled to the side and up onto her hands and knees, using what always worked with JD—distraction. She wiggled her ass suggestively and tossed a come-hither glance over her shoulder. Gathering her courage, she looked him straight in the eye and dropped the equivalent of a sexual bomb.

"I want you to fuck my ass."

Her words had the desired effect, erasing her previous slip from his mind. The heat of JD's gaze slid over her bottom as he blindly reached for the nightstand, fumbling for the lube she kept in the drawer with her toys.

A pink vibrator, her favorite, rolled across the sheets and settled next to her knee, followed closely by a butterfly-shaped clit teaser. Silver Ben Wa balls sailed right off the end of the bed. A flash of red caught her eye a split second before the leather tails of her flogger snapped against her ass. The heavy thud stung for only a moment before warmth spread through the fleshy globes. Rissa moaned and lifted her ass into the next swat.

"Damn, baby. I would have done this sweet ass weeks ago if I'd known you had a flogger hidden away with your toys."

JD landed several more heavy swats then his hand rubbed over her stinging ass, spreading the heat. "So pink and beautiful," he praised.

The leather tails connected with her upturned ass over and over, and Rissa was lost to the decadent thrill. She had bought the flogger on a whim, more as a novelty, never expecting to feel the thuddy sensation on her bare flesh or to be so turned-on by it. Mere minutes ago she had been sated, yet after a few swats her desires roared back to life. With each lash her body rocked, breasts swinging, pebbled nipples dragging across the sheets. Her clit swelled, throbbed, needing attention. Hot fluids gushed from her pussy, the walls clenching, emphasizing its emptiness.

"JD," she moaned. "Please."

He dropped the flogger and a big palm smoothed over her flaming flesh, making her even hotter. "Please what, baby? What do you need?"

Something blunt pressed at her opening and she gasped, arched her back and thrust her hips, impaling herself on the vibrator he held. Strong muscles flexed, drew the toy deeper.

"Fuck, Rissa. That's hot!"

He flicked the switch and the toy started to oscillate as he fucked her with it, rasping over her G-spot with each pass. Lost to sensation, she squealed as cold liquid sluiced down the crease of her ass and a well-lubed finger thrust deep. Soon one finger became two, scissoring, stretching. Burning pleasure-pain had her grinding against the toy and his fingers. The two pulled out and on the next pass were replaced with three. It was too much, not enough.

JD was in limbo, somewhere between heaven and hell. Rissa's responsiveness blew him away as he watched her ride his fingers and the vibrator. He couldn't wait to thrust his cock into her hot, tight ass.

She cried in frustration when he removed his fingers. He grabbed a condom and rolled it on, squeezed a generous pool of lube into his palm and fisted his throbbing cock. When he was nice and slick, he pressed the head against her tiny hole and grasped her hip. With his free hand, he reached around and rubbed her clit. The stimulation to the engorged nub relaxed the tension and her anus fluttered open.

"Nice and easy, Rissa. Take a breath. When you blow it out, bear down."

Following his lead, she breathed and relaxed. The head of his cock slipped past the dense ring of tissue and into the blistering heat of her body.

His control nearly faltered as JD gritted his teeth and held perfectly still. If she changed her mind now it would kill him but he'd pull out. Endless moments passed in sheer anguish as her ass fisted the first inch of his cock and Rissa panted. When she finally moved, pushing back slightly, he hissed at the heady combination of ecstasy and agony.

Her shy, tentative thrusts ripped away at his resolve, but digging deep, he forced his body to comply, remaining rigid as she took more of him. After what felt like excruciating hours the rounded curves of her ass nestled in snug against his pelvis and her body engulfed him in glorious, tight heat.

"JD," she gasped. "Move, damn it."

Calling on every ounce of discipline and control, he eased back through the heated grasp of her body, hissing from between clenched teeth. "Not...going...to...last—"

His fiery temptress had other ideas. She dropped her shoulders and cheek to the mattress then reached back under her body to fondle his balls, which were already drawn close to his body.

"No," he shouted, barely holding on.

"Yes," she growled and thrust hard. "Fuck me."

A man's endurance and strength has limits—a line that when crossed will snap the strongest of wills. Rissa's verbal and physical demands pushed JD far past his restraint. He lost any semblance of control, taking her hard and fast with wild abandon.

"Yes...yes...yes," she cried, punctuating each punishing thrust. Unable to bear leaving her intense heat, he pulled out only halfway, the vibrator partially withdrawing with him. He slammed back into her and so did the toy, fucking her pussy and ass simultaneously almost as if he had two cocks.

Her ass spasmed and clenched, she screamed and panted, riding an almost continual orgasm, forcing his own climax to arrive much quicker than he wanted. He couldn't hold back, her body milked every pulsing jet of cum from his balls and he continued to thrust until exhaustion claimed him.

JD dropped against her back, rolling them both onto their sides so he didn't crush Rissa. Her body continued to contract, forcing out his deflated cock and the vibrator. The device skittered across the mattress and disappeared over the side.

He felt a powerful need to care for Rissa—wash her body, see to her comfort—but he couldn't move. He managed to remove the condom and toss it into the wastebasket. Intending to rest briefly, JD gathered the last of his strength, pulled a blanket over them and cuddled her into the curve of his body.

He woke with a hard, insistent pounding echoing in his head. Cracking one eyelid, JD cursed as sunlight pierced straight through his skull. Rissa shifted in his arms and he realized that neither of them had moved a muscle since they'd fucked each other into a coma. A goofy grin split his lips but the constant pounding intruded on his happy thoughts.

He glanced at the bedside clock and wondered who the hell was knocking down the door at seven twenty-nine in the morning.

"Make it stop," Rissa grumbled and pulled the blanket over her head.

He rolled out of bed, pulled on a pair of boxers and shouted at the unwanted visitor as he stomped through the condo. "Do you have any fucking idea what time it is?"

He unlocked the door and threw it wide. "This had damn well better be good!"

Standing on the doorstep was a wide-eyed teenager. The boy's mouth opened and closed several times but nothing came out. JD gave the stunned kid a quick once-over. Thick mop of brown hair, familiar dark brown eyes, high cheekbones, full lips and a wide mouth. The spitting image of his mother.

"Aw, fuck!"

* * * * *

A sliver of moonlight fell on JD's handsome face and sparkled in his pitch-black eyes. God, those eyes. He didn't even try to hide the growing emotions reflected in their depths. If she stared into the dark pools long enough, she'd lose herself. And she couldn't let that happen, although her reasons why seemed less and less important. Especially in such a romantic setting.

She glanced around, praying the condo association had not installed a security camera near the hot tub, which according to the sign was closed after midnight. Not that JD let the association's rules or an unknown witness stop their naughty water fun. The mere idea of someone watching created a wicked thrill that had her fucking him faster, harder.

"Rissa!"

"Oh yeah. Almost there."

"Rissa!" JD's tone turned sharper and he shook her shoulder.

"What?"

"Wake up, baby."

Wake up? What the hell was he talking about?

"Come on, Rissa. Wake up." He shook her again. "Robby's here."

Her son? In the hot tub?

Rissa's eyes snapped open and she blinked against the bright light flooding her bedroom. Damn it! She was still in bed and it had only been a wet dream.

"I'll start some coffee." JD headed for the door, muttering under his breath, "We're going to need it."

Robby's visit wasn't that big of a surprise. Ever since Mariah had talked to JD on the phone, Rissa had been expecting one of them to pay an unexpected visit. Apparently, Robby had drawn the short straw.

And right now her son and her lover were together, possibly talking.

Dios!

She rolled out of bed and raced around the room, threw on some clothes, brushed her teeth and pulled her hair into a ponytail. She saw no point in trying to cover the love bites on her neck with makeup since she and JD had obviously been in bed when Robby arrived.

Taking a deep breath, Rissa squared her shoulders and walked into the kitchen as if it was just any regular day and nothing of particular note had happened.

Robby sat on a stool at the counter with a steaming mug of coffee. "Good morning." She stopped to kiss his cheek and headed for the coffeepot. JD leaned casually against the cabinet dressed in jeans and a shirt. As she moved closer, he reached out and pulled her body flush with his.

"Don't I get a good morning kiss?"

She laughed and spoke softly so her son wouldn't overhear. "You've already had several but another would be nice."

JD took her mouth in a scorching-hot kiss, his tongue sliding past her lips to tangle with hers. But they had an audience and she had no intention of putting on a show. She pulled back and nipped his lip. "You've made your point, now play nice."

"Baby, I always play nice." He kissed the spot behind her ear that never failed to turn her core to molten lava.

She grabbed a mug, added a liberal amount of flavored creamer and sighed as she took a tentative sip. Mirroring JD's relaxed stance, she faced her son. "I wasn't expecting to see you this weekend. Don't you have exams coming up?"

Robby had matured at an early age and regardless of the unfamiliar situation, she was proud of the calm composure he displayed. Thankfully, Mariah had not made the trip, because her daughter had an innate flair for drama and would have made a scene.

"Mariah's been pretty crazy. She threatened dismemberment if I didn't get in the car and come check on you." He shrugged. "Besides, I figured you'd prefer to avoid one of her manic fits."

JD shivered. "Thank you! I have an older sister and several female cousins so I know how insane girls can be."

"You haven't met my sister yet. Add in her Latina temper and she redefines psycho."

JD shot her a knowing look then began speaking fluent Spanish, teasing Robby and making Rissa choke on the sip of coffee she'd just taken. He slapped her back and kept up the chatter without missing a beat.

"Are you okay?" he asked when she'd regained her composure.

"I didn't know you spoke Spanish."

"There's a lot you don't know about me."

True, but did he have to stress that point in front of her son? She'd been so busy keeping their relationship casual and avoiding personal subjects that she really didn't know her lover at all. Regardless of her efforts to keep her life and her affair separate, the two were bound to collide at some point. She began looking at JD through fresh eyes as he quickly put her son at ease and they got to know each other. When they began making plans to go kayaking, Rissa knew she'd lost the battle. She longed to spend some time with her son but she had made plans for the day.

"How long can you stay?"

"Not long." Robby raked a hand through his thick hair and sighed. "I need to head back by tomorrow morning."

"Well damn. I have an appointment at the salon in an hour and then I'm supposed to meet some friends for lunch."

"Don't worry about it. I'll catch up with some friends."

"No." Rissa had missed Robby and wanted to spend time with him. "I'll reschedule."

"You don't need to do that, baby," JD said. "I'm off work until tomorrow morning. Robby and I will go kayaking and hang out—get to know each other."

She nervously chewed on a fingernail and her gaze shot to Robby to gauge his response.

"Really!" He shot JD a wide-eyed, hopeful glance. "You wouldn't mind?"

"Yeah, man. I've been dying to get some time on the river. Besides," the two shared a conspiratorial grin, "your mom's not big on kayaking."

"Did she freak out? Tip the kayak?"

JD clapped Robby on the back and the two of them meandered toward the living room. "She held it together pretty good but the snakes and gators made her really tense."

"Hey," she called after them. "You didn't warn me about the snakes and gators."

Not good. Already thick as thieves, they ignored her ranting. Rissa rubbed at her temples as they began to pound. She had not imagined her son and her lover becoming buddies and taking off to spend the day together without her. No, this was definitely not good for her chances of keeping things with JD casual.

Chapter Eight

ॐ

For those who reside in the sunshine state, hurricanes are a fact of life. Hurricane season runs from June first through late November with August and September being the busiest months. A late July storm, Alex, had thrown weather forecasters into a frenzy. No one had expected Hurricane Alex to become so strong or move so fast.

Being a veteran of many storms, Rissa didn't worry until a storm approached Cuba and either stayed in the Atlantic or headed into the Gulf of Mexico. The warm waters of the Gulf strengthened the storms and put the Tampa Bay area in the potential strike zone.

Lucky for her, Alex had stayed in the Atlantic. Unfortunately, the residents in the southeastern part of the state got hammered by the formidable force of nature. Curled up on her couch, she watched the reports as Alex crossed the Everglades and moved into the Gulf. All the computer models were now showing the storm had finished with Florida and headed straight for Mexico.

She'd stocked up on water, canned goods and batteries, and as a precaution the condo association had hung plywood over all the windows. The entire situation made for a rather depressing fortieth birthday, sitting alone in her boarded-up condo watching for the latest news.

The fire department had been put on emergency activation yesterday, which meant the crew had to be there whether scheduled to work or not. Although now that the storm had passed things would go back to normal.

JD hadn't even called today, not that he knew it was her birthday. He didn't. Rissa wasn't sure why she'd kept it a secret, but the longer she remained in the condo alone the angrier she became, which was ridiculous. She shouldn't be mad at him for not knowing.

And yet, over the past six weeks, JD had forced his way in and become a big part of her life. He'd practically moved into the condo with her and had even befriended her son—all while she'd sat by and let it happen. In another two weeks school would start and she would soon have to face the inevitable breakup. Their summer fling had almost reached the end. But how was she supposed to break it off?

Needing some advice, she booted up her computer and opened the instant message program, glad to see Cam was online.

Rissa: Hey

Cam: Hey stranger! Please tell me you're not in the path of that storm.

Rissa: Nah, I'm good. It stayed far south of me and is supposed to go after Mexico next.

Cam: Good! Well, not for south Florida or Mexico, but you know what I mean. So what's up? How are you doing? Or more appropriate, who are you doing? *G*

Rissa: LOL! I'm good. It's my birthday. The big four-oh today.

Cam: Hey, happy birthday. You have plans to celebrate?

Rissa: Not really. I'm still seeing JD but he's on emergency duty.

Cam: That sucks.

Rissa: Yup. So listen, I need some advice.

Cam: Sure. What's up?

Rissa: Well, school starts in a couple of weeks. It's time to get back to real life and end this summer fling.

But I've never had to break up with anyone before. How do I do it?

Cam: WTF! I don't get it. I thought you and JD were solid. He and Robby became friends, right? And isn't he living with you?

Rissa: Yeah but this was never supposed to be more than a summertime thing. I don't want it to become permanent. So how do I end it without hurting him?

Cam: Too late for that. If you didn't want to hurt him then you should have left it at a one-night stand. Why do you think you have to end it? Why not ride it out, see where it goes? You never know, it could be the real deal. Something permanent.

Rissa: I've had that. Went right from my parents' house to my husband's. From daughter to wife then widowed mom. This is my first time living alone, being on my own. And that only lasted for a little over a week before JD started moving himself in. There are a million reasons he doesn't fit into my real life.

Cam: So you've never lived alone. So what. You're going to pass up a possible future with a good man because you want to be alone? Are you crazy?

Rissa: Maybe I am. I'm not sure of anything anymore.

Cam: Then my advice is until you get your head on straight don't do anything rash. Don't break up with JD. Take this chance to be happy and hold on tight.

Hold on tight.

That was the one thing she couldn't do. If anything, all her conversation with Cam did was add to her frustration. She didn't want a permanent relationship with JD. At least, she thought she didn't. Right now she wasn't sure of anything and feared making the wrong move. The fear fed her temper to the point Rissa was spoiling for a good fight. All she needed was a target for her anger.

The phone rang and she snatched it up. "Hello."

An automated recording began a sales pitch for term life insurance coverage. Rissa listened only long enough to identify the company. She found a phone number for the organization online and placed a scathing complaint with the poor soul unfortunate enough to be on the other end of the line.

She hung up feeling less than satisfied.

In need of a distraction, Rissa picked up the book she'd been reading. It was written by one of her favorite erotic romance authors. No matter how great the story, Rissa wasn't able to concentrate. When she'd read the same page five times and still didn't remember what it said, she closed the book and tossed it aside.

Someone knocked on the door.

"Well, all right. Fresh meat." She made it to the entryway before the third rap sounded. She yanked open the door, ready to rumble, but found herself taking a reflexive step backward, one hand covering her throat. Her jaw hung open for a moment before she recovered from the shock of seeing JD decked out in full camouflage military uniform.

"*Dios!*" she cried. "A little early to be dressing up for Halloween."

"This isn't a costume, Rissa." He sighed, took off his hat and rubbed a hand over his head. "I only have a minute. The guys are waiting." The problem was he had no idea what to say.

Rissa's hands fisted at her sides and her cheeks were flushed red. Her anger irritated the hell out of him. He'd lost count of how many times he'd tried to tell her about his life. She hadn't wanted to listen, always keeping him at a distance. And she didn't appear any more receptive now.

He took a breath and forged ahead. "I'm a member of the National Guard and my unit has been called to the areas hit by Hurricane Alex. I'm not sure how long I'll be gone. A week— maybe ten days." He shrugged. "Could be longer."

She cursed him in Spanish then switched to English. "You lied to me. Let me believe you were just a firefighter. I should have known. You're an adrenaline junkie so the military makes perfect sense. *Dios!* I have no restraint. Should have resisted that damn cougar challenge."

Cougar challenge? Exactly what had she been keeping from him?

Her right fist flexed and JD shifted his stance, steadying himself for a blow that never came. "Well, see ya. Don't let the door hit you in the ass on your way out." She grabbed the door and swung it forward.

Hell no. He wasn't about to let her just end things by slamming the door in his face. JD thrust his foot out to prevent the barrier from closing, barely flinching as the solid wood crashed into his booted foot. "Uh-uh. Not so fast, baby."

She shrieked and stepped back as he stormed into the condo, ignoring the honking of a horn, his ride's way of telling him to hurry up. There would be no rushing this. He didn't plan on leaving with so much unresolved between them.

"I didn't lie to you."

"You lied by omitting important facts. Facts that would have changed everything. My husband was in the Army and died while on duty. He was in an accident during a vehicle transport."

Ah, now here was the reason for her anger. She was trying to protect her heart from being hurt in the same way twice. He decided to push her a bit, release some of his own frustration. "I've tried to tell you about myself hundreds of times, Rissa. You've never let me, never wanted to listen. And if you're going to pin my balls to the wall for lying by omission then you're a hypocrite. Tell me about the cougar challenge." He hoped to hell it wasn't what it sounded like.

Rissa's spine stiffened, her lips compressed to a thin, pale line and she glared at him. He really shouldn't be getting turned-on by her fiery temper but there was no denying the potent effect she had on him.

"You can't handle the truth," she yelled.

He didn't say a word, knowing doing so was akin to lighting the fuse on a stick of dynamite. The explosion wasn't long in coming and completely blew him away.

"Fine. A friend invited me to join a blog, *Tempt the Cougar*. It's for a group of women who lust after younger men." She paused and her fists moved to her hips. "By the way, I turned forty today."

There was nothing he could say since he hadn't known when her birthday was. If he had, he would have definitely done something to mark the occasion.

"The blog started after a group of women met at an erotic romance conference and one of them challenged the others to become cougars by sleeping with a significantly younger man. It doesn't have to result in a permanent relationship. A one-night stand is sufficient. Some of them even had more than one younger guy at a time." She crossed her arms under her breasts and arched her brow. "You made great cougar prey."

The words stung, bad. JD took a deep breath and thought the situation through. Rissa's intention may have been a quick notch on her bedpost but he'd become a bigger part of her life than she realized or would admit. He had no doubt she cared about him or she wouldn't waste the effort to argue.

Several loud horn blasts had him cursing. The guys wouldn't wait much longer. He hated to walk away like this but he didn't have much choice, he had to do his duty.

"I have to go but this isn't over, baby. Not by a long shot."

Rissa swallowed hard and her eyes sparkled with tears she fought to hold back. She would not let him see her cry. The very idea he could push her to the brink of tears renewed her temper but when she spoke, the words lacked her earlier conviction. "Don't bother. By then I'll have found other cougar prey."

Her back slammed into the wall, driving the breath from her lungs and before she could suck in a breath, JD's lips smashed down on hers. It was a hard, potent kiss. A claim. A promise. She was held captive between the solid wall and his hard body as he poured all his anger and frustration into the punishing kiss.

JD lifted his head, keeping her pinned, and stared into her eyes for several long moments. She saw too many emotions passing through his black gaze to grasp yet one came through loud and clear—love. God help him, the fool had gone and fallen in love with her.

"Don't you see this can never be permanent? I'm forty and you're what, twenty-three?"

"Twenty-six, but what's that have to do with anything?"

"It's everything. You're young, one day you'll want a family. I've already raised my children and that's not something I can give you."

Two more loud honks intruded on their argument.

"I've got to go. We'll discuss all this when I get back. And make no mistake, baby, I will be back."

Rissa sighed and shook her head. "It's pointless."

"Do not go out looking for some other guy because I will tear him apart. Don't test me on this, Rissa."

A fist pounded on the door. "Shit!"

"Just go, JD."

He kissed her again, this time a soft and tender brush of his lips. A kiss full of love. Then he turned and stormed out of her life without looking back.

Chapter Nine

ॐ

Excited chatter hit her the moment Rissa opened the door and stepped into the teachers' lounge. She sighed deeply. The first day of a new school year the air always seemed to crackle with electricity.

Until this year.

For the first time in twenty years of teaching at the Bay Academy, a private elementary school, she wasn't anticipating greeting parents and getting to know a class full of bright-eyed, curious children.

It had been fifteen days, seventeen hours and a handful of minutes since JD had walked out of her life, and she had thought of little else during that time. Today was the first time she'd stepped away from her television, broadcasting CNN all day and night as she waited for any small bit of news about the aftermath of Hurricane Alex, foolishly hoping to catch even a fleeting glimpse of JD during one of the reports. Utterly pathetic.

He hadn't called, not that she'd expected him to since utilities and cell towers were still out in the hardest-hit areas. He'd be busy working and it wasn't as if she'd encouraged him to stay in touch.

Her condo was no longer the sanctuary it had once been. Every room, piece of furniture and item within its walls held memories of JD. She'd tried to exorcise his spirit from her space by packing up all his things and cleaning the place from top to bottom. It didn't work and eventually she put each item back where he'd left it to await his return.

Surprisingly enough, it had been a visit from her daughter that made Rissa finally face her true feelings for him.

Mariah saw through the false cheer she put on and forced her to open her eyes by dragging her in front of the mirror to look at herself. What she saw was sunken eyes surrounded by dark circles from a lack of sleep, and the expression of someone who had lost their best friend.

"You have to snap out of this," Mariah demanded. "*Dios!* I never thought I'd see the day. You're lovesick."

Mariah was right, Rissa had done the unthinkable. She'd fallen in love with a man she couldn't keep. No matter how she tried to convince herself she didn't love JD it failed to work. He was a good man with so many wonderful qualities and they fit together perfectly—with one exception. He loved children and because of complications in Robby's delivery it was the one thing she couldn't give JD. He deserved to have the experience of being a father. Deserved so much more than what she could give him.

And now she had to move on with her life, get back to reality. Pasting on a smile that made her teeth ache, Rissa moved through a sea of familiar faces to the coffeepot. The only way she'd make it through the day was with large quantities of caffeine.

"Oh. My. God. Rissa! Have you seen the new teacher yet?"

Wanda Weaver, one of the kindergarten teachers, held out a steaming mug, which she gladly accepted. "We have a new teacher?"

"Heck yeah. His name is Jeffrey Harmon and the man redefines the word gorgeous," Lynn Fuller added.

Rissa glanced around the room but there were no new faces. "Who? Where is he?"

"He's brand-spankin' new, just got his certification, and he's more nervous than a virgin getting her first kiss," Wanda said.

Amy Brighton leaned in closer, joining the conversation. "He just got into town late last night and is setting up his classroom. I think we should show pity on him and offer to help."

They all shared a good laugh.

"What?" Amy asked. "He's hot as hell, young and single. No ring, I checked. I am definitely making a move on that fine hunk."

"Oh, the things I'd like to do with that rock-hard body." Wanda all but drooled as she spoke.

Since she had no interest in hearing about the hot new teacher that had all the women worked up, Rissa tuned out the conversation, her mind wandering back to the question that ran through her mind in a continual loop. What the hell was she going to do about JD if or when he came back?

The day dragged forward slowly. Rissa found her patience severely tried by the drama of tearful goodbyes, rough adjustments to a new situation and willful testing of her authority by the rambunctious children. By the end of the day she had a raging headache and visions of a long soak in her tub, along with a big glass of wine.

She pushed in the last chair and was straightening the supplies on top of the desk as her classroom door swung open. Some of the others had talked about going out for drinks tonight but she wasn't in the mood. Rissa turned with an excuse on her lips that strangled in her throat.

In dress pants and a button-down shirt with the sleeves rolled up, revealing muscular forearms, JD looked more extraordinarily handsome than she remembered. She wanted to run straight to him, throw herself in his arms, but she couldn't move and was afraid to breathe.

"Hello, Miss Cross. Some of the other teachers thought you might be able to give the new guy some pointers on how to survive the sheer insanity of first grade. Although I do have to say that I did pretty well today regardless of how hectic everything was."

Her mouth dropped open as she tried to form some sort of response. Her arms and legs tingled and chills raced through her body as her head swam.

"Wow, I don't think I have ever seen you at a loss for words before." His dark eyes shone and he gave her a tentative smile. "Can I come in?"

"Y-you...you're the new teacher? Jeffrey Harmon." God, she hadn't known his first name and had forgotten his last, otherwise the pieces would have clicked into place this morning. And he was a teacher? That's something she definitely should have known.

He nodded as he took a step forward. "Yeah, that's me. Jeffrey Daniel Harmon. JD to my friends."

He continued to move closer, slowly closing the distance between them. "We have a lot to talk about. The way we left things—" His lips pressed into a thin line and he shook his head. "Are you ready to talk, Rissa?"

"I—you—you're a teacher?" She was stuck on that concept, unable to fully wrap her mind around it.

"Yeah, I am. Don't be so shocked. I'm not stupid and can do more than jobs requiring physical strength."

No, he definitely wasn't stupid. She didn't doubt his intelligence. What she'd done was put him in the same category with her late husband as all brawn and no ambition. She hadn't taken the time to actually find out if he was different and wanted more in life. "I know you're smart, but a teacher? Why a teacher?"

"I love working with kids and wanted to settle down with a stable career. Teaching's a good fit. I worked hard, took classes on my days off, graduated and landed the job here just before we met. I didn't know you taught here.

"My time in the Guard was up last month, although I do still plan to work at the fire station during summer breaks." He shrugged as if it were nothing special, but satisfaction shone in his eyes for all he'd accomplished.

Rissa's chest tightened, her knees weakened and tears pooled at the corners of her eyes. This was why she'd held back. She'd already thought the world of JD and now her heart swelled with pride and love she had no right to share with him since she'd kept him at a distance. She had to be strong now, encourage him to find someone capable of giving him everything he deserved, regardless of how much it would hurt to let him go. It was the right thing to do for him.

"Come on, Rissa. Let's go home."

Home? Good as that sounded they couldn't have a home. Not together. *Dios*, what a mess she'd made.

He reached her just as her legs gave out and pulled her cold, weak body into the warm support of his solid frame. "Are you okay?"

The tender concern in his sexy rasp made her heart ache for things to be different but she had to face reality. "I can't," she hiccuped, took a breath and started over. "This can't be, JD. I can't give you what you want. What you deserve."

"Aw, baby. You are everything I want."

She shook her head, trying to ignore his intoxicating scent and the warmth of his body. "I'm fourteen years older than you. I've had my family, raised them, seen them head out into the world. You're young and will want to have a family one day. I can't give you that."

"Rissa, age is a number and it doesn't matter. Not to me." He shook his head. "Is that why you've kept me out of here?" His palm pressed flat over the upper curve of her left breast and her nipple beaded in response to his touch. "You don't want to have more kids?" His voice turned cold and hard. "Or is it that cougar thing? You want to get more young men in your bed?"

"The challenge is irrelevant and what I want doesn't matter." Unable to look him in the eye, she lowered her gaze. Rissa didn't want to tell him but he deserved the truth. If anything would set him free the truth had the power to do so.

She took a breath and forged ahead before second thoughts formed.

"When Robby was born there were...complications, I hemorrhaged. They had to do emergency surgery. I—I *can't* have any more children." She still didn't meet his eyes, afraid she'd see pity she didn't want, and continued to stare at his chest.

"Jesus, Rissa. I'm sorry you had to go through that. It must have been horrible. But have I ever said I want to have kids?"

Well, no. But they hadn't discussed important issues like having a family.

He gently lifted her chin and she lost herself in his stunning black eyes. What she saw was warmth, understanding and something tender. Was it affection?

"Sure, I love kids. Other people's kids that I can give back when they've worn me out. I have more than enough nieces, nephews and cousins to keep me busy without having to change diapers or stay up all night when they're sick. Those are not things I need."

"Oh." Rissa felt the barriers she'd so carefully erected between JD and her heart start to crumble. The primary justification for keeping her distance fell away with a few simple words. "Then what exactly do you want?"

"All I want—all I need—is you! I love you, Rissa. I'd like to see where that can take us. I just want you to give us a chance."

He what? Her mind stuck on the part where he said he loved her. It didn't seem possible with the lengths she'd gone to make sure that didn't happen.

"Is there a chance for us?"

He didn't wait for her to respond, not that she knew what to say. JD turned her numb body toward the door and began walking out of the building with his arm wrapped securely around her waist. Several other teachers watched with stunned expressions and a million questions brewing in their eyes. She'd have a lot of explaining to do...tomorrow. Right now, hard as it was for her to comprehend everything that had happened, the only thing she cared about was within her grasp.

Overwhelmed by his reappearance and finding out they had a lot more in common than she'd thought, Rissa remained quiet and let JD talk, greedily taking in all the details of his life, feeling the undeniable bond between them grow stronger with each passing moment.

She decided that JD wasn't asking for too much and maybe she could actually give him what he wanted. Relax and let things develop between them. After all, a teacher was stable and fit in with her normal life much better than a thrill-seeking fireman. Rolling with the tide and seeing where it took them sounded good. Damn good. Maybe they'd last a few months or a few decades. There was no telling unless she gave them a chance to find out.

Rissa was quiet. Too quiet! Her usual chatter nonexistent. JD watched her from the corner of his eye as he drove, trying to gauge her mood until he couldn't take it anymore. "Are you okay?"

"Um-hmm."

The mumbled response failed to reassure him.

"Everything okay with Robby and Mariah?" Robby was a great kid. He'd like to meet her daughter, who was probably a lot like her mom—strong, confident and stubborn with a wicked temper. He hoped the two of them had ironed things out between them while he was away because they seemed to have a close relationship.

She sighed heavily. "Mariah came home last weekend. It was awkward at first but we had a nice talk. She...umm," Rissa rubbed her palms on her slacks and avoided meeting his eyes. "She's busy with school but wants to come down for Thanksgiving week."

Her hands fluttered about and she chewed on her lip. He'd never seen her that nervous and wondered what she was afraid to tell him. "And?"

"Well…she wants us to spend the holiday together, cook a big traditional meal. Umm…you know. The four of us?"

Did he dare hope her daughter wanted to include him? He had to be sure. "Four?"

"Yeah. Robby, Mariah, me…and you. If you're interested."

His heart swelled and slammed into his ribs as he parked the truck and turned in the seat toward Rissa. Her big brown eyes finally met his to reveal a wide variety of emotions. Fear, restrained optimism, self-doubt and longing all swirled together, increasing his own desires for the future.

Taking her hands, he stilled their nervous motion and brushed a kiss across her knuckles. "What about you? Is that what you want too?"

"I would like to have all the people I love together." She searched his expression, apparently finding the encouragement she needed to continue. "I missed you. Worried and thought about you the entire time you were gone."

His pulse raced as he waited her out, knowing how hard it was for her to say what was on her mind.

"I was stupid and scared. Tried to maintain distance between us and only let this be an affair. It's not our age difference but my own insecurities. I wanted to prove I'm capable of standing on my own two feet. And I didn't want to risk my heart, to feel such loss again as I did when my husband died. I tried to keep you out so I wouldn't lose you. And you know what?"

Jesus, she was killing him. He needed her to say it, to return the emotions she sparked in him, more than he needed his next breath. "What?"

"It happened anyway." She nodded. "When I wasn't looking you became a part of my life. A vital part. It took being apart for me to see that and realize how much I love you and want to be with you. I can't sleep without you in my bed, your legs tangled up with mine, your snores ruffling my hair."

"Aw, baby." He cupped her face and slid across the bench seat. "I'm right here and I'm not going anywhere."

"Good because I need you here."

He pressed a chaste kiss to her lips. "There's just one more thing. I want you to tell me about the cougar challenge."

She sighed. "It's stupid."

"I don't care. I still want to hear it."

"Fine," she huffed. "A friend got me to join a blog, *Tempt the Cougar*. It's a group of women who have a thing for younger men. One of the members, Monica, challenged us all to become cougars."

"Go on."

"There's not much more to it. We talk about our experiences, post pictures we find or take of hot guys and we're all going to meet up at RomantiCon, an erotic romance book conference."

"Does this challenge require you sleep with a certain number of younger guys?" He practically growled the question but it was a sensitive subject for him. The idea of Rissa sleeping around pissed him off. He wasn't into sharing. The idea of another man touching her, holding her, fucking her made him absolutely insane.

"What? Um…no, just one. Although some of the girls had ménages and got sandwiched between two guys at once, that's not part of it."

"So you're done with it? You completed the challenge?"

"I really don't want to talk about this now."

"Rissa," he gritted from between clenched teeth. "Answer the question. Are you done?"

She leaned back and blinked. "Of course I'm done. I conquered the challenge the first time we fu—"

He narrowed his gaze and shot her a warning glance.

"Uh, I mean the first night we made love it was finished."

"Good because I'm going to be the only man in your bed. Understand?"

She swallowed hard and nodded. "I kind of like this possessive side of you. It's sexy and really turns me on."

He sealed the agreement by claiming her lips in what started as a soft and tender kiss that quickly turned into a blazing-hot possession. When he pulled back they both gulped in air.

"Come on. Let's go inside."

"Wait!" Rissa's voice was higher, almost frightened. "One more thing."

"Okay. What is it?"

She bit her lip and stared at her fingers before looking up and meeting his eyes with none of her usual confidence. Whatever she had to say was important. JD sat up straighter and his pulse raced.

"I want us to be together. All the time. Will you move in with me?"

He laughed and gave her hand a reassuring squeeze. "Won't take much. Most of my stuff is here already."

"Is that a 'yes'?"

"Yes, Rissa. There's nowhere else I'd rather be. Now let's get inside before two fine, upstanding teachers get arrested for having sex in public."

"Ooh, that sounds delightfully naughty."

"Rissa," he groaned and shoved his door open. "Get out of the truck and up those stairs, baby. I need to be in you, no condom. Nothing between my hard cock and your tight, wet pussy. Skin on skin."

"*Dios*, yes! Hurry."

Feeling as if a huge weight had lifted from her, Rissa jumped out of the truck and raced up the stairs, squealing as JD landed a swat on her behind. She shouldn't enjoy the heat spreading through her bottom as much as she did.

She had to slow down to get the door open. As soon as it slammed shut they were all over each other. It had been way too long since she'd been in his arms and had his cock inside her. She was primed and ready.

Arms tangled as they tore at their clothes, frantic in their need. Their lips were just as busy kissing every inch of bared flesh. Neither one cared about foreplay. By the time they were naked, the bedroom was still too far away. JD's hands closed around her waist and lifted her, placing her back against the living room wall. She wrapped her arms around his neck and her legs around his hips. Their bodies lined up perfectly, with his hard length nestled along her wet slit.

"Hurry," she repeated on a gasp. Tremors racked her body and her pussy clenched in anticipation.

JD moved his hands to her ass, palming the cheeks as he lined his cock head up at her needy opening. His eyes locked on hers like dark lasers. Regardless of their urgency he slid into her slow and easy, making sure they both felt every wonderful inch.

"Oh god. So hot. So good," he hissed. He paused for the space of several wild heartbeats then started shafting her blessedly hard and fast. Tender lovemaking would come later. Right now they both needed hard and fast.

"Yesss," Rissa moaned, lifting into each thrust as much as possible. "Perfect."

Having him inside her without a barrier was amazing. She was dying to feel the hot spurt of his release fill her, making her complete. Tension coiled tight in her belly, rising in waves of pure bliss. She was so close.

"JD," she gasped. "Now. Come now."

She raked her fingernails over his sensitive scalp, knowing he loved the tingling sensation. He shifted her hips, changing the angle, his piercing tapping against her cervix on each forward thrust.

Her body went rigid as she crested the peak. JD shouted her name and his movements became erratic. And then it happened, sizzling-hot cum filled her, breathing new life into her orgasm, extending the pleasure.

God, it was perfect. And she was right where she wanted to be — where she belonged — in the arms of her sexy fire stud.

Also by Samantha Cayto

ℰↃ

eBooks:
1-800-DOM-help: Mistress Mine
Cougar Challenge: Locked and Loaded
Illegal Moves (*with Dalton Diaz*)

About the Author

ℰↃ

Samantha Cayto is a Boston-area native who practices as a business lawyer by day while writing erotic romance at night—the steamier the better. She likes to push the envelope when it comes to writing about passion and is delighted other women agree that guy-on-guy sex is the hottest ever.

She lives a typical suburban life with her husband, three kids and four dogs. Her children don't understand why they can't read what she writes, but her husband is always willing to lend her a hand—and anything else—when she needs to choreograph a scene.

She is a member of the Romance Writers of America and the New England Chapter and credits RWA, NEC and the wonderful friends she's made there with helping her become a published author.

Also by Lexxie Couper

စာ

eBooks:
Cougar Challenge: Copping a Feel
Stone's Soul
Timeless Wrath

Print Books:
Passionate Peridot (*anthology*)

About the Author

৪১

Lexxie's not a deviant. She just has a deviant's imagination and a desire to entertain readers with her words. Add the two together and you get darkly erotic romances with a twist of horror, sci-fi and the paranormal!

When she's not submerged in the worlds she creates, Lexxie's life revolves around her family: a husband who thinks she's insane, a pony-sized mutt who thinks he's a lap dog, and her daughters, who both utterly captured her heart and changed her life forever.

Living in Australia makes it a bit tricky for Lexxie to pop by for coffee, but she still loves to chat! Contact her by email or find her at her website or her blog (http://lexxiecouper.wordpress.com/).

Also by Nicole Austin

ಬಿ

Print Books:
Ellora's Cavemen: Dreams of the Oasis I (*anthology*)
Holding Out for a Hero
Passionate Realities
Predators 1, 2 & 3: Predators
Savannah's Vision
The Boy Next Door

About the Author

ഇ

Nicole Austin lives on the sheltered Gulf Coast of Florida, where inspiration can be readily found sitting under a big shade umbrella on the beach while sipping cold margaritas. A voracious reader, she never goes anywhere without a book. All those delicious romances combined with a vivid imagination naturally created steamy fantasies and characters in her mind.

Discovering Ellora's Cave paved the path to freeing them as well as manifesting an intoxicating passion for romantica. The positive response of family and friends to her stories propelled Nicole into an incredible world where fantasy comes boldly to life. Now she stays busy working as a certified CT scan technologist, finishing her third college degree, reading, writing, and keeping up with family. Oh yeah, and did we mention all the hard work involved with research? Well, that's the fun job—certainly a labor of love.

ഇ

The authors welcome comments from readers. You can find their websites and email addresses on their author bio pages at www.ellorascave.com.

Tell Us What You Think

We appreciate hearing reader opinions about our books. You can email us at Comments@EllorasCave.com.

Why an electronic book?

We live in the Information Age—an exciting time in the history of human civilization, in which technology rules supreme and continues to progress in leaps and bounds every minute of every day. For a multitude of reasons, more and more avid literary fans are opting to purchase e-books instead of paper books. The question from those not yet initiated into the world of electronic reading is simply: *Why?*

1. *Price.* An electronic title at Ellora's Cave Publishing runs anywhere from 40% to 75% less than the cover price of the exact same title in paperback format. Why? Basic mathematics and cost. It is less expensive to publish an e-book (no paper and printing, no warehousing and shipping) than it is to publish a paperback, so the savings are passed along to the consumer.

2. *Space.* Running out of room in your house for your books? That is one worry you will never have with electronic books. For a low one-time cost, you can purchase a handheld device specifically designed for e-reading. Many e-readers have large, convenient screens for viewing. Better yet, hundreds of titles can be stored within your new library—on a single microchip. There are a variety of e-readers from different manufacturers. You can also read e-books on your PC or laptop computer. (Please note that Ellora's Cave does not endorse any specific brands.

You can check our website at www.ellorascave.com for information we make available to new consumers.)

3. *Mobility.* Because your new e-library consists of only a microchip within a small, easily transportable e-reader, your entire cache of books can be taken with you wherever you go.

4. *Personal Viewing Preferences.* Are the words you are currently reading too small? Too large? Too… ANNOYING? Paperback books cannot be modified according to personal preferences, but e-books can.

5. *Instant Gratification.* Is it the middle of the night and all the bookstores near you are closed? Are you tired of waiting days, sometimes weeks, for bookstores to ship the novels you bought? Ellora's Cave Publishing sells instantaneous downloads twenty-four hours a day, seven days a week, every day of the year. Our webstore is never closed. Our e-book delivery system is 100% automated, meaning your order is filled as soon as you pay for it.

Those are a few of the top reasons why electronic books are replacing paperbacks for many avid readers.

As always, Ellora's Cave welcomes your questions and comments. We invite you to email us at Comments@ellorascave.com or write to us directly at Ellora's Cave Publishing Inc., 1056 Home Avenue, Akron, OH 44310-3502.

MAKE EACH DAY MORE *EXCITING* WITH OUR

ELLORA'S
CAVEMEN
CALENDAR

✝ WWW.ELLORASCAVE.COM ✝

ELLORA'S CAVE
Romanticon

Annual convention
for women who
refuse to behave

www.JasmineJade.com/Romanticon
For additional info contact: conventions@ellorascave.com

*Discover for yourself why readers can't get enough
of the multiple award-winning publisher
Ellora's Cave.*

Whether you prefer e-books or paperbacks,

*be sure to visit EC on the web at
www.ellorascave.com*

*for an erotic reading experience that will leave you
breathless.*

CPSIA information can be obtained at www.ICGtesting.com

261634BV00001B/34/P

9 781419 963681